D1461213

An Angel's Heart

Book 1 of the *Ray of Light* Series

Raven Gregory

Fulton Books, Inc.
Meadville, PA

Published by Fulton Books 2020

ISBN 978-1-64654-394-6 (paperback)
ISBN 978-1-64654-395-3 (digital)

Printed in the United States of America

This book is dedicated to my boys Lucas and Hunter for giving me more reasons than I can count to never give up on anything, for the many hours of playing with wooden swords, for endless amounts of time watching silly reruns and eighties fantasy movies. For being the inspiration, I needed to want to give you more.

I love you both more than anything.

To my love, Greg, for believing in me, even when I couldn't believe in myself, for loving me enough to push me out of my comfort zone, for showing me love beyond compare, for giving me wings when I wanted to fly. Without you, I am nothing.

You are my soul mate and my twin flame.

I love you endlessly. You are the Drake to my Rhea.

Prologue

There is magic all around us every day, some of light and some of darkness. There are those who are good and those who are evil, and there are those that are both. The world overlooks magic or magical beings for something out of stories or lore. Most people are oblivious to its presence and carry on with their day-to-day lives believing in very little. Those who are aware that it exists either pretend it doesn't or embrace it and realize just how special magic really is and what wondrous miracles occur when it is used for the right purposes.

Rhea was just such a girl. She was plain and ordinary but saw in things what others didn't. There was nothing special about Rhea, just like most of the girls in her village, and she had come to terms with that a long time ago. At seventeen, the world is supposed to open its door and wonderful things are supposed transpire, but Rhea's life was already predestined. She was to live in Hearts Prairie for the whole of her life, a small, little village with no real connection to world, a pin-prick on a map that no one has heard of. She was to help heal those of her village just as her parents and grandparents had before her. She was to marry a boy from a good family and have babies and live on the family property. This life didn't appeal to Rhea's sense of adventure. She wanted to see new places and explore all that there was to offer beyond the village borders. She wanted to meet new people and have a greater purpose than to be a mom and a wife.

Her sister, Rosa, was meant for that life, and it was likely to happen if Derik's heart stayed true. Rosa was young still and had time, but Derik had been in love with her every moment from the time they reached for the same apple in the orchard. Rosa would get it right on the first try, just as their mother, Rene, had with their father, Richard, when she was younger. Rhea, on the other hand, had a series of courters none that ever seemed to stick. Even at seventeen, she was strong-willed and determined to do things her own way.

She longed for a suitor that would be able to keep up with her spirit and allow her to fly. She couldn't imagine settling down, let alone with any of the boys in the village. They were all dull and mundane. They would all try to tame her. There was Travis… Oh, Travis and how his daring ways called to her heart, but she didn't love him, at least not enough to consider marrying him. They had talked about running away together to some far-off land, but that was just the talk of impetuous teenagers with nothing better to do.

She lay in the meadow, the spring moon bouncing slivery threads off the thousands of wildflowers that had just bloomed with the season. She loved the meadow. It was one of the only places she could ever be alone with her thoughts. She and her family didn't see eye to eye on anything, but the topic of her future had been a constant discussion as of late. She couldn't take it anymore. She had to get out the house; somehow the meadow always called, and she answered. At times, she had felt more at home in the meadow than in her family's house. The members of her family were good people, but they felt entitled to control her life, and she disagreed. A lot.

She looked up to the sky, stars twinkling. She wondered what it was like to be star, but then she decided that being a star was not much different from the life her family had plotted out for her. The same thing day after day. Routine was not something she fancied. She sighed and closed her eyes. "Goddess Ariadne, please give me a better, more exciting life" was her silent prayer as she drifted off to sleep. It wasn't long before she began to feel very strange. She felt like she was rising out of her body. Still asleep and not able to wake, she began to panic. She heard a voice, sweet and melodic, gentle and loving, but commanding. The voice was female and familiar, but she didn't know why.

"Beautiful Rhea, believer in all things magic and mysterious, I am the goddess mother, Ariadne. You asked for my help, and now I offer you my services. I have come to make you an offer." Rhea tried to speak, but there were no words. Ariadne continued, "I seek an angel of the earth, someone who is of the light, someone who can heal others and who can find her magic within. I have watched you for a long time and have felt your struggles, but I offer you the escape for which you long. Take my offer and become an angel of the earth. The only other option that can be offered is that of an early, untimely death. You are not meant for the life your family has planned for you, but the only way I can help is if you accept my offer and be of my service."

Rhea again tried for words. This time she heard them, but in her head. "Goddess Ariadne, thank you for hearing my call. What does it mean to be an angel of the earth?"

She felt the goddess's presence on her skin. "It means to serve me as I see fit, to go where there is a need, to heal and put others above yourself, to protect those that you love at any cost, to give selflessly to those around you even if your heart should break in the process, to love beyond compare but set them free when the time is right, to uphold a sense of balance—good versus evil, light versus dark, love versus hate, male versus female. Knowing that each plays a part in our world and, without one, the other is incomplete but knowing that in battle, good always conquers evil and love always prevails."

The goddess was quiet as Rhea mulled this over in her dream state. There didn't seem to be any other way but to accept the offer. She was not ready for death, and going back to the life her parents deemed worthy would surely kill her before her eighteenth birthday. She had no idea what it meant to be an angel of the earth, but anything was better than the alternative. She supposed she would figure it out as she went along. She would do anything if it meant freedom. Ariadne waited patiently for a response. "Goddess, I don't really understand what you ask of me, but I will gladly become an angel of the earth, and I will serve you as you request. How long until I can leave and venture out into the world?"

The goddess was delighted; this was a special creature and was bound for greatness. "Rhea, be patient. It is not yet time for you to go forth out into the world, but it won't be long, and you can rest assured that when I am ready for you, I will call. You will be a great healer, and your powers will come from the light. You will be blessed with many gifts, but these gifts will never be understood by your family, and because of this, there will always be a sense of disconnect between you. You will always love them and they you, but you will never agree on what is to become of your life path. There are things you must try to understand as they come and not before. Your path is of the goddess divine and that of the feminine, but you will be surrounded by forces of the masculine. You crave unconditional love, and you will seek it in the most unlikely sorts of fellows. None will be good enough for you, and none will withstand your zest for life. You will try and try again but will not succeed. Your match will present himself when the time is right and when you need the power of love the most. Try not to despair about this, but know it is part of a greater destiny. I leave you now, but we will speak again." With that, Ariadne was gone, and Rhea felt herself return to the ground and to her body.

It was three years later to the day that Ariadne called for Rhea to leave all she had ever known and find her place out in the world.

Chapter 1

He was a creature of the night, and usually, the darkness was his greatest companion, but tonight, the dark was unseemingly cold and harsh. The wind bit at his body, causing it to ache and throb.

The wind blew the long black traveling cloak away from him, giving his shadow the appearance of having wings. He held the hood tight around his face, leaving only his piercing blue eyes visible to any passers. He looked frightening in the faint glow of the occasional moonbeam. He walked along the lifeless streets, longing for shelter and desperate for company. His thoughts filled with light and warmth as his memory drifted to her.

She was once the love of this demon's life, the one thing that was good and true in his meaningless affair of never-ending darkness. His heart began to cry, and he cursed her and himself. His harsh words fell to the wind, and he quickened his step, trying to find anything else but her to focus on. She was gone, and there was nothing he could do about it. It was his fault she was gone, and he had eternity to live with that. All he wanted was to forget her—forget her beauty and charm, forget the shape of her body and the gentleness of her heart. He wanted to forget the light that radiated from her entire being and the way she looked at him with her emerald-green eyes. He wanted to forget her laugh and her tears, the way she could ease his pain and suffering with just a simple touch. He wanted to push her out of his mind and never remember what it was like to have the love of someone so pure and good. But more than anything, he wanted to forget her smile. Her smile had brought him to his knees the first time he saw it. It was the strongest, most enchanting force of magic he had ever felt. It had burned a hole into his dark heart. Her smile was her best feature for it was sincere and endearing. It made her eyes dance and her face shine like the stars. He loved her smile almost more than anything else about her.

Now alone in the dark hell of this unfamiliar town, her smile was all he could see, and it hurt him down to the core of his stomach. His haunting blue eyes glistened with the faint mist of a tear. Who was he kidding, their love was never meant to last. He was selfish, and his thirst for women was almost greater than his thirst for blood. There was nothing in his immortal being that would ever allow him to be a good husband, and she deserved a good husband. Rhea had wasted so much time on him that she was blind to this. Another tear rolled down his cheek. He blamed it on the cold.

The little inn was not the most ideal of places for men of his kind, but the fire looked inviting and the crowd was small. He crossed the street to the corner where the inn stood. It was small and quaint, the type of place you would imagine finding a lone barkeep overseeing the whole place. An old wood cottage tucked away in the farthest corner of the little town, the last known building for miles. The outside of the little inn was surrounded by shrubs and bushes that might bloom flowers in the spring. An old rickety pinewood fence encompassed the cottage. An old Welcome sign hung loosely on the swinging gate. He unhooked the latch, and the wind swung the gate wide. He stepped through and gave a shiver. The path was well beaten, and he hated that. He avoided places with well-beaten paths. It meant people and questions, and he was in no mood for either. There was a sign that looked older than the one on the gate reading the inn's name: "The Dragon's Cauldron." The front door was a heavy oak door with a serpent dragon carved in the middle. He pushed the door open and stepped inside. The fire was the main source of light; only a few candles were lit throughout the rest of the main room. There were only five other guests, and none of them gave the newcomer much notice. He scanned the room for any source of danger. There was none to be found. The hand that held his hood eased off the cloak and revealed his face. He was good-looking by nature, and being what he was enhanced those good looks. Travis had a long oval face, no hard lines or harsh features, except the icy blue of his eyes. He had black hair and wore it long. His skin was not pale, but not olive either, which intensified the blueness of his eyes. He wore a goatee that was as black as his hair and framed in his mouth and set jawline. His chin was slightly pointed but strong.

The barkeep looked up at him and gave a half smile as he finished drying the beer mug in his hand. The room smelled of stale smoke. The tables were more like picnic tables looking of pine log and benches to match. The bar was a long counter wrapping around the back half of the cottage. There were matching stools tucked neatly under the bar ledge. Behind the bar was a wall of every alcohol imaginable. The more expensive bottles lined the top two wooden shelves. He approached the counter in front of barkeep. They surveyed each other briefly. The keep was old and tired; he had lines on his face showing age and wear. Balding slightly from the forehead, his hair was the color of ash with specks of white scattered here and there. His bushy eyebrows almost hid his wise eyes that were the same color as his hair. His eyes might once have been blue, maybe even green. Time had made his long fingers withered, but not weak. He stared at the stranger while he spoke. His voice was gruff and low as if from smoking for many years but welcoming as well. "What can I do you for?" he asked.

Travis gave a small weak smile and said, "Whiskey, and keep it coming." The old man nodded and turned toward the wall of bottles. He reached for something in the middle, but Travis stopped him. "No, I want the good stuff tonight!" The tone of his voice left the old man feeling cold as if the chill from the air outside had drifted in on this man's words. He grabbed a bottle from the top shelf and turned back to face this dark stranger. He set the bottle down gently on the counter, steel in his eyes. Not often did anyone come in and demand of him his finest whiskey. He wanted to keep a close watch on this man. He pulled a glass up from below the bar and set it next to the bottle. Travis nodded in thanks and took the cap off the bottle. It smelled strong and inviting. He poured the caramel-colored liquor into the glass, three fingers full. The barkeep watched him as he downed the glass in one long swallow. This man had something he needed to drink away and fast. He turned and went back to drying glasses.

Travis was grateful for the old man leaving him to his whiskey and his thoughts. The whiskey was smooth as silk and hot as fire going down his throat. His thoughts were still of her. He poured another glass, more this time than the first. He sat on a stool and faced the fire. This time he sipped the whiskey. The smell of it filled his nostrils. He watched the fire, searching the flames for anything but her face. It blazed red and orange swaying to a rhythm which he could not feel. It cackled as if mocking his suffering. He was glad she was not there. The people in the bar gave him enough sense of company to not feel totally alone but were few enough not to make him feel trapped.

The hours passed slowly. The fire began to die down, and the whiskey was almost gone. He sat alone on his barstool staring into nowhere, blinking very little. His hunger had increased, but not for anything the old man could offer him. The inn was almost empty except for him, the barkeep, and two men arguing about something which Travis could hear, only because being what he was intensified all his senses, but he gave it no notice. When the front door burst open, the wind blew in the rain (which had started to come down after he entered the inn) and some leaves. Travis looked up, and there she was. He closed his eyes and opened them again, but she was still there. He thought for sure the whiskey and the flames of what was left of the fire were playing tricks on him. He rubbed the backs of his hands over his eyelids to clear out any clouds. It didn't change. She was still standing there cold and tired and just as beautiful as ever.

She pushed the door shut and stood there for a moment trying to shake off the bitter cold. Her hands ached, and her shoulders throbbed. She had healed eight people along her travels that day, including aiding in the birth of breech twin baby girls. Both the babies and mother were well. She was blessed with gifts by the goddess, but she was still human, and she was exhausted. She shivered and looked around. She didn't notice Travis at first but had a strange feeling as her eyes darted around the room. Then they stopped at the center of the bar. He knew she saw him and knew she was just as surprised to see him sitting there as he was to see her. She, too, closed her eyes and reopened them. He was still there. Her heart skipped a beat, and her breath lodged itself in her throat. This made her shiver again. She pushed back the hood of her cloak to make sure it wasn't causing a strange shadow. Her long auburn curls fell around her shoulders. She didn't know what to do. She wanted to turn around and head straight back into the storm. She feared the storm would be much less painful then being here with him. It had been a long time since she had seen him, and he had made it very clear that he did not want to see her ever again. His words had almost destroyed her. They had broken her heart, and now he was sitting in the place she sought for shelter.

He sat there watching her. His haunting eyes were locked on hers. She hated that, after all this time, he still had a spell over her. She had never been able to resist him no matter how she tried. He was truly one of her weaknesses. The two men were still arguing in the far corner closest to the fire. The old barkeep glanced at her briefly then went back to his work. It was just the two of them. That's how it always had been when they were together—everyone else just disappeared. She was pondering moving in his direction when, fast as lightning, he was off his stool and walking right toward her. Her heartbeat was so loud she thought for sure he would hear it hammering against her chest. Without realizing it, she had clenched her fists into balls at her side, her anger winning out over the soft spot in her heart that belonged only to him. His stride was quick and powerful. He was not tall but still was a couple of inches taller than she was, and when he moved, he was almost intimidating. She had never been afraid of him even after she found out what he was. In a strange way, it made her love him more. She could feel his anger as he got closer to her. She wanted to run but had nowhere to go. The storm was getting fiercer behind her, and he was in front of her. She was trapped by the man she had loved off and on and the old oak door of a deserted old inn. He stopped less than two feet away from her, his blue eyes burning holes throughout her body. He was mad, and she knew it. Though she was not sure why. It was only by chance they had come to the same old inn. Or was it? Nothing with them was ever by chance. He, too, had his fists clenched at his side, causing his whole body to tense and stiffen. She could smell the whiskey even before he opened his mouth to speak. His words were rough and harsh, and she wanted nothing more than to hide.

"What the hell are you doing here?" It was more a demand than a question.

She searched his eyes for anything that would let her know, somewhere, he still cared for her, but between the whiskey and his anger, there was nothing there to reassure her. She took a deep breath and let it out slow. Choosing her words carefully, she answered him. "I am only passing through. I needed a drink and the warmth of the fire. There was light from the window. Had I known you were here, wasting away with a bottle of whiskey, I would have kept going, taking my chances with the storm. I am not here to ruin any wallowing you may be doing." Her green eyes flashed in the firelight, making her emotions very clear.

He hated her for being rude; it was not her style. He knew the words she had just spoken were just to bite back at him for his unpleasantness. If she would just give him a smile, he would forgive her intrusion on his thoughts and his space. He decided to try again. He did not want her there; this was true, but there she was. He spoke again, this time with a little less hostility. "Rhea, it has been a long night, and I have had a lot of whiskey, and you look tired. I did not mean to be so gruff. I am sorry." His fists softened, and so did his eyes.

She searched his face questioningly, but it was blank. She was still right mad about his greeting, but glad the anger was fading. He was much easier to handle when he was clam and out of temper. She wanted to smile at him but feared it would cost her too much. She was not ready to allow him that power over her, not when she had worked so hard to block him out of her memory and her heart. He stood there waiting for her to say something, anything. The silence was worse for him than any slap in the face. Finally, she decided to respond to him. Her words were gentler but still full of caution. "Travis, I am sorry I invaded this place. I am cold, tired, and hungry. I will get a quick drink and bite to eat then retire to a room. I will be gone before first light so that we won't have to encounter each other again. You have made it very clear that you wish not to ever see me again. I will grant you that wish and leave you to your bar and your whiskey. Now, if you'll excuse me, I will get a table so that I may hurry and get out of your sight." She sidestepped, passed him, and hurried over to where the old man stood.

While she made her request, he stood there watching her, part of him wanting to scream at her for how she treated him and the other part of him wanting to scoop her up in his arms and carry her to a bed above them and make love to her through the remainder of the night. What he did not want was for her to sit and eat alone and leave without saying goodbye. He wanted her to forgive him and act as though he hadn't stomped on her heart. He knew she would not. He watched her move to a table away from the counter and away from the men arguing. She sat down and untied her velvet cloak. She pushed her hair away from her face then put her hands over the emeralds that were her eyes as if crying. He hated to see her cry. The eyes that were of strange green became more like a freshly polished emerald when she cried than that of an emerald that had long since been neglected. Her eyes were next in line for her best feature. Everything you ever needed to know about the woman was there in her eyes. They told her story, and they told it loud.

After a minute, she removed her hands and placed them on the table. If it were possible, she was even more beautiful than his memory allowed. She had a slender, small body that she kept very well-toned. The dress, which was made for traveling, was a dark shade of red. The velvet material hung to her every curve, making it impossible for him to forget how the shape of her body felt against his. He had not moved back to his stool but stood there watching her. He could not help but recognize that his hunger had intensified. He might be a demon but was also a man, and she was the one thing that could make him weak.

He was angry again, but this time not with her but at him for letting her go. It was for her own good, he had told himself. If his secret wouldn't hurt her, his lust for female flesh surely would. He was not built for fidelity, not even before he became a vampire. He knew, though she was already hurt, and it was his fault that she was hurt. He knew his words had ripped her heart to shreds. He had been drinking too much to try to find words that might soothe the jagged edges of her heart. Slowly he returned to his stool, not taking his eyes off her. He had wanted to drink her away, and now all he wanted was for her to glance in his direction. The old man took her a mug (which Travis knew to be hot cocoa and whiskey, topped off with a little milk) and a plate of food. She granted the old man the smile that he longed for. It was a tired smile, but nonetheless potent. She touched the old man's hand and talked with him about something inaudible. Seeing the angel for the first time that night made his anger start to melt. The old man returned behind the bar. She glanced toward the bar where Travis sat watching her.

When he caught her eye, she quickly brought her stare down to the plate in front of her. She was not about to let him see her fall to pieces. It killed her having him there. She was torn between the only version of love she had ever really known and hate, though she could never hate him. She also knew she could not ever truly love him. He was no more hers than she was his. Just two people whose stars got crossed a long time ago. Her mind battled with her heart over Travis for many years. Her mind deemed him unworthy, and her heart deemed him the only one who was worthy, even though she knew that was not the truth. She knew her heart did not belong to Travis. Tonight, her mind was finally winning even though he had not given her much choice in the matter. He wanted no part of her, and because she had loved him to whatever extent, her heart let her mind win. Time eases all pain.

She picked up her fork and started to pick at her food. Upon arriving, food had been her first concern, but after her encounter with Travis, her appetite dwindled. She knew he was watching her even still. She could feel the intensity of his eyes poring over her. She ate quietly, wanting him to go away. The food was warm but not going down easily. The hot chocolate and whiskey, on the other hand, was going down altogether too easy. It made her insides hot. It only took her a short time to finish the meal and drink. She wiped the napkin around her mouth. She grabbed her cloak and hung it from one arm. She scooped up her used dishes in her hands and walked over to the barkeep. The old man looked pleased with how much she ate and thanked her for bringing the dishes to him. He handed her a key and patted her hand. She nodded in appreciation and turned to make her way up the stairs but stopped. She turned her head slightly over her right shoulder and glanced back in Travis's direction. She looked at him for a moment then said quietly enough for only him to hear "Good night."

Before he could respond, she had turned back and was making her way up the stairs. *Damn it*, he thought. What kind of game was she playing at? That simple "Good night" had caught him off guard. He grabbed the bottle of whiskey and slammed the remainder of it down his throat and crashed the bottle back onto the counter. The old man was watching him closely. Travis knew the old man was a little scared. He looked at the old man and shrugged. "Women."

The old barkeep moved a little closer to Travis but kept a cautious distance. "She asked me to give you a message, sir."

Travis had had too much to drink, for the old man caught him off guard as well. "She asked you to give me a message?" He was confused, and the look on his face told the old man so.

With a small smirk, he replied, "The lady has asked me to tell you that she apologizes for her outburst and that she hopes you can forgive her for intruding on this place and wishes you well. She also says to tell you that she hopes the wind blows you both in different directions so that forgetting each other will be easier from here out." He paused for a brief minute and continued, "She also paid the cost of your bottle of whiskey in hopes that it will help the fact that she invaded your thoughts." Travis was baffled. He knew not what to say, so he turned away from the little man. The bartender walked over to the far end of the bar.

Travis stared at the dying fire. She had paid for his drink, wished him well, and apologized for stumbling across the same inn he occupied. He didn't understand it. He didn't understand how she could possibly think any of this was her fault. Being too kind and loving was her only fault. Her heart had always been too big, and he had always been greedy and selfish with it. He hated himself more now than he had on the night he told her he never wanted to see her again. As his thoughts spun around in his brain, the fire died.

He climbed the stairs of the inn sometime before morning, and he felt everything but drunk. The whiskey, which started out working so well, had turned on him and was now making him think more clearly than he had in months. She had single-handedly put the blame on herself instead of on him. He was to blame not her; all she ever did was love a monster. He reached the top of the old stairs and leaned on the rail, hoping it would break with his weight and he would crash to the bottom of inn. He looked up and down the hallway. The upstairs was lined with doors, four on one side and three on the other. Seven rooms, and she held one of them. Which one, he thought, held the woman he longed to forget and longed to embrace. His head started to hurt. He needed to lie down. His room was the last of the three.

He pushed open the door. It was cold and musty-smelling. There was wood in the brick fireplace. The bed was small but inviting. It had heavy blankets and a lone pillow. He stared at the room for a moment before removing his cloak and throwing it over a chair that was the only other piece of furniture in the room. The floor was made of wood and covered with straw for a little bit more warmth. He sat down on the edge of the bed and pulled off one of his boots. He couldn't help but imagine her lying on her own bed, auburn curls sprawled over the pillow, her soft olive skin tucked beneath the goose down blankets. He cursed as he pulled off his other boot. She had wanted him to forgive her, but it was he that needed her forgiveness. If he could just talk to her and try to explain, then she might be able to understand why he had sent her away. He wondered for a moment whether she would see him if he went to her to try to explain. He dropped his boot to the hardwood floor and fell back upon his bed. It was rather hard and not particularly comfortable, but it served the purpose. He did not move his head to the pillow or crawl under the blankets. Instead, it suited him to lie there, his legs hanging off the side of the little bed, his feet touching the floor. His thoughts swirled around in his aching head. He wanted so much to touch her soft skin and taste her lips. Visions of this clouded his eyes, and he drifted to sleep. His visions of her became his dreams.

She was standing before him, the velvet of her dress hugging to her body, her hair spilled over her shoulders in dark cinnamon curls. Her little body stood there, making no movement except for her slow and steady breath which caused her perfect round breasts to heave delicately up and down her chest. Her emerald-green eyes were softly scanning over him. He could almost taste the smell of her. It was sweet and mild as of rose soap and a bit musty from the rain. She had always smelled of rose soap, but this, mixed with the rain, was pure bliss. It was sending him straight into oblivion. His hunger growing stronger every second, he needed her in a way that was both passionate and cruel. He heard her whisper his name ever so sweetly; it was agony of the best kind. She called his name a little louder this time, singing straight to his groin. He was burning with passion. She repeated his name a third time, this time louder than the first two. He didn't move, just smiled in his sleep. *Damn*, she thought. He was dreaming. He was a deep sleeper only when he drank and didn't enjoy being rudely awakened.

She was well accustomed to his behavior no matter what state it arrived in. She needed to speak to him, and if she had any intentions of getting sleep herself, she had no choice but to wake him. She bent down and shook him gently. "Travis, wake up." He shifted to his side but did not wake. She looked at him briefly, longing to touch him. His black hair fell across his face when he turned. She wanted to brush it aside and kiss his cheek. She shook him again, this time a little harder. He groaned a little but was still sleeping soundly. She thought for a minute that there was no point; he wouldn't hear her out anyway. She stood up and started to back away, but the urge to touch him became much too great. She knelt back down. Her knees hurt a little against the hardwood floor. Her heart began to beat faster, and her breath quickened. She bent her head to his and brushed aside his hair. She ran her hand lovingly down the side of his face. He was always cold to touch; his skin was like a frozen river rock, smooth and hard. He moaned a little more. Her hand moved again to his hair, and she tangled her fingers into it. He was so handsome. Her heart was already breaking as she moved her lips to his. He would shatter her again when this was done, but she didn't care; he had done it many times before. That was just the way of it with him. Though this last time had, by far, been the worst, he had left her in tears, alone and weak. She pressed her lips to his cautiously. Those, too, were always cold. He tasted of whiskey and nothing more.

His eyes fluttered open, looking at her cloudily. It took him a moment to realize what she had done before he was fully awake, bolting upright so fast you would have thought it was a bee that had stung him instead of a simple kiss. He looked at her, dazed and confused for a short time before he found his voice to speak. Sleep muddled his words. "Rhea? What the... How did you... What are you..."

She loved how flustered he looked; it took some of the edge off his intensity. She sat there watching him search for any signs of what had just happened. He was so cute when he was confused, and it didn't happen very often. Rhea could not help giving him the smile he had longed for. Her eyes twinkled and danced like stars, her face soft and gentle. Still kneeling on the floor beside his bed, she dared not touch him again for fear she wouldn't be able to stop.

He slowly came to his senses and sat up. He sat taller than she did, therefore making it easier for her not to reach up and kiss him again. He stared at her with the utmost interest; he was unsure whether the kiss had been in dream or if she had really kissed him. He wanted so much to speak, but his voice had not found its way back awake entirely. He stared at her, blinking back sleep and the fog of whiskey. The one being who had ever shown him love was kneeling on the floor of a worn-out old inn, looking at him with eyes so sweet and understanding; her smile was making his heart ache. He wanted to know what was going on in that mind of hers.

Rhea could not take this scene any longer; the silence was making her even more uncomfortable than she already was. She had to say something. "Travis, I am sorry I woke you." Her eyelids closed and opened again slowly. He knew all anger had since seeped from her veins and she was back to being Rhea, the honest and pure; Rhea, the good and kind; Rhea, the healer and light bearer; Rhea, the beautiful and loyal; and Rhea, the keeper of the keys to his heart. Even now with so much hurt inside her, she sat there holding the keys that could unlock his entire soul.

"Travis, we need to talk. I can't sleep with this much animosity between us. I know you don't want to see me again, but please give me a chance to explain." Her words were simple, yet they were pleading with him at the same time. He could not bear it any longer; she had overpowered him and didn't even realize it. He was weak and falling to the bottom of an endless hill that was his love for her. Without a second thought or hesitation, he reached down and pulled her into his arms and pressed his lips to hers before she could protest. He pulled her in tighter and tighter until her breasts were smashed into his chest. His long fingers dug into her arms, chilling her slightly. Her pulse was beating in his ear, and it was causing his hunger to rise to its peak. He had not known desire like this for a very long time, and he was not sure he could stop it. He kissed her with all his might. It was hot and wild and hungry, yet passionate and gentle and longing.

She could not pull away for he held her too tight, but he was not hurting her. She fought his kiss until there was no use and finally could not fight the urge any longer. She was used to the frozen touch of his lips on her own. She melted into him and put her arms around his neck. He kept kissing her, all the while pulling her deeper and deeper into the spell that he had cast upon her so many years before. She was helpless in his embrace; anyone else would be shivering from the cold his body emitted, but for her, it was the best warmth she had ever known. He had shattered the last link of her strength, and she was his in that moment, whether he wanted it or not. The kiss seemed to last forever. He did not want to let go, for he would then have to face her, and he wasn't ready for that again. He held her in his arms, and that was all he needed. If he could just keep her there pressed against him, he might not have to feel the pain in his heart. He needed her there and now. If he were to have her, he knew words were in order. He somehow had to pull himself from her lips of silk and peel his chest from hers. If he didn't, all would be lost. He braced himself with all his might and pulled back from her. Her eyes had closed sometime during the kiss, and they flew open, her cinnamon lashes curling over her eyelids. Her mouth was parted slightly, and she gasped for breath. He could tell she was just as shocked by the abrupt stopping of the kiss as she was by the kiss itself.

She looked at him as if almost hurt that he had stopped what he had begun. He needed to bring her back to the here and now. "Rhea, I... I am sorry." It was all he could manage; she was so beautiful and enticing. She took a deep breath and pulled herself out of his arms. She sat beside him on the bed, hardly looking at him. She didn't want an apology, not now and not ever. For her, an apology was as bad as the things he had told her the night he left. Didn't he know by now that she would forgive him anything? She always had. This was no different. The moment had passed, and they were back to not knowing what to say to each other or how to say it without making the other angry. They sat in silence. The storm raged its war against the glass of the inn window.

Travis looked at her in hopes that she would meet his eye. He knew he had hurt her again for it was there in her eyes that looked at the ground. No matter what he did somehow, he always managed to cause her pain. "Rhea, I don't know what came over me. It has been a long time since I have had the urge to be with anyone, let alone you. I am sorry I should not have kissed you like that. You came in here to talk. Please look at me."

The words hit her hard. He still had all the power over her. She was weak around him, and now more than ever, she hated it. She slowly looked up at him; the room was dark except the candle she had brought in with her. His eyes flickered in the single flame when her eyes met his. She looked at those eyes for a second and then started to cry. She had let him get the best of her, and now her foolishness was causing her hurt that she had tried so hard to vanquish. No matter what he said or did, she would always have some love for him. Tears spilled down her cheeks, staining them red. She looked away and buried her face in her hands. How could she let him have this much effect on her? It had been so long, and she had moved on, hadn't she? She was confused and hurt.

He sat there watching her cry. It was the worst kind of agony. It was as if someone had just stabbed him in the stomach. Had he been mortal, the stab would have been fatal. He hated to see her like this but didn't know how to console her. The world was in a state of war against a powerful being, who aimed to wipe out all the goodness in the world, a being that had hidden in shadows for a century and was now making a grand entrance upon all mankind, a being which Travis belonged to till the end of time. Here in a deserted inn, the most beautiful woman he had ever known sat there in tears because of years and a broken heart. The war was his reason for telling her he had never wanted to see her again. He was afraid she would get hurt or worse. Now, alone with him in the darkness, she sat there not knowing anything of a horrible battle or the part in that battle in which he played. She was just woman who loved a man, and not just any man—him. She had loved him off and on for as long as he could remember.

He gently put his arm around her slender shoulders, trying for some way to comfort her. He held her like this for a few minutes that seemed like hours, and her sobs began to soften. Her hands finally fell from her face, and she moved closer to him. Her little body had always fit perfectly into his, as if made to be there like a piece of a puzzle. She let her head fall to his shoulder, and he wrapped his arm tighter around her, trying to make her feel safe. The storm was slowly starting to let up as if it were mirroring their moods. They sat there for a long time not saying anything or even moving, just being. They had not shared the same space for many months, and it had certainly not been this awkward. He couldn't help but move his hand from her arm to her hair. He loved her auburn curls, the way they smelled and the way, when they were wet, they could spring into perfectly tight coils. He loved the way she would curse them when it rained or when the wind blew. She very rarely wore them tied back. He loved how they felt gliding through his fingers. He let his fingers run all through the mass of curls as they sat there, just the two of them, while the world around them disappeared.

After a while, the rain outside was nothing more than a sooth-ing shower. The night was getting ready to turn into day. Rhea lifted her head and looked up into Travis's face. She had regained her composure and decided that this needed to be settled once and for all. With dawn approaching, her time was slipping away.

"Travis, there is a reason I came in here tonight. I am sorry I had to wake you, but it is a matter that needs to be settled between us." Her eyes were now blazing into his, and he tried to interrupt her, but she continued. "Travis, the last time I saw you, you single-handedly tore out my heart without so much as an explanation. I know time has always taken us in different directions, and I have come to expect that, but to have you tell me you never want to see me again and have you turn and walk away without even a glace backwards has hurt me more than words can ever say. I deserve an explanation." She stopped for a second to make sure her thoughts were in order before she went on. She was undeniably beautiful even if she was on the verge of being angry. "Travis, for as many years as I can remember, we have crossed paths along our individual journeys. In that, we have formed a bond of friendship, of trust, and of love. We have shared the same thoughts as well as the same bed." Taking her to bed was the only thing he could think of. "We have traveled many roads together and many apart. The loneliest one of all has been this last." He knew she was right; the last few months had been torture. "I will walk out of this room and never look back or give you a second thought if you tell me right now that is truly what you want in your heart. If not, then I ask for a reason for your unkind departure and a reason to make me stay." She sat back, watching his face for the slightest change, but there was none. He sat there staring at her, face as blank as it had been before she had begun to cry. He could see the wheels in her head turning. Her face stern but loving, she moved slightly away from his side, not wanting to be too close. If distance was what he sought, it would be easier to give it to him without touching him.

He thought long and hard about what to say to her. When he saw her move away, he thought for sure she was leaving and had to act quickly. Leaving was the last thing he had wanted. He formed his words carefully in his mind. "Rhea, I know I have hurt you beyond compare. I also know that the way I treated you was cruel and heartless. For that, I will never fully be able to apologize to you. I don't want you to go, nor have I ever wanted you to go. I cannot help the fact that you are my weakness. You are the only creature of good or evil that has the power to bring me to my knees." Rhea searched his eyes but still moved away. He hated that she kept moving farther and farther away from him as if he were a monster. It would be the death of him for sure if she felt that way, though he was a monster, only she had been able to look past it. He spoke again, this time looking into her eyes. "Rhea, you are right. Everything you say to me now is true. I acted like a coward and a fool. I gave you no reason for my behavior or for my harshness towards you. I only did I what felt I had to. There is so much I long to tell you yet I fear that only more pain would come of it. There is so much about me that you do not know, yet you sit there watching me, knowing me better than I know myself. All I have ever wanted was for you to be happy and safe. Now, because of me and the things I will tell you if you ask, I am afraid you may not be either happy or safe."

His eyes locked on hers; she could tell he was sincere. She needed to know what filled him with such worry and fear. He had often feared for her safety, but he had never feared for her happiness. Now they almost felt like the same thing. What burden was he carrying? She had to know. "Travis, please tell me what is weighing on your mind. You are so full of strange thoughts, and it is not like you."

"Rae, please don't go. I will tell you all there is to tell, but please don't go. These last few months without you have been more misery than I have ever known. No matter what I tell you, please promise you won't leave me."

She looked at him, seeing for the first time that night the man she had loved, the man who had won her over more times than she could count. For the first time in a long time, she saw the man he was and not the creature of darkness that he had become. "Travis," she touched his cheek with her hand, rubbing gently with her thumb, "I promise you I will not go. Maybe I can help you with your troubles. Just confide in me the way you once did. Tell me your secrets. Please, I must know."

He took her hand from his face and held it in his own. It was as warm as he remembered it being. He knew she would stay for as long as he needed her to and that she would listen to what he was going to tell her without judgment; that's the way she was. She would do her best to understand and offer advice where she could. In the end, while she would comfort him in a way no one else ever could, he would not be the man to hold her heart any longer and he would not be the man to offer her the happiness she deserved. That was the hardest revelation he had ever come to.

Chapter 2

The night had melted into day. The first rays of sunshine were making their way through the remaining clouds. There were birds somewhere singing a morning song in the distance. Rhea swept around the room, creating an artificial night for Travis. He lay on the bed, watching her create darkness for him so that he could tell her everything. He could be out in the daylight, but it made him a little woozy, so he preferred the night. He loved that she never complained about the dark or that he was at his best at night, though he knew very well she was a creature of light. The room was, in an instant, completely dark. She looked around, making sure no light could seep in anywhere. Satisfied with her work, she decided to go and get breakfast. It was easier for her to handle the weight of the world on a full stomach. She walked to the door. "Travis, I am going to get us some breakfast. When I return, I will be ready to hear your troubles." With that, she flew out the door and made her way down the stairs of the inn. Travis sat there thinking long and hard about how he was going to tell her what was causing him such distress. He didn't even know where to start. He couldn't just begin by saying, "I am a soldier in war, and not just any solider, but second-in-command." His mind was racing again, but he knew she would not let him out of this. He had to tell her. He knew he was going to lose her forever when all this was said and done, and that scared him more than anything any other vampire could ever do to him. If he were to be lost, he was glad it was to her. Their time together had given him so much hope.

She was back faster than he had anticipated, carrying two plates of eggs and some form of smoked meat he assumed to be ham. The food smelled good, and he was hungry; he just wasn't sure his stomach would allow him to eat. Unlike most vampires, Travis still liked the occasional human meal that was not of blood. He tried to maintain some sense of humanity even if it were in small fractured shards. Anytime he was with Rhea, he made sure his desire for blood was tucked away. She had offered him the chance once to drink from her, but he would not allow himself to do so. He knew that he if he tasted her blood, he would not be able to stop. He could not change her into what he was, not without destroying her very radiance, no matter how much she tried to convince him otherwise.

She was smiling this morning, and that seemed to ease his anguish a little. She had managed to go to her own room and change into a new dress. This one was of sapphire-blue velvet with a black ribbon around the waist. She had a matching ribbon tied around the end of one long thick braid that fell down her back. She had on black riding boots and looked like a queen. She set the plate of food down on the bed for him and sat in the chair where he had thrown his cloak the night before. He sat up and took his plate of food. They ate in silence. He finished his plate before she did, and he needed something to busy himself, so he set to work building a small fire in the brick hearth. He kept his back to her while he worked. He did not want her seeing his anxiety before he was ready to share it. When the fire was lit, he turned to face her. She had finished her breakfast and had set the plates aside. She was curled up in the chair, with her legs tucked up underneath her. Her braid was draped over her shoulder, and her hands rested across the arm of the chair and into her lap. She had the urge to toy with her braid, but fidgeting was only her coping mechanism when she was nervous or bored. She was trying to refrain from showing her nervousness. She looked as if she could stay there for hours. He knew that if this were a different time and place, she would have a book in her hands and be buried in the words of someone else instead of his own. He returned to the bed and sat facing her; he took a long breath to calm himself.

She smiled at him. "Take your time. There is no hurry. Just relax. You and I have shared many secrets as well as hardships. Have faith and trust in me." Her words were exactly what he needed; he knew he would get through this.

With one more breath, he closed his eyes and then opened them. He looked into her eyes and began to tell her his burdens. "Rhea, you know what I am, and you know what I am capable of, yet knowing this, you have never turned away from me. You have stayed by me no matter what, and now I hope that when I am done telling you all I have to say, this will still be the case." She didn't move or make a sound; she just sat watching him.

"The reason that I told you, the last time we saw each other, that I never wanted to see you again was because I couldn't bear the thought of you being in danger. I have always been weak when it comes to you. You have always brought me to my knees on many occasions, and I was afraid, if you knew what I was doing, that you would want to help, and in that I would be weak and would not be able to complete my mission. Rhea, there is no easy way to tell you any of this, so forgive me for being blunt. The world is at war." She looked at him with very loving and knowing eyes. This information did not seem to be new to her. But she did not speak, so he went on. "I am a part of this war. You see, I am in legions with the great vampire Jeremy. He has become king to all vampires willing to follow him, including myself. With that, he has declared war on humanity and is now prepared to come out of hiding to try and conquer the world."

At this, Rhea's face changed drastically. She went from understanding and loving to concerned and confused. "Why would you want to follow someone so dark and evil? You yourself have said, many times, that you would never follow suit with the other vampires. You have told me all these years that you didn't want to be like them. Now you join forces with them as they make their mark on the world. Is this about power?"

Her eyes glistened with tears. He had to finish just to keep her from crying. He had had enough of that earlier, and it stung that she thought this was about him obtaining power. "Rhea, please understand I am not doing this to be like the others or for the sake of power. Believe me, it has been offered in abundance. I am doing this to try and save the world as we know it. Jeremy trusts me and listens to me. He takes my advice, and in that, I can convince him that this war is wrong. He came to me about a month before I told you good-bye. He wanted my council and my services. He told me of a great war that he was planning against all mankind and how he was going to burn it down in a tirade of flames. He was creating armies of loyal vampires for the cause. These vampires are willing to die for him if that's what it takes. He told me he is tired of lurking in the shadows and he is tired of hiding away in *hell*. He said he wants the world to know his name and cry it out with their last breaths. He came to me because of my connection with the mortals. He knew that I inter-acted with them as if I had never changed. You, too, know this of me. You have known me when I was still a mortal man as well as after I became a vampire. When Jeremy came to me, I refused his offer. I did not want any part of a war, especially one against all mankind. He promised me power and wealth beyond my wildest dreams, yet I turned him down. For days he would send one of his men to ask me to join him, for days I told him, "No." I was not going to sink to the level of monsters. All the time I was thinking there had to be a way to stop him. Then it came to me—the way to stop Jeremy and his war was by joining forces with him. I was getting in on the ground level, learning his plans and his movements, watching, and listening to all that was said. Every being, mortal or not, has a weakness. All I must do is find his, and I can do that by being his right-hand man. He has made me second-in-command. He has given me power to control his army when he is not there. They trust me, as does he, and they will follow my commands. You see, Rhea, this is a matter of life and death to all involved, including you. If I join him, I can stop this battle and save lives in doing so." The weight was lifting from his shoulders with each word he spoke. He was feeling more at ease now having told someone what he was really trying to do.

Rhea sat there not sure of what to say. Surely, he realized how dangerous this mission was to undertake, especially doing it alone. She could not bear the thought of him dying for a cause that was too great for any one man to accomplish. The thought of him taking on the entire vampire world, and their monstrous king, scared her, and it hurt her to breathe. Her breath was shallow. How was she going to talk him out of this one? Without knowing it, she blinked her eyes, and a single tear fell down her cheek. The man she had loved, for one reason or another, had just told her he was going to go head-to-head with the most powerful vampire in a century. She had already known of a war on the world. It was her job to know about things like that, and she had heard whisperings for a while now. But the war she was most concerned with was the one Travis was fighting alone.

Travis saw her change expressions and saw the tear roll gently down her face. He knew she did not understand, and he felt he needed to continue so that she would. "Rae, don't you know this is my chance to do something great? I have wanted a chance like this all my life, and here it is. I get to be the savior of mankind and all that is good. That includes you."

Her thoughts were racing wildly around in her head. She didn't know what to say or do. She looked at Travis, and for a moment, she did not see the vampire he had become but the boy she had first met many years before. He was young and attractive. He was full of life and all things that went into being a boy in adolescents. At sixteen, the world was his plaything, and now as a vampire, trapped in immortality at twenty-five, the world was now his quest. She looked at him, trying again to find the boy and the man she had once known over many years. All she could see now was a vampire unlike any other with a purpose to save the world. He looked older than he should have. Though it killed her deep inside, she could see his death. She knew in that moment that this war would be the end of the man who had shared so much of her journey, the man who, on many occasions, had earned her love. How could she make him understand this? It had been her job to protect him, and now, she saw there was nothing she could do to save him from his fate. Nothing had ever hurt her more, not even having him tell her he never wanted to see her again. That would be more bearable than knowing he was not going to make it out of this battle. She could feel her eyes welling up again; she did not want to cry. She couldn't let herself enter that state of mind. But, maybe, there was something she could do. But what? There had to be something. She had to speak before her thoughts consumed her.

"Travis, I understand what you are telling me. I have known of this war for some time. It is part of being a light bearer and part of having a connection to you. I have known that Jeremy is creating armies, preparing them for battle, and preparing to march out of the darkness and into the eyes of the world. What I am having a hard time understanding is why you feel it is your job alone to try and stop him?" She paused, fighting back her tears. "Travis, why do you have to do this? Please tell me."

"Rhea…" Trying to make her comprehend this was going to take great care, but when he spoke, he realized he could never make her understand. "Rhea, I know I can never make you understand why I must do this. All I can ask is that you stand by me no matter what." He looked at her longingly, praying that she would not desert him. He needed her to be on his side more than he had known.

She met his eyes with her own; they were full of hope. She could not turn away from him now, not even if she wanted. She looked into his eyes and saw his heart, and without words, she understood why he had to do this. It was because of her. His love for her was so strong he felt he had to save the world to prove it. There was nothing she could say to him to change his mind. All she could do was stand by his side and pray to every goddess and god that he did not fail. She reached out her hand for his; he gave it willingly. She bent down and brushed her lips to his knuckles, sweetly kissing his hand. With this simple gesture, he knew she understood and that she would be there till the end. Matters of the heart are often best explained without words.

"Travis," her voice was nothing more than a whisper, "your mission is dangerous. I don't think I need to tell you that. You are entering uncharted waters, and you need to tread lightly. As your guardian, I will do all in my power to protect you and guide you. I will surround you in light, and my wings will embrace you. If I am not able to keep you safe, I will send someone who can. When facing Jeremy, you must always remember to think first and fight second, for if you fight first, you will lose. Remember above all else, you are not alone. I will fight with you, though you did not ask me to."

Travis looked at her with admiration. "Rhea, I cannot allow you to fight this battle with me. It is not yours to fight."

"It is mine because you are fighting for everything I stand for, it is mine because I make it mine, and it is mine because I am bound to you not only to be your protector but as your friend and onetime lover. Therefore, I fight for lovers everywhere, and that in itself makes this my battle. I know you would not have me be any part of this, but it is too late for that. You see, when you made your alliance with Jeremy, you, without knowing, dragged me into this. So now I step forward, willingly, and fight beside you."

There was no changing her mind; she was as strong-willed and determined as he was. He knew she was right the moment he gave his word to Jeremy that had pulled her into this. She was bound by contract to protect him, and nothing he did would ever change that. The goddess Ariadne had pulled Rhea into her service to guard and protect. It is why her heart always got in the way. So, they would fight side by side till the end. He leaned forward, put his free hand around her shoulders, and pulled her into him, keeping his eyes on hers. He pressed his lips to hers; the kiss was full of passion, and so it was with a simple exchange of love that this battle would not be fought alone. It was in that moment he knew this might be one of the very last times he ever kissed her. He also knew with everything that he would die saving her, fighting for her so that she could live and love.

Chapter 3

Travis needed sleep, and so Rhea picked up the breakfast dishes and went downstairs. The inn was alive with people for being midmorning. Rhea loved people and loved watching them. To her, humans were fascinating. She decided that she would go get her book and read for a bit while she enjoyed the many people of the inn. She set the dishes down on the end of the counter and made her way back upstairs. Her room was larger than Travis's, holding more furniture, including a writing desk and chest of drawers. The room smelled of mesquite. The fragrance was mixed with the smell of rain, but not overpowering. Rhea thought to herself, as she moved around the room, that if they intended to stay in the inn for a spell, she would have to convince Travis that her room was far more suitable than his. He would put up a little fight, saying that his room was smaller and therefore cozier, but in the end, he would give into her reason. She couldn't help but smile as she played the scene out in her mind. He always had loved giving her a hard time in arguments, but in the end, she was usually right and that inside she would always gloat slightly. She grabbed her book out of her satchel and gave herself a quick glance in the mirror and decided to untie her braid, her mass of curls falling around her shoulders. She was pleased with her reflection and turned to leave her room, closing and locking the door behind her. Though she was a bit on the flighty side, she never was too careful when traveling, especially alone.

At the bottom of the stairs, she surveyed the room for the perfect place to read but still have a view of most of the room. She chose a table close to the fire, sitting with her back to it, so she could see almost the entire dining area. People were chatting away among themselves. Some gave Rhea a friendly nod or greeted her with a smile. She sat and watched for a while, but before opening her book, Rhea heard the innocent sound of a child crying. She looked around and saw a woman holding a baby sitting at a table. At her feet, a child no more than four was crying and, holding his sides, doubled over in pain. Rhea watched as the young mother tried to soothe her son. The baby in her arms was swaddled. She was trying to sway the babe while consoling her other child. She looked tired and worn. Rhea set the book down on her chair and made her way over to the young family.

The mother looked up as Rhea approached. Rhea smiled at the mother, and she eased in an instant. "It must be hard to have such little tikes," Rhea said, easily not wanting to startle the poor girl. She rested her hand lovingly on the woman's shoulder. She had straggly long blond hair and soft pale skin. She was still carrying a little extra weight from the baby. Her clothes were simple with no hint of luxury. She was lovely and looked at Rhea with specks of hope through sleepless gray eyes. She could not have been more than twenty-two. "My dear, you must be exhausted. Your husband is out hunting, and you are left alone with the littles." The girl nodded. Rhea continued, "My name is Rhea. I live in a small village not far from here."

The girl nodded again and, this time, spoke in return. "My name is Sarah. I do travel with my husband. He has been gone for several days. The baby is still new and still nursing. The boy has been doubled over in pain for the last two days, and I don't know what to do."

Rhea smiled again. "I am sorry to hear that your son is not well. Would you mind if I had a look at him?"

Sarah shook her head. "His name is John."

Rhea nodded and looked down at the little boy who had not bothered to see whom his mother was talking to. He was dressed in his bedclothes, a white cotton shirt that was dingy from wear. His hair was a mess of blond like his mother's. He had a face round with cheeks meant for pinching, a little button nose in the middle of his face, and eyes the color of wheatgrass in the fall. Rhea would venture to say they were his father's eyes. He was cute and floppy, just as a little four-year-old boy should be. "John?" She allowed the sweet, motherly voice to come out. He still clutched his sides but looked up at the new voice that was not his mother's. "John, my name is Rhea. Would it be okay if I looked at your ouchies?"

He looked at her, cross-eyed and skeptical for a moment. Then, because the brain of a four-year-old can only hold so much, he lifted his arms up for her to pick him up. She sat down on the floor beside him and scooped him into her lap. Sarah watched as this stranger interacted with her son. There seemed to be no real danger, so she let Rhea proceed. John wiggled in her lap. Rhea could feel the heat coming from the boy's side. The energy flowed into Rhea's hands. She let the power of the goddess guide her to where the infection was and rested her hands gently on his sides. John tugged at the coils of her hair, pulling them straight and then letting them go so they sprang back up into curls. He found this really amusing and giggled each time. She cuddled him in lovingly and let her healing powers pull the toxins from his tiny, little body. Her hands were on fire, but she let the magic flow. John calmed down and stopped pulling her hair. He snuggled into Rhea's arms, and before long, he was asleep. Sarah watched this curiously. Rhea looked at her. So young and innocent to the ways of the world.

"Are you magic?" she asked as if this were something out of a story.

Rhea smiled at her. "Sarah, I am a healer. I have gifts given by the goddess Ariadne. I am a light bearer. I can sense pain in others, and I work to remove the pain and allow for healing energy to replace it. John has an infection in his stomach. I am just trying to pull out the infection and make him feel better." Sarah nodded. She shifted the baby to the other arm and didn't question Rhea anymore.

Rhea sat there holding the tiny, little cub. Oddly enough, in all her travels and all her adventures, she never saw herself settling down and raising a family. She loved kids, they filled her with pure and innocent joy, she liked when children were present, she liked the way they viewed the world. There was always a sense of imagination and wonder in the eyes of children. Rhea continued to let the healing powers course through her hands; John rested in her lap. At the other end of the tavern, a man watched this scene. He had followed her for days. He would bide his time.

After about thirty minutes, Rhea felt the infection finally lift, and his little body stirred. He looked up at her with sweet baby eyes. "Are you a fairy?"

Rhea could not suppress the giggle that bubbled in her chest. She scooped John up and brought him up so his nose touched hers; she nuzzled it playfully. And he laughed. "No, John, I am not a fairy, but I do know they hide in the flowers in gardens of this very land."

His eyes lit up, and he looked at Sarah. "Mama, can we go find a fairy?"

Sarah smiled to see her son's health revived. "Mistress Rhea, I am grateful for your services. John looks as if he were never ill." She dropped her head quickly and looked full of remorse.

"Sarah, my dear girl, why do you look so glum? Your baby is in good health, and John will be good as new before day's end. Have I offended you in some way?"

Sarah shook her head; straws of blond fell into her face, and she started to cry. Rhea didn't understand.

"Sarah, I do apologize for any grievances I may have caused. I was only trying to help."

Sarah looked up, tearstained cheeks and rosy nose. She sniffled. "Mistress Rhea, I have no means by which to pay for your services." She dropped her head and started to cry again. John squirmed in her lap, and Rhea set him down.

She knelt in front of Sarah. "Sweet Sarah, my gifts do not come with a price. They come from a place of service to the goddess and from my heart. It was my pleasure to help your family." She lifted the delicate chin of the young mother and smiled kindly. "You owe me nothing."

Sarah looked at Rhea. "Such kindness, my lady. Thank you. I will find a way to repay you, somehow. Of this you can be sure."

Rhea left the matter alone. "Come, let us go outside and see if we can spot a fairy." She offered John her hand, and he took it, pulling her toward the door. Sarah got up and followed them.

The air was fresh, with puddles left over from the night before. They all wandered the grounds of the tavern. John was bobbing up, to, and fro, touching everything he could reach. Sarah's cheeks brightened in the sunlight. Rhea enjoyed her time with the family. It was nice to be even, for a moment, away from the inn and Travis. Rhea knew that last night and this morning was just the surface of what was to come for her and Travis. Rhea spotted an iridescent butterfly floating past and landing on a bush. Its delicate gossamer wings twitched as it rested. Rhea grabbed John's hand. "John, I think I see a fairy," she whispered so John would not get overly excited and scare off the butterfly. They inched closer to the plant. John saw the butterfly and squealed with glee in excitement. "Shhh, don't scare it away." They got a little closer. As if the butterfly knew what was going on, it spread its wings and lifted off in flight and gently landed on John's tiny hand. He beamed from ear to ear and tried to hold as still as he could but was trembling with joy. Rhea bent beside the little boy. "You have magic powers, John. Fairies only show themselves to those who have magic."

"You have magic too, right?"

"Yes, I have magic too." She smiled.

Sarah touched her arm. "Thank you, Mistress Rhea, for everything. You are an angel."

"Sarah, don't ever let John lose his belief in fairies and magic. Encourage him always to believe in things magical and mysterious. He is a very special little boy and has a gift for seeing things for more than what they are. I think he gets that from you." With that she turned, heading back toward the inn, leaving the lingering traces of whimsical fancy behind her.

Rhea returned to her table and her book. There was still a lot of day left. She felt satisfied with the work she had done. A little boy's health returned, and he found a fairy. All was right in the world of a four-year-old. As for her, all would be right in her world someday. She sighed and curled up in her chair. Rhea loved to read, almost more than anything else, especially the great works of Shakespeare. He could hold her entranced for hours and hours. At times, she felt as if she knew him and he knew her like they were old friends. She always traveled with a book, and on this trip, her companion was *Othello*. She had not yet read this tragic play. Opening to the first page was like opening a beautifully wrapped Christmas package, adored by a child, the contents inside a wonder and awe.

Before long, Rhea was enthralled by act 1. The crowd around her drifted into the background. The noise was pleasant for her as she read, not so loud where she couldn't concentrate, but not so quiet where she was in silence. Rhea hated silence; it drove her mad and made her extremely restless. In silence, her mind was louder than she cared for, and it was truly a terrifying place to be. The people of the inn moved around, never troubling her and carrying on with their own affairs. Hours passed by, and she fell deeper and deeper into the story of Othello.

It was the beginning of the third act when Rhea happened to glance up from her pages to find a curiously good-looking man sitting across from her. He sat there at her table, staring at her. He had not asked to sit down, nor had he made any sound in doing so. He had not moved or cleared his throat to get her attention but sat there fixated on her and her book. She couldn't help feeling a little apprehensive. She traveled alone, and times were rather dark; this stranger could be anyone. Rhea set her book down and gathered her courage. She looked at him as pleasantly as she could, though she was rather annoyed with him for being so rude. "May I help you, sir?" Her words were strong and confident, and she felt better that they had not come out in a squeak. She studied him carefully; he was handsome, but not in the striking way as Travis. His hair was short, the color wheat in sunlight. His eyes were blue, but not the clear color of frozen water as Travis's were, but more like the sky on a warm spring day. His features were strong but gentle.

He did nothing during this inspection as he was surveying her in just the same fashion. He could see that her beauty was beyond compare; long flowing curls of red and brown combined to be the perfect shade of auburn, reminding him very much of fresh-cut cedar. Her eyes were the color of pine trees, and her face was soft and feminine. Their eyes met momentarily before she blinked away. He could see she was going to be hard to resist and even harder to convince that he was sent to save her. He could tell she was used to doing things her way and on her terms. She wasn't going to like it when her way had to include him, but he liked a challenge, and he'd be damned if he let some stubborn female get in his way of the job he had been given, even if she was as beautiful as the setting sun.

"Are you the lady they call Rhea?" She looked at him, both curious and concerned, but it didn't faze him. He asked her again, this time with a more domineering tone. "Are you the lady they call Rhea?"

Bold and confident, she replied, "I am Rhea, lady of light and protector of life. I am only Rae to my friends, and since, good sir, you have not properly introduced yourself and have quite rudely sat down without an invitation, you will be so kind as to address me henceforth as Rhea."

His eyes widened, and a look of shock spread across his face. He had watched the interaction with Rhea and the little boy and saw her sweet, kind, and loving. He had been expecting a lot of things, but *feisty* was not one of them. He was in no mood for feisty; he had been following her for days in unspeakable weather. He was not one to argue with a lady, but this woman was already becoming a pain in his ass. "Listen, lady, I don't really care what I can and cannot call you. I have been following you for days. The storm you dragged me through last night nearly made my horse go lame. If you are the lady they call Rhea, then I am here to discuss some business with you. If you be not the lady Rhea, then go back to your book and forgive my intrusion."

Rhea was taken aback. Was it not he who sat down at her table and he who had interrupted what was turning out to be a wonderful reading session? And now he had the right to make demands? Not if she had anything to say about it. "Sir, forgive me, but are you always this rude when talking to ladies? I have done nothing to offend you, and you would be good to remember such things, and in the future, it is customary for a gentleman to announce himself before he sits down at a table occupied by a woman. I am the lady they call Rhea, and frankly, whatever business you have with me is now concluded. You will be so kind as to remove yourself so I may get back to my book. Good day."

Blake was used to being told off and put in his place. It had happened to him many a time, but never by a woman. He had a new respect for her. She was not the meek counterpart to his masculinity like most women. She was strong and not afraid to speak her mind. He liked that in a woman. She was going to be a challenge, and if she kept this up, it would be impossible for him to resist her. Her eyes were burning holes into him; he could feel it. The pine-tree-green color of them was intensifying to a dark shade of jade. He liked her eyes this hew of green but did not like the cause of it. He knew he had to calm her down or it would be back to trailing her again, and he was not quite ready for that. He hated not getting the last word; he had to stuff his pride in his pocket or this woman's scorn would have him traipsing across God knows where.

"Lady Rhea, forgive me. You are right, I have been very rude. My journeys have been long and tiresome. Please allow me to get drink and food and sit with you awhile and discuss what it is I have been sent to discuss with you. Will you join me in a late lunch?"

Rhea looked at him. He seemed sincere in his apologies, though she was still a little annoyed, but he obviously had something on his mind that required her attention. Therefore, it would be equally as rude of her not to allow him to speak his mind. Maybe someone needed healing; on top of that, she was getting hungry. It had been hours since she and Travis had breakfast. She would find out who this man was and what he wanted with her during a peaceful meal. In the end, she really had nothing to lose. Besides, he was rather nice to look at; she couldn't help but smile at the thought of this. She was a sucker for handsome men. She found the company of most women hard to keep, but men, she could relate to.

"Sir, I would very much like to join you for a late lunch as I have not eaten since early this morning, but first, I do not share meals with men whose name I do not know." She smiled again, and he returned the smile. She was even more beautiful when she smiled. She was a strong, independent woman; that much he knew for sure. She also seemed to have a good sense of humor, and he liked a light-hearted woman.

He reached out his right hand to her in a gesture of greeting. "I am Blake Larson from the Glenn of Elden Springs, and you are?"

Rhea laughed. Good-looking and charming—that was nothing but trouble. She took his hand and shook it. "I am Rhea Edwards, lady of light, healer, and friend to faeries. I am from Hearts Prairie, which is not very far from your Glenn, as I am sure you know. My friends call me Rae. I am pleased to meet you, Blake Larson."

"Well, Ms. Rhea, my friends call me Bull. What can I get you for lunch this afternoon?"

She laughed again. She would not be calling him Bull; that just didn't roll off the tongue nearly as nicely as Blake. "Surprise me, I am not picky."

He nodded his head in a slight bow and stood up. He turned and walked to the old innkeeper. Rhea watched him go. He was nicely built, about the same height as Travis, but had a more powerful frame. He looked like he could easily put his hands around her waist and still have room to spare. He wore plain trousers and tunic the color of mud, but his riding cloak and boots suggested an air of wealth. The cloak was colored dark blue with strange red-and-gold embroidery along the edges. His boots were brown leather and worn high over his pants. His arms had muscle and a lot of it. She could see his biceps stretch the simple cloth of his tunic. She hated herself when the thought of him running his hands up her body entered her mind. Travis was asleep upstairs, and no, they had not been lovers for a long time, though she still felt a pang of guilt. She was picturing another man's hands upon her. How could she let a perfect stranger cross her mind in such a way? What would Travis say? She knew that her and Travis's time was long since over, but to love someone for as many years as she had loved him leaves one feeling selfish when someone else might come along. She knew the time had come for her to move on. She had tried many times to convince herself that she had. Maybe this new stranger was here to help her move beyond the remnants of teenage fantasies and delusions; maybe he wasn't. Only time would tell. She knew Travis had never been faithful to her, not for one minute, but he was familiar and comfortable. Dark and light were never meant to last though, and she knew that.

She watched Blake from across the room. He was here on business, and that's the way she would keep it. She didn't have time to entangle herself with anyone right now. She had a vampire army to contend with. Still there was no harm in looking at another man; she was a woman after all, and looking was just part of human nature. Blake returned carrying two glasses of what looked like mead. Rhea loved a glass of mead in the afternoon.

"The innkeeper said he would have our food out to us shortly." He set the goblets down and slid onto the bench, once again facing her. "I hope you like mead?"

She smiled. "It just so happens that I love mead, especially in the late afternoon." She lifted her glass. "Cheers." She raised her glass to her lips and sipped her wine. He couldn't help being enticed by this. Her lips were rose pink and full. The mead moistened them ever so delicately. This was going to be one hell of mission to keep his mind on, being as she was very alluring, but business came first. He watched her sip the wine seductively one last time before he spoke. "Rhea, while we are waiting for our lunch, maybe we should discuss why I have been following you these past few days and what matter of urgency my business is with you." She set her glass down gently and looked up at him. Her long lashes fluttered over her eyes as she blinked. Her expression was warm and tender as if nothing he was about to tell her would faze her. This was very arousing for him. He had only known her a short time, and already he knew he had never met another woman who even remotely came close to her. She was unique and something of a mystery, and he liked that.

"I think that is a great idea," she said with a smile. Getting down to business would keep her from being distracted by his good looks. "Please tell me what could possibly use so much of my attention that made you follow me for days. I am very curious." She folded her hands in front of her on the table and leaned back against the stone wall of the little inn.

"Rhea, I do not expect any of this to make sense to you as it barely makes sense to me. I have been sent here on a mission to protect you." Her face changed at this, her eyes widened, and a small hint of mocking crossed over her lush lips. She could not help a chuckle, which she smothered by pursing her lips together. He was not very pleased with this sort of reaction. "Rae, please, this is not a laughing matter."

She could see the distress written all over his face. "Blake, I do not mean to laugh. It is just rather amusing to me that someone has been sent to the one sworn to protect those whom she encounters. That is my gift and my curse, and I bear them well. Please, maybe you had better give me a bit more information about this mission of yours, including the one who sent you."

Her face was serious now. He really did not care for the serious side of her. She was much more enchanting when smiling and happy. "Rhea, I told you, none of this makes sense to me either. This is the first time anything like this has ever happened to me, so I was not sure how to handle it—"

She cut him off before he could go on. "This is the first time what has happened to you? What are you talking about?"

"I… I, well, I am not sure how to explain it."

"Well, I suggest you try." She was starting to feel a little uncomfortable with this handsome stranger. People came into her life often for one reason or another that was part of her gift to help those in need or find their course. But this man was claiming that he had been sent to her to do the one thing she did best: give protection.

Blake shifted in his seat. He, too, was getting uncomfortable. "Rhea, I don't even know where to start. I was in my shop one day pounding out some shoes for a man's horse when I fainted. I am not sure if it was the heat from the fire or from lack of water that day, but I fainted." He stopped to check that he had her full attention. He was not one for nonsense or whimsy, and he was about to tell her about a vision or at least the only logical explanation he could come up with to describe what had happened. He could tell by her body language, and the intensity of her eyes, he had her undivided attention. "While I was out, I had a very real but very strange dream, a dream of war and evil and of all things good and of well…you."

Rhea understood what had happened to him even if he had not. Visions were a thing of great power and a force not to be reckoned with. They spoke of things to come or things that could come to pass. She herself had had many, and they had set her on many a similar quest. "Blake, I think I understand what you are trying to tell me. I need to know every detail of this 'dream.'"

Blake looked at her as though he could not begin to comprehend how she could know what he was talking about, but he went on hoping she really did know what he was trying to get across. "When I saw you in my dream, you were standing in an open space surrounded by blood. You were crying, and there was this brilliant light all around you. I didn't understand, but then I heard a voice telling me that you were most precious to the world and to this war and that, no matter what, I was to keep you as safe as I possibly could. I asked how I was supposed to do this, and the voice told me that I would just know. When you needed me the most, my inner powers would take hold and I would know how to keep you out of harm's way. The voice said I was to find you and tell you of my quest, so I asked around about you in local markets and pubs. You are a very well-known woman, Rhea of Hearts Prairie. It was not hard to track you down."

Rhea nodded her head, in full understanding. "Blake, did the voice ever once tell you who he was?" Of course, the voice had told him who he was; he was an intelligent man and knew it would be best to know who was giving him such random instructions.

"I asked him his name, and at first he didn't want to tell me." She was very intrigued by this. "I kept asking him who he was, and finally he said, 'My name is Clinton, and I am friend and guide to the lady Rhea.' He then said that the mention of his name would really help clear things up for you." He looked at her; her face and eyes were rather sad as if she might cry. She nodded again and looked away from him. She was biting her bottom lip and looking into the crowd of the inn as if someone she knew were there.

Several moments went by before she looked back at him, still sad, but this time, she spoke. Her voice was soft and almost small, like she was saying a prayer into the wind. "Blake, are you very certain that the voice talking to you said his name was Clinton?"

If Clinton truly had sent this man to her aid, this war was going to be worse than she thought, and Clinton always had her best interest in mind and at heart. Blake took a long, slow drink of his mead. The innkeeper was approaching the table with their food. Blake could see him out of the corner of his eye. She, too, saw him coming, for she quickly put on a smile as the innkeeper came closer. The old man seemed to enjoy his meetings with her, for he was warm and pleasant when he set down the plates. "Will there be anything else this afternoon?"

"Yes, sir, if you please, we would like a bottle of this sinful mead."

He bowed and backed away. "Yes, milady."

When he was out of earshot, she spoke again, still soft. "Mr. Larson, I need you to be 100 percent sure the voice you heard was named Clinton."

He looked at her. Did she truly know this Clinton fellow, and why hadn't he gone to her first? None of this seemed to matter now. "Lady Rhea, I am a man of virtue and honesty. I would not lie to you about this or any other matter. Clinton was the name he gave to me in this 'dream,' as I believe you called it."

Rhea's heart fell to her stomach; Clinton would not send a man to her aid, or anyone to her aid for that matter, unless he foresaw that she was in the gravest of danger. He must have known that she would give her life to stand by Travis and fight for what she knew to be good and just in her soul. This man sitting in front of her was the man her great friend, guide, and once companion had sent to be her guard. She didn't like the thought of having to be rescued even if she trusted Clinton more than anyone else in this realm or any other. Her face was sad, and her eyes had the look of reminiscing. Clinton would not lead a man into battle unless he knew the outcome was in her best interest. She wondered if Blake truly realized what kind of quest he was on and wondered if he knew that his own life was now at risk. She looked at him. He seemed like a good man, well-tempered, and hardworking. The question, however, was he willing to die trying to save her? A woman he had barely met whose heart belonged to the goddess and who shared the secrets of now the most second powerful vampire in the world, a woman who believed in all things good and pure but had loved a man of evil. None of this needed to be discussed with him at this moment in time. She saw Travis coming toward them. Had the sun set already? Travis had his hair tied back in leather, as black as his clothing. Rhea could remember very few times that he wore anything but black. He approached the table, studying her companion. Blake looked up and saw Travis standing over him. Rhea knew she needed to be the one to speak first or there could be trouble. The goddess had blessed her with many gifts, but handling the ego of a male was not always easy.

"Good evening, Travis. Did you rest well?" She smiled at him as he looked away from Blake and focused on her. She knew he could not resist her smile. She knew she was not his nor he hers, but Travis was a jealous man just the same.

"Won't you join us, sweets?"

Sweets? thought Blake. *Were she and this dark man a couple?* He could not understand why a man of no consequence to him would appear to him in a vision and tell him to protect a woman who, first off, didn't seem to need protecting and, second, who already had a male escort. There must be more to this woman than met the eye.

Travis sat down next to Rhea, turning his glare back to Blake, staring holes through every ounce of him. It made Blake uncomfortable, like being at a funeral. The old barkeep had appeared with another bottle of mead. Travis said to him, without moving his eyes from Blake, "We will need whiskey as well."

Rhea interrupted him quickly, "The mead will be all for now, good sir. Please just put it on my tab." She looked at the old man sternly but pleadingly. The old man nodded once again, left for his counter. "Travis, I don't feel whiskey is going to do us much good tonight. We have things to discuss and not a lot of time to do so. Also, this here is Mr. Larson, he will be joining us from here out." Her tone was challenging yet final. She knew he would fight back. She had taken away his whiskey and told him that another man would be joining them. He was not going to be pleased, and she was well ready for the fight. His smoldering stare gave Blake one last pierce and then rounded on her. His eyes were fierce, but not like they were when she had entered the inn the night before. She knew it was going to be a good go-round and was full ready to take him on.

"Rhea, I do not think this is the best time to tell me what is going to be going on this evening. I will have my whiskey, and this man, Mr. Larson, will not be joining us. We leave tonight, and that is that." She could feel his body go rigid beside her. He hated being told what to do.

"Travis, if I am to accompany you on this journey as I have agreed, you will be doing it sober. I had enough of you and your whiskey last night to last me a very long time. I need you to be focused and clearheaded, not drugged up by a substance that does nothing for you except drown out the hunger that drives you. As for Mr. Larson, Blake, I mean, it is not up for discussion or debate whether he comes with us or not. He is here on a mission, and that mission includes me. I will keep watch over him, and he will be in my command. He will be no trouble to you." Her eyes were focused on his, and there was an air that said this is final to them. She was not going to budge.

"Damn it, Rhea this is not a game. We have work to do. I have no patience for your demands." He waved his hand to the old barkeep, but Rhea grabbed it down. Blake sat there watching this power struggle between the two of them, but he was not sure who would win out. It was best not to interfere, even if he wanted to tell her that he was in no one's command.

Rhea held tight to Travis's arm and stared at him, her eyes with fire in them. He stared back with the same flames in his eyes. "Travis, I am in no mood for this. We have work to do, and there is no time for us to be arguing over minor, little things." Travis looked at her like he wanted to lash out at her. Part of her wished he would. He had her recourse coming to him after the way he had treated her last August. She smiled at him coyly and eased up on his arm. "Travis, please, we can do this on the road if you really want to get into this deeper." Her voice was calm and cool, but still very much in charge.

He pulled away from her and hissed out a long breath. "Fine, we will finish this later. As for you," he looked at Blake, "I don't know your mission, nor do I care, but I warn you, do not cross my path more than you must. I am not one for undesired company, and you are undesired. Do I make myself clear?"

Blake returned the challenging stare. "I hear you quite clearly, and don't worry, my mission does not involve you, so our paths should rarely cross." He was not intimidated by Travis in the least and made sure his expression said so.

Travis looked to Rhea again, still challengingly, "I am going out for a while. You and Mr. Larson need to be ready to leave immediately when I return. This is not over between you and me, so you know. I will not be told what to do by you or anyone else."

Rhea looked at him as if he were ill. "I guess you should have thought of that before you made a choice to enter into this in the way you did." She was cold, and he hated it. He knew she was right, and that made everything worse. He had made his decision to enter this war and knew very well he would be told what to do by Jeremy, and he knew very well that he would have to obey till he was strong enough to flip sides. That was different. Taking orders from Jeremy was much easier than taking orders from the woman he had often loved. Somehow, he knew she would be giving him orders a lot over the next few months and he would obey them because his love for her was greater than his ego. He loathed how things had gone between them, especially in front of this stranger. He glared at her one last time before getting up and storming out of the inn.

Rhea followed him with her eyes till the oak door was shut behind him, then she looked back to Blake apologetically. "Blake, please forgive the scene Travis and I have just made. He does not do well with strangers, and he really does not handle being ordered about, especially by me. It drives him mad when he knows I am right, and in this case, he knew he was in the wrong. I do not care for him when he is drunk and whiskey is his poison. As for you, he may never warm up to you, just so you know." She was sweet and endearing in her apology. Her eyes were bright and sparkling once again. She truly was an amazing creature.

He, too, had a few things he needed to say to her. "Rhea, I trust there is a reason for us to travel with Travis, so I will do well to avoid him unless necessary. I am sure over time you will entrust me to more of this story so that I may understand my mission more completely, as you seem to know more about it than I do, which makes me slightly uncomfortable. I am a practical man, and following a dream or vision is very out of character for me, so at this moment, you lead me blindly into the unknown. Lastly, I will say this once and only once, I will not take orders from you or Travis. I am here on my own accord and, therefore, will answer to no one. If there are things I need to be told, I will expect them to come from this Clinton as he is the reason I am here. Now I ask you to trust in me as a friend and tell me where we are off to. Do we understand each other?"

Two men, very strong-willed, as her traveling companions were going to be quite difficult for her; keeping them apart was going to be even harder. If anyone could do it, it was her. She smiled at him and poured them each a glass of mead. "Blake, we have an agreement, and there is much to tell you before Travis returns. Let's drink, and then you may help me gather my things in my room, where I will proceed to tell you what you need to know." She drank her mead in one long, slow drink, set her glass down, and grabbed the bottle, getting up from the table.

Blake drank his own glass in a hurried gulp, then stood up, and followed her up the stairs to her room, where she told him of Travis being a vampire and of a war that was about to begin between good and evil. She filled him in briefly on the part about Travis being second-in-command on the vampire side and of his plan to overthrow Jeremy. At the end, Blake not only felt confused but angry. There were many things he did not understand, but she promised it would all make sense as the journey went on. Finally, he looked at her and said, "Enough. I am here on a task I do not understand, and you are the center of that task, and whatever I must do, I will do it. You are in good hands, lady of the light. I will guard you with my life, and that is all either of us need to know. You can fill in any holes when needed, but for now, I need some air." He turned and walked out of the room and down the stairs and out of the inn.

Chapter 4

She sat alone in her room. Her stuff was all ready for them to depart. She knew she had overwhelmed Blake with information he could not possibly understand but knew it necessary to fill him in so he knew what he was heading into. She decided it best to send a letter home as well. She knew the only person back home who would even come close to understanding was her best friend, Selene. They had known each other since they were girls, and she was the only one who really, truly comprehended Rhea's gifts. She took out a piece of parchment and her ink and quill. The letter was not short for she had put in as much detail as she could. She trusted Selene to inform her family that she was well. She found writing to her family caused undue stress. It was a way for them to tangle things up and confuse her words, and she didn't have time for that. She folded the letter and sealed it shut with the letter *R* in red wax and grabbed her things. She would wait for Travis's return downstairs. She checked the room and shut the door behind her. She stopped at the counter to pay the innkeeper for her and Travis's tabs. She left him several silver pieces for his kindness. She gave him the letter and asked him to make sure it was delivered as soon as possible. He assured her it would be done, and he smiled at her sweetly as she walked away. She chose a table overlooking the front door so that she may see either Travis or Blake when they entered. This was going to be her longest, most challenging journey yet. Though she knew she had no choice, she was not sure she was prepared for it.

While she waited, she happened to catch a glance of Sarah and little John. He was tugging her hand, pulling her toward Rhea's table. Sarah smiled as she saw where John was taking her. Rhea's face brightened as they approached her table.

"Ms. Rhea, Ms. Rhea!" John exclaimed with glee. "My tummy no longer hurts, and I got to see to see a fairy today, and it's all because of you." His words spilled out of his mouth quickly and jumbled, but Rhea understood them perfectly. She scooped him up into her lap and tickled his sides. He wiggled and giggled in little shrieks. Rhea set him down, and he toddled back to Sarah's side.

Sarah spoke softly, "Rhea, I promise our paths will cross again one day, and when they do, I will repay your kindness somehow, someway." With that, they moved on, and Rhea was again waiting for her traveling companions.

Blake sat on a hay bale inside the stables. His mind was spinning in more directions than he could handle. Rhea had just told him he was about to take on vampires and mass evil, something he had only heard about in stories, and that his traveling companion was none other than the second most powerful vampire in the world. He was to set out on a fool's journey to save the life of a woman whom he did not know from what was sure to be sudden death. He pulled his knees up to his chest and laid his head upon them. He closed his eyes, hoping the dizziness would subside. He could smell the horses and the manure. The hay smelled wet from the storm the night before. His mind was easing up when he heard a voice. He looked up, expecting to see someone, but no one was there. The voice called his name, and he knew it was Clinton. "I am here." Blake's voice was a whisper.

"Blake Larson of Elden Glenn, I know Rhea has just given you more information about your quest and that you do not understand most of it. You will make sense of this in time. It is most important that you stay by her side. She needs to come out of this war alive. I know the fate of Travis, and so does she. It does not end well for the dark and conflicted vampire she befriends. Rhea will do all in her power to try and change his fate. You must not let her get in the way of what is meant to be. He will not survive this war. Travis will die in front of the face he loves. Her heart will break, and she will be weak. It will be then that she will need you the most. Also, you will be tested not only in strength and bravery but also in matters of the heart. She will become your weakness, but not in a romantic matter as Travis is hers. Travis will try to fight you for a place at her side. He knows he must let her go, but it is not his way to walk away without a fight. He loves her, this is true, but will do all he can to deny it so that she doesn't make him weak or give her any sense of false hope that maybe he will finally be good to her. One sure way to kill a demon is to have the love of someone as pure of heart as Rhea. It is the one thing that will break them, and when that happens, it is much easier to kill them, and he won't allow anyone to have that chance. As for Jeremy, that is a matter I wish I could speak to you of now, but it is not the time. I must leave you now, Blake Larson. Your path is set. May the light of her guide you in times of darkness and the power inside you guide her to safety. The goddess is with you. Tell her not that I have come to you again for I will visit her another time. But, do give her this." Blake felt a chill run down his spine and felt the gentlest touch on his cheek, as if the wind had kissed him. And then it was gone, and he was alone. He called for Clinton, but there was no reply. What was so important about this woman that he was to risk everything, including his life, to keep her safe? What did Clinton mean when he said she would become his weakness and be tested on matters of the heart? All this, he gathered, would be shown to him in time. He was not a patient man and hated uncertainties. He was entering this quest without patience or certainty. What the hell for? He got off the hay bale and brushed himself off. If it was to be his destiny that he saves this woman's life, it was best he not let her out of his sight.

Travis wandered alone in the dark, trying to find anything that would cure his hunger. He was irritated with her for the way she treated him when he awoke. If he had whiskey, at least he wouldn't be so famished. Whiskey filled him like food could not. It was the nearest thing to blood he had found, but it was true he was not very well-tempered when drunk. Who was this stranger she insisted upon bringing with them? Were they involved? He could not bear the thought of another man's arms holding her even though she was not ever going to be in his arms again. They did not seem to be affectionate toward each other. What difference did it make to him if she had a suitor? He had no claims on her. He had had claims on her once a long time ago, but that didn't matter now. He could not forget the taste of her lips when they had kissed the night before. He yearned for her as much as he did blood. He wanted to feel the curves of her body under his own but knew this wouldn't happen. He would let her be collateral damage in the time he had left on this earth. His vampire instincts heard the cat crossing the road. It was not his favorite type of blood, but it would suffice. He grabbed the cat by the scruff of its neck. It was a brown tabby, mangy-looking. The cat had yellow eyes and looked at Travis, seeing the monster he was. The cat hissed as Travis bit into its neck, draining it of all life. It was bitter but went down smoothly. Travis threw the body off to the side of the road. It made him sick to think that he had not had human blood in days, nor would he allow himself to do so while she was near. He headed back up the path to the inn, brooding and suffering in silence.

The inn was busy and full of life. Rhea sat watching the door, waiting for one of the men to reenter. Each time the door opened, she was sure it was one of them. Finally, Blake walked in; he looked like there was weight on his shoulders, but he stood tall and carried himself confidently. He saw her and joined her at the table. She smiled sweetly as he sat. He smelled of horses, so she assumed he had been in the stables. That was good because she knew he had not encountered Travis. She feared that if they met alone, it might turn out badly, and if she could help it, they would not be left alone. She would make sure she was always with one of them. As she knew the way of it, it would be Blake that would be easiest to stay by. He was sent to protect her, and therefore, he would be much less inclined to leave her. Travis, on the other hand, worked best alone, so she knew that he would take advantage of this as often as he could, even if she had sworn her allegiance to stand next to him and fight. She knew he would take solitary confinement, especially with Blake traveling with them.

They sat quietly for a few minutes before she decided to speak. Her voice was gentle and caring. It was what he imagined an angel would sound like. He was already drawn to her; he could not help it. Any man that breathed air would be drawn to her. "Blake, when Travis returns, we will set out on a long and tedious journey. We shall travel mostly at night while Travis is with us. He will venture off on his own from time to time, only then may we travel by day. We will have to take in as much ground as we can cover in a night. It will serve us well if we rest when we stop. We will plan and work out strategies during the day. Travis will inform us when needed. Otherwise, he will stick to himself. If he feels it necessary, he will share any information with me alone, and I will then share it with you. I will ride with you for the most part. Travis will cover more ground than either of us, but he will wait for us before he moves on or he will send word where our next meeting point will be. Do you have any questions?" She was truly radiant. Light really did emanate from her. It was as if she were the flame of a soft candle. He could not help but be in awe of her. She looked at him in a way that could not be described, but it was a look he hoped to receive more often.

The door to the inn burst open, and her attention shifted quickly from him to the door. He walked in covered from head to toe in black. Blake saw Travis enter and saw how people shuddered as if a terrible cold had entered the inn. This did not faze Travis one bit. He was used to it. He strode over to where they sat, not looking at anyone except her. He reached the table in less than the blink of an eye. "Rhea, gather your things. We are ready to set out. I have told the stable boy to get your horses ready to leave. I have few things I need to get from my room and settle my tab with the old man. I want you in saddle by the time I get back."

"Travis, I have already settled your tab. All you need is to get your things. Blake and I are ready now." The look between them, Blake could tell, was very much love-hate. Travis turned away and practically flew up the stairs.

Rhea touched his arm gently. "It is time for us to go." Her touch warmed his skin and sent his blood almost to a boil. Clinton was right about one thing: she was going to be his weakness. He was not going to be able to resist her long. Before he finished this thought, she was standing with her riding cloak fastened around her neck. She had pulled her hair back while she told him about his mission. Her hair looked pretty in the long braid, but he had already experienced her curls that fell below her shoulders and framed her face ever so perfectly. He wanted to run his fingers through her curls at first sight. Now was not the time for these kinds of thoughts though. He had a duty to protect her. He had to keep his desires in check, or she would be out the door and gone before he knew what direction to follow her. They walked out of the inn in silence. The horses were tethered to the post in front of the stable. His rowan was shabby compared to her pure-white mare. Her horse was the color of snow on the mountains he loved so very much in wintertime. He was going to miss those mountains as much as he was going to miss home. She stood by her horse. He came up behind her. "May I help you, my lady?"

She turned her head and faced him. She nodded and smiled. He lifted her with ease as if she were a feather. He knew she could very well mount her horse probably moving if she really had to, but nonetheless, she allowed him to help her into her saddle. "Thank you, Blake." She liked a man who was chivalrous and treated her like a lady. Gentlemen were few and far between anymore. He mounted his own stead after untying their reins.

They sat waiting for Travis. Blake noticed that there was no horse for him. Rhea sensed him noticing there were only two horses. "Travis finds horses slow him down. If he decides to ride, he will either ride with me or I may need to ride with you. He will not ever take on his own horse. He has a thing about keeping things that could serve as a meal for him, but as Pixie was once his, he will take her if he feels the need. She is fast as anything and trusts him. He will get her back to me like he always does." She did not realize that Travis was standing there, nor did Blake. It was Pixie who felt his presence. Her ears twitched, and she whinnied softly. Rhea looked around and saw him standing by the post. He blended into the night the way he liked it. There was a slight breeze that caught Travis's cloak and made it rustle. It was then that Blake finally saw him. He had his arms folded over his chest. He took a step forward and reached a hand for Pixie. She smelled him and then nuzzled his hand for more affection. "Hey, old girl, are you behaving for Rhea?" He was talking to the horse but looking at Rae. He loved her in the moonlight.

Rhea smiled. "She's missed you." Travis nodded. "Will you ride with me tonight?"

He looked at her as if she had just given him a present wrapped in gold. "I will indeed." He came around the post to the side of the white mare and pulled himself up behind her on her saddle. It had been a long time since he had ridden with her, and he loved that she refused to ride sidesaddle. It felt good to be behind her, his body close to hers. He looked at Blake. "We ride quick and steady, so do your best to keep up." With that he took the reins, clicked his heels, and they were off. Blake clicked the side of his own stead and was off, only trailing them a little. Riding was by far his favorite thing in the world to do, and now he got to do it by moonlight, following the most intriguing woman he had ever met. He could not help the roll of jealousy that went through his stomach when Travis mounted behind Rhea, but there was going to be a time and a place, he knew, when it was going to be his body pressed against hers, so he would bide his time. They flew on the winds back through the darkness.

Rhea leaned back into Travis, her back resting on his chest, her head even with his own. The velvet of her cloak was tickling the nape of his neck. He put an arm around her waist. She looked at him and sighed. They had much to discuss, and she knew it was now or never. "Travis, are you mad with me?" Her voice slipped through him like silk.

"Yes." He was, in fact, very mad with her.

"Why are you mad, love?" He hated when she sweet-talked him. It made it hard for him to stay mad.

"Because you gave me orders in front of a stranger and made me look weak. Because you invited another man into a battle that is no more his than it is yours. Because you were not there when I woke and because I know, no matter what happens, I will not be able to touch you without going mad."

This surprised her very much. She turned her head so that their eyes met. "I understand the first three things, but I do not understand the last two. You are mad with me because I was not there when you woke. I thought you preferred to wake up alone, and as for you not being able to touch me, who says you can't? My heart still holds space for you."

"Rhea, don't you see? The more I touch you, the weaker I get. I can never hold you again, or at least not until this war is done and I have defeated Jeremy. I cannot allow myself to be weakened in any way or he will bring me down and we will lose."

She saw the pain and truth in his eyes, and it tore at her. She had already seen his fate, and to know that he would never again hold her in his arms saddened her greatly. She would never again feel his hands slide over her body or feel his breath on her skin. She turned away from him at this.

"Rhea, what is it?"

"Nothing," she whispered, and a silver tear fell down her cheek. "I am sorry I gave you orders in front of Blake. I didn't mean to make you seem weak. I cannot stand it when you drink. It makes you someone I do not know, and we have got to stay focused, and when you drink, you focus on nothing. As for Blake, he has been sent to me by Clinton, and I will not travel without him." Travis knew this to be true for Clinton was her guide and friend for many years before they met. He knew she trusted him fully, and if he sent her this man, then she would not refuse it.

"Fine, but make sure he stays out of my way."

"As you wish." She would not look at him, so he knew something else was troubling her. He bent his head to her neck and pressed his lips to her bare skin. She did turn this time, and the moon reflected sadness in her eyes.

"I will ask you kindly not to kiss me. If you cannot touch me, then I cannot bear it if you kiss me. You still don't realize how much of an effect you have on me. If I must live without your love and your touch, then I will have to live without your kisses too. It kills me a little deeper each time we touch or kiss or even lock eyes. It will eventually kill me completely. I will not be your weakness in this war as you have asked. That means you cannot be mine on this journey. If it is not meant for us to love each other on this path, then so be it. You may have all of me or none of me, and that is a choice I have never made you come to." She knew the answer even before he had a chance to respond; their destinies were not together, and it was finally time she realized that. "Rhea, I—"

She cut him off, "Don't. I do not wish to hear it. I will always and forever have love for you, but I can no longer go on with the possibility that someday we will be together forever. That is not in the stars for us. It never has been, you know it as well as I do. We will never again be the star-crossed lovers of our youth. That is not our destiny. We will always cross paths, and we will always share wonderful things, but I know now that you will never love me as much as I have you and that I need to stop being the foolish girl who lets you in and then has to let you go. I am tired of always having to let go. Until last night, I was sure there would be a time when I would be over you, and you would be just a memory that I cherished, but once again, the gods have thrown us together, and we now must save the world. There is something more sacred to me than the world that also needs saving, and that, my dear, is my heart. There is someone out there who will love me endlessly and without condition." She looked away from him again.

He could not bear the pain in her voice, and he could not bear the pain in his own heart. She had no idea how much he loved her and how much he wanted to hold her and kiss her and never ever leave her. Jeremy already knew he had a weakness for a woman, but he was not about to let Jeremy use that weakness against him, nor was he capable of being more than what he was. He whispered in her ear, in the seductive way that only a vampire could, "I promise you, if we come out of this war alive, there will never be a reason for you to have to let go again."

She looked back at him, still sad. "Don't make me promises you cannot keep." Her words chilled him to the very core of his being. She had never spoken so callously toward him, and he did not care for it. If this was going to be her mood, then he would match it beat for beat. It would be easier for him to be cross with her than to play nice. He knew that had this been any other time and any other place, this passiveness would turn to lust and desire between them and, before daybreak, they would make love. Tonight would be a first of many to come where he did not take her to his bed. As much as he wanted to, he would not give in to her, especially now that she had shattered his dark heart. He now knew exactly how she had felt all those months ago on their last parting when he had told her he had never wanted to see her again and turned from her without a second look. He had smashed her heart to the ground that night, and she had now done the same to him.

He removed his arm from her waist and returned it to the reins. He shook them harder. "Yah!" he shouted to Pixie. She was graceful and agile and obeyed his commands precisely. He could feel her body move beneath him. Rhea looked over her shoulder and saw Blake trailing slightly behind them. He rode as well as her or Travis, his stead working hard to match Pixie's speed. They rode through towns and villages, through the night. Travis slowed the pace as they neared the little town where they would stop before daybreak. He found a nice little inn and pulled Pixie to a stop. Blake pulled in right beside them. Travis dismounted.

"It is almost daybreak. I will go in and get us three rooms. I trust you can tend to the horses." He was colder than Rhea had ever known him to be. "By the way, I will go my own way tomorrow night. I have a meeting with Jeremy. I will send word to you here of what is to be done next. It would be ever so much easier if you were here to receive my message." With that he turned and walked into the inn.

Blake dismounted and helped Rhea down. He could not help but notice the sadness in her eyes.

"Thank you, Blake," she said to him with a small smile. She took the reins and walked Pixie into the stables.

The young boy was half asleep when she entered, Blake right behind her. The boy bolted up. "Forgive me, good sir and lady, I did not mean to, uh… I must have fallen asleep."

Rhea smiled at him gently. "It is no matter. It is very late. If you'd like, we can put the horses to rest ourselves."

"No, miss, I will do it for you. I am awake now, and I promise you, the horses are in good hands."

She handed him a silver piece and walked out of the stables. Blake caught up to her quickly. "Rhea, you look sad. Is there anything I can do?" He was sweet to be so concerned.

She put a hand on his arm. "Thank you, no, I am just tired. We will talk more in the morning when I have rested. It seems two nights of no sleep has finally caught up with me. Rest well, Blake Larson from Elden Glenn. May your dreams be sweet." She then quickened her pace and entered the inn.

The innkeeper was already with her key when she walked in. This inn was so different from the Dragon's Caldron. It was small and very quiet, not a soul around but a kind old woman who owned it. She was tall with short reddish hair. Her smile was more welcoming than anything Rhea had come across in days. Rhea took the key from her soft old hands, bowed, and headed down the hall to her room. She liked the feel of the place; it felt like what she imagined home would feel like if she had one.

She entered her room and shut the door. For the first time in many years, her thoughts would not be of Travis; her dreams would belong to her instead of to him, and she would rest knowing that what lies ahead of them will be nothing more than a common goal to save mankind. Never again will she long to look into those icy-blue eyes of his or crave his kiss and his touch. Her heart hurt much less than she had imagined it would. Tonight would be the first night Rhea Edwards, lady of light, would let go of her love for Travis, the vampire, and start living in the present rather than in the past. She and Travis had had their last romantic interlude that night, and she had finally gotten closer to something that had ended many years ago but she could not bring herself to accept. She fell upon the large down bed, pulled the blanket over top of her, and fell fast asleep.

Dawn was quickly approaching, and he needed to sleep. He closed his shutters tightly and sealed off any light from his room. Sleep was going to be hard for him tonight. He had a broken heart, her to blame for it, a war plan, a monster to destroy, and very little time to accomplish this in. The war was set for the evening of the spring equinox. And all that mattered to him was that she came out of this alive. The world would not miss a lone vampire, but the world without an angel would be a dark place. If they were to be on the outs, that was fine; it would make concentrating on battle that much easier, but he would give his own immortality to see her safe and unharmed. Maybe she was right; perhaps it was time for them to let go. He could no more promise her forever than he could promise Jeremy that he would help him bring down the world. She knew he could not keep such a promise. Every promise he had ever made to her he'd broken. The only vow he had ever made to her that he has kept was to love her eternally. There was nothing that anyone, not even her, could say or do that would change that. He hoped she still knew that. He dropped down onto the bed. He was weary; the cat's blood was wearing off and his hunger creeping up on him. He had a four-day journey ahead of him. Rhea was not going to be pleased that he was taking Pixie, but the road ahead would be much more challenging without her. In the end, Rhea's gentle disposition would give in, and he and Pixie would be off. He didn't even realize he had drifted off to sleep thinking of her and only her.

Blake lay on his bed staring at the ceiling; his thoughts were of her as well. He was sworn to protect her in a war that she had no business being in. Wars were meant for men that wanted power, not for women who wanted peace and found the good in everyone, including vampires. He didn't understand how a woman like her could give her heart to someone with no soul. What was more intriguing to him was how, in a matter of several hours, she could go from loving him and taunting him to be coy and playful in inviting him to ride with her to being so very sad. What had he done to her that made her whole-body drop? Why did women always go for the men that wound up hurting them in the end? He could never understand it. He cursed at himself for being a nice guy and then cursed Travis for hurting her. He did not know what it was about her that he was drawn to, especially in such a short time, but he would be damned if he didn't find out. What was so magical about this woman that not only would make him leave his home and follow her into war but also make him want to hold her in his arms and never let go? How could she hold so much power over him in only a day? He sighed; nothing had ever tugged at his heart more than when he lifted her from her horse and saw tears in her eyes. Even in sadness, her beauty was beyond compare, maybe even more so. All he knew was, he didn't care for her being sad and he would make sure he made her smile before the days end.

The sun was high in the sky when she awoke. Close to the eleven o'clock hour, she was sure. Sleep had not been so peaceful in many years. Her heart grieved slightly, but that was to be expected after loving the same man for more than nine years and finally realizing that nothing was going to ever come of it. It made her sadder to know that he would not survive this war than it did that she had closed the door on their romance. A part of her would always remember the times they had shared, but now it was time for her to start anew and create a life that was hers. The day was bright, and she felt refreshed. Time to move on. What better way to make a new beginning than by reading Shakespeare in the outdoors under a tree or by a stream. She quickly washed and changed into a different dress. She traveled lightly, usually only bringing two or three gowns with her; this time, for whatever reason, she had four or five. They were lightweight and practical and did not take up much space in her saddlebag. The dress she chose matched her eyes, a dark green. She left her hair down for the most part, pulling back the sides in a ribbon of lavender that she tied in a knot instead of her normal bow. She grabbed *Othello* and opened her door.

The inn she barely saw a few hours prior felt more like home than she had realized. It smelled like spring flowers and apple pie. The inn had five rooms, three of which she and her traveling companions occupied. She gave a brief thought to which one was Travis's then turned and walked into the main room. It was as quiet now as it was when she entered before dawn.

The kind old woman was sweeping the floor from the breakfast crowd. She looked up as Rhea entered. Her smile made her think of her nana. "Good morning, dear. Did you sleep well?"

Rhea smiled. "Yes, thank you kindly."

The old woman looked at her with knowing eyes and replied, "An old woman knows when a young woman's heart has been broken, and that time will heal your pain."

Rhea bowed her head in gratitude. "Thank you, ma'am. You are very kind. I think time is already healing the pain." The old woman nodded and went back to sweeping. Rhea watched for a minute and then headed for the door.

The air was sweet-smelling and fresh. The soft breeze felt good against her face. Birds were singing pleasantly in the sky. It made her sadness and troubles melt away. She walked along the garden path, brushing her hand along the winter-grown shrubs. She was ready for the spring even though winter was her season. It had already been a harsh cold November, and December was shaping up in the same fashion. This morning was one of the warmest days they've had in quite some time. Winter meant Christmas and her birthday and *snow*. She loved snow as much as she loved anything. It was calm and peaceful and extremely serene to watch; it was almost romantic in a nongooey sort of way. It was like watching a sunset or going for a long, slow horseback ride; something about these things just made her very sentimental. There had not been much snow this season but a lot of rain. Rhea loved rain, especially the smell, but too much of it made her feel gloomy. She was tired of feeling gloomy. She knew, though, that with a major war creeping up, gloom would be hanging about the way the gray clouds lurked in the sky. She followed the path fondling shrubs and bushes, with her hand along the way, to a small brook that ran the edge of the property of the quaint little inn. It flowed over smooth river rocks, making a gentle gurgling sound. She breathed the air in deep; it was cold on her lungs. She let the air out slowly. She decided the large lone pine that stood at the banks of the brook would be her spot to read. No one around to interrupt her or her thoughts. Travis would sleep the day through; as for Mr. Larson, she was not sure what he would do to occupy his day, but now she did not care. She wanted to find out what happens to the Moore of Venice. She sat down and opened her book. The pages turned easily, as did the story. Scene after scene, the tragic plot of *Othello* unfolded. Time went by as quickly as the narration.

Blake woke shortly after Rhea had with all sorts of strange thoughts of wars and vampires running around in his head. He splashed some cold water on his face from the little basin on the dressing table. He felt groggy from restless sleep. His thoughts kept drifting to her and saving her from an evil vampire called Jeremy.

How in the hell was he going to save her from such a creature, a being that aims to destroy all that is good, all that he held dear, and all that she stood for? It was going to be a feat just traveling with a vampire, let alone conquering one to save a woman. He wondered what it was she was doing at this moment. He hoped to find her in the sitting room down the hall. He hurried and dressed in the same clothing he had on the day before. He was not one for carrying with him a lot of unnecessary items, including clothing. He headed out of the room, barely shutting his door.

The place was deserted, and it gave him the chills; he would rather have the busy inn of the day before than that of this tiny, little place of solitude. The old woman sat in a rocker by the fire knitting. She was benign-looking, very maternal, he sensed, like a mother hen. He scanned the room for Rhea, but she was not there. The old woman looked up and smiled at him. In a quiet old voice that echoed age and wisdom, she said, "You won't find her here. She set out with a book along the garden path about an hour ago. I reckon she's down by the brook. Her eyes weren't as sad this morning as they had been last night." Blake looked at her, knowing she was reading his mind. He bowed to her sincerely and walked out of the inn.

He, too, felt the warmth of the air; it also made him crave the spring. Not really paying much attention to the path leading to brook as she had, he made his way down the narrow little path. Normally, this would have given him a sense or relaxation and tranquility, but the lack of sleep was seriously affecting his mood. He reached the brook in no time at all. He saw her under a large pine tree, her back nestled against its trunk; her legs were stretched out in front of her, crossed at the ankles. Her hair blew softly in the breeze, falling into her face every now and again. She would push it away with one hand, never taking her eyes from her book. He had never met a woman who read as much as she did. He liked watching her read; he got a sense of emotion from her and could almost tell what was going on in the story without having to be reading it. He stood there silently watching her for a long time. She was such a mystery, this woman, yet she seemed at peace. He did not want to disturb her, so he sat on the path quietly and just watched her be.

The story was reaching an end, and Rhea was ready for it. The story had given too much away for her not to know how it would end. Though she knew death was inevitable, it still made her sad, and it made her think of Travis. She knew this war was going to be the end of him; she had seen it. She would not allow herself to wallow in this anymore. She pushed him back out of her mind and finished the story of *Othello*. She sat for a long time on the last page, not wanting to close the book. She thought about her parents' home. It had been so long since she had been to Hearts Prairie. She thought of her family, who were all healers of one kind or another, and how, out of all of them, she was the only one ever to leave. She couldn't make them understand that she had wings that needed to be spread. It had hurt them the day she left, not really knowing where she was going. She was always on the outs with her family. They would encourage her in one breath and tell her she was making a huge mistake in the next. Her parents were supportive but still didn't understand why she had not returned home yet after so many years. As she got older, the more she realized how different she was from her family and how she was never really her own person when she was with them; she was some strange version of herself, but in the light her family wanted her to be in. No matter what light she was in, it was never good enough for them. Christmas was the only time she ever ventured back through her parents' door. With December quickly approaching, she didn't foresee herself in front of their little hearth and fire this year. It would be the first year ever she would not spend a Christmas with her family. It hurt to think of this, but she had a war to stop and had no idea how much time she had to do it in; Travis had not given her that much information.

She thought of all her friends and how much she missed them all, Selene particularly. Selene was Rhea's only real female friend. Girls were threatened by Rhea and her gifts; that was why her company was usually kept with men. Rhea knew that Selene would come and fight beside her if she had asked it. Rhea wasn't sure yet if she was going to need Sel or not. Her thoughts drifted from one friend to another whom could she count on if things got out of hand.

Without warning, her thoughts fell upon someone she had not thought about in a very long time: Drew. Drew was one friend she could not bring herself to say goodbye to. There was always something there that she could not explain between the two of them. They had met through her old flame, Thomas, and became instant friends. When the spark died out for her and Thomas, she and Drew were still able to be friends. There was a certain unspoken attraction with them. Drew, however, had never been single long enough to test the waters. They had worked alongside each other at the old carpenter's shop for a while before she had left. He oversaw building, while she was never sure what she was in charge of while there. But the old carpenter William paid her well in silver pieces, and she was able to be around people.

She thought back to one day at the little shop. William had left them alone to go home to his wife, who was with child. He had never left them alone at the shop before, so Rhea wanted to make sure everything was just right when he got back. She spent the morning busying herself with sweeping and tiding. She crossed through the work area where Drew was working to empty the trash bucket. Drew watched her go out the back door and watched her return. When she walked past him, he reached out his hand and grabbed her wrist. She turned and faced him, and before she could retreat, he had both her wrists in his grasp. She didn't try to get free but stood watching him. He was backing her up. In a moment's notice, she had her back against the workbench. He had released her hands but had put his own on either side of her, pinning her to his workspace; the smell of passion and sawdust filled her senses. She did not know what he was thinking or what he was going to do, but the moment was full of fire and lust. The unspoken attraction between them was now burning her face hot; she felt her cheeks flush and her heart quicken. She wanted him to kiss her more than she had ever wanted anything. She could feel his breath on her neck; it was as hot as her face. His soft-brown eyes never left hers. He had the longest eyelashes she had ever seen; they curled up and gave him this sweet, innocent schoolboy appearance, but in this moment, there was nothing innocent about the way he was looking at her. His eyes were full of hunger. Her breath returned to normal, and her heart started beating at a normal rhythm as he backed away from her. She wanted so badly to know what he was thinking, but she couldn't bring herself to speak. She returned to the front of the shop, glancing back to him only once.

From that day on, they flirted with each other every chance they got. They had spent some time together outside work; they spent most of their time talking, but when they weren't talking, they were kissing. He was a great kisser and made her lips tingle every time they touched her own. It was fun and comfortable being with him. Their conversations flowed easily but were not much more than idle chitchat. Sometimes they would spend time with Thomas, and when that happened, they had to keep their feelings in check because neither of them wanted to hurt him. She hated these times.

She and Drew had grown close, and then suddenly, he stopped coming around as much and then just stopped altogether. Rhea felt it was because he knew she was leaving. She made sure, before she left, she had said goodbye to everyone, and she walked past the old shop probably a dozen times, but she could not bring herself to go in and tell him goodbye. The last time she walked past the shop was the day she left. She stopped, blew a kiss and whispered, "You will always be a thought away," and turned and walked out of the little village where she had spent her whole life. She hadn't thought about him often, but whenever she did, it always brought a smile to her face. She sat under the large pine tree smiling, knowing very well that he would tell her this was a foolish, crazy mission that she was heading for but, at the same time, want to be right there with her in the action. He was as crazy as her, if not more so, and that was one of the things she liked best about him. In her heart, she knew there was not ever going to be anything more than youthful flittering for the two of them.

Her thoughts were shattered when she heard footsteps behind her. She turned to see Blake walking toward her. She cursed under her breath. This guy was going to be hard to ditch. She sat up and tucked her legs up under her dress. This was the second time in the short while they had known each other that Blake had intruded on her serenity. She looked up at Blake, who was now standing at her side. She gave him a half smile. He returned the gesture and sat down next to her. He seemed to always have a calmness about him, and Rhea liked that. Travis was never calm. Damn it, she had let her mind drift to him. It was hard not to when he was one of the only consistent people in her life for so many years.

"Good afternoon, Blake," she said, quickly recovering from her mind slip.

"Same to you, Rhea." He wondered if they would talk about the events of the evening past. He partly hoped they would talk about them only to know the cause of her sadness. But at the same time, he knew a woman's emotions were a delicate line and was not sure he wanted to know what this woman was like when her emotions were set free.

She spoke, answering his thoughts. "Thank you for not pressing me last night." She smiled at him, and he could see in her eyes that this was the beginning and the end of this conversation.

"You are welcome. If you decide you want to talk about it, I am not going anywhere. By the way, it would be a whole lot easier to keep you safe if I didn't have to come searching for you all the time." He smiled a big cheesy grin.

She laughed. It was like the tinkle of wind chimes, and it made her eyes dance in merriment. He might not be so bad after all, she thought. "I guess you are right. I will try and let you know before I go wondering. Fair enough?"

"I suppose that will be okay." They both laughed.

For the next few minutes, they just sat enjoying the outdoors. The breeze picked up to a small wind. The world, for the time, was as it should be: peaceful. Wars and vampires could not touch this moment. She was comfortable sitting with Blake. It felt to her like sitting with an old friend. She wanted a friend so badly. She had left all of hers behind, and now even she and Travis had lost the friendship they had always shared.

"Blake, can I ask you something?"

"That depends on what you want to ask!"

She nodded. "I was just wondering if maybe we could be friends?"

Friends? He thought about this for a minute. He liked the idea of being friends with her, but he was also very curious as to what it would be like to be more than her friend. He wanted to know what it was like to hold her in his arms and make love to her until they were both numb, but he supposed for now he could be her friend. "I think we could be friends, Ms. Rhea. It might make things easier since we are on this mission together." He turned and looked at her. It might kill him to be her friend and never touch her, but it seemed worth it to him.

"I would really like that. It has been such a long time since I have had a friend."

"Rhea, what made you leave Hearts Prairie?"

"Hmm, that is an interesting question. Well, I was given a task, same as you. My task was to go out into the world and protect and heal all those that I encounter."

He looked at her quizzically. "I am not sure I understand."

"I didn't figure you would. Let me explain to you. I am what one calls an angel of the earth. I have all the powers of a regular angel minus the wings. All whom I encounter are there forth bound to me and my protection, until they no longer need me or until I no longer need them. Each person I come across, I am meant to cross paths with, for one reason or another. This is the wish of the goddess Ariadne. I carry out her orders as she sees fit and go where she needs me. The only real problem with this is that when I care, I have a hard time letting go. Travis is a good example of that."

"How did you two meet, if you don't mind me asking?"

"I don't mind. Maybe it will help you see the whole picture a little clearer. Travis and I were very young when we met. I was seventeen, and he was fifteen. He was still mortal at that point. We met through an old friend of mine. Shawn was very hesitant about letting us meet. One day, by chance, I happened to be at Shawn's house the same time as Travis. Shawn introduced us. Travis and I locked eyes, and that was the end of it. It was inevitable that my heart would be lost to him. We never said a word to each other that day. Then we met again about a year later. He was a very carefree mortal boy, with hopes as big as the sea. Nothing had changed. He still had my heart.

Even at a young age, he was not capable of being faithful to just one girl, and his fate was in the arms of the one who turned him. The night before she changed him, I stumbled upon them in a lovers' embrace. Embarrassed and heartsick, I walked away without a word or a second glance. She changed him the very next night. We have crossed paths many times on our journeys, and each time we pick up right where we left off, very much wanting to love the other.

"Doomed by the fate of what we are and wanting different things, we are not able to be together for longer than a month or two. Each time we part, it gets harder and harder. Then late in the summer, we had spent a lot time together again, longer than we had ever spent together. I had thought briefly that maybe, just maybe, things would be different. Then one night we were to part ways like normal, and he looked at me as if he had never seen me before. It tore at me, but not as much as him telling me he never wanted to see me again. Nothing had ever hurt more. You see, angels are not meant to be in love like that. It becomes unbearable. For a vampire to love someone so pure of heart becomes a great weakness. The love of an angel is a sure way of killing off a demon. Nothing affects them more."

"I am following your story, but how could someone love such a creature?"

"He wasn't always a vampire, and when he became one, my heart was already lost, so I overlooked what he was on the outside because I was able to see the man he was inside. It's like opposites attract. We were perfect for each other, like fire and gasoline, destined to explode or burn out. The night he told me he never wanted to see me again, he very well could have ripped out my heart and drunk the blood from it. It damn near destroyed me. It took a lot of healing for me to recover. I was well on my way to being over it until two nights ago. When I walked into the Dragon's Cauldron and he was there drowning his misery in whiskey, just like that, I shared once more the burdens of a demon trying to ease the pain. I am now on the same mission he is, to save the world."

"How can you be sure that he will keep his word and try to stop this war?"

"Travis and I may not always see eye to eye on anything, and we may be of different realms, but one thing I know for sure is that Travis has a good heart, hates Jeremy and the other vampires more than anything. He would never take orders from Jeremy unless there was an ulterior motive behind it."

Blake looked at the brook, pondering all she had said. It made sense enough for him, but he just still could not grasp how she could have given Travis her heart. He decided Travis was not to be trusted even if she thought he could be. "Rae, what is our plan of action? I would feel better knowing we have some sort of strategy."

She looked at him. "Blake, I don't know yet. I was thinking of people I know who would join my army when you walked up. I know that eventually Clinton will appear to me and fill in any blanks that I am not seeing. Until then, we just wait it out." She knew he was not reassured, but it was all the information she could give him right now.

"Rhea, do you think we will win?"

"Blake, I hope so for all our sakes." At that they did not utter another word to each other. They just sat side by side, pondering the fact that the world rested in the hands of an angel, a farm boy, and a vampire.

The day passed by quickly. Before either of them realized it, the sun was starting to set, sending pinks and golds around the horizon. Rhea stretched out her arms and leaned forward to stretch her back. Blake, too, was starting to stir. He had his arms up over his head. Rhea looked at him. "I think we should get back to the inn. I have not eaten a thing all day." Blake nodded his head in agreement. They both got to their feet and made their way back up the little path to the inn.

The inn was still quiet. A handful of people were eating supper in the main room. It smelled of smoked meet and fresh bread. Her stomach rumbled.

"Rae, why don't you go sit down and I will see what smells so wonderful." He smiled at her and walked away.

She shook her head and chuckled to herself. There was a table by the fire that was calling to her. She made her way through the room and seated herself by the window. The fire felt good after being outdoors so long. The inn was peaceful. She liked places like this; they gave her a sense of balance. Blake was following the kind old woman toward the kitchen. Rhea sighed and looked out the window. The world was turning gray. She sensed his presence before she knew he was standing there. She did not turn to face him. He stood there watching her. She was at peace as she should be. He knew the mishaps of the night before would still be in her eyes, and he was not sure he was ready for that, but he was in a hurry and needed her to cooperate. He moved a little closer to the table. She slowly turned and faced him. He was dressed in his usual black. His eyes were a fierce shade of blue, almost the color of the ocean before a storm. She knew he needed her for something but was not going to be the one to break the silence. She was not ready just yet to be in confrontation with him. She needed a few more days of recovery first.

Travis broke the silence. He had no time for idealness. "Rhea, I need Pixie. Jeremy is waiting for me. I have a long brutal road ahead of me and would make better time with a little help from Pixie. Please, Rae." He had the weight of the world on his shoulders again, she could tell. She knew Pixie would be of great assistance to him.

"Okay, Travis. Though, I expect her to return to me in one piece when you are done with her. I don't want her to be lost to the world of vampires. It would break her spirit."

"Rhea, thank you. I will make sure she returns to you. I need a couple more things from you." He looked more serious now. His eyes grew stern. "Rhea, I need you not to talk to anyone of this war. Jeremy has spies all over, and it would be detrimental to all of us if he were to find out that others knew of his plans. I need you to wait here and talk to no one. As far as I am concerned, Mr. Larson knows too much of this war, but he is not my concern. You, on the other hand, need to know the great importance of this battle and treat it with great care. There is nothing more dangerous for you than being my acquaintance. Keep your ears open and your mouth shut."

She did not like being talked to like a child but knew at this point it was better not to argue with him. She, too, had things on her mind that required his attention. "Travis, I will say nothing to anyone, but I need to know, what is our next move? Better yet, when and where is Jeremy going to wage this war?"

"Rhea, I don't know very much as of now. I do know the war is to unfold on the eve of the spring solstice. I know nothing other than that. I am in a hurry, and it looks as if Mr. Larson is heading back this way. One more thing, please stay here. Try not to go wandering away from this place. Until you hear from me, I need you to stay put."

She looked at him with mischievous eyes. "I cannot stay in one place for very long. You should know this as you are the same. I promise to stay here as long as I can before I get restless and bored."

He knew she would not wander far or for long, a day or two at most, but she would keep this tiny, little inn as her home base until further notice. That was good enough for him. Blake was approaching, and he did not want a conflict. "The last thing I need from you before I go, I need you to keep your mind open to me, especially in dreams. It will be the easiest way for us to communicate." Her hopes of him not invading her sleep flew out the window. It looked like he was going to still have a part of her thoughts for the time. She wasn't happy about it but nodded in agreement. "Rhea, take care, and I will get word to you as soon as I can."

"Travis, safe travels. Angel wings are with you always, mine or otherwise."

With that he gave her a bow and headed for the door. A small ping hit her heart for the man she was letting go, and a new beat leaped at the return of her new friend.

Chapter 5

Travis walked to the stables, half hoping she would follow him out. He knew it was not likely. Night was quickly approaching, and he knew the road ahead was going to be long and unbearable, but that was the choice he had made, his own cross to bear. The stable was cold and dark. The stable boy was nowhere to be found, not that it mattered. Travis didn't need some teenage boy getting in his way.

Pixie whinnied as he approached her stall. She was still loyal to him after all these years. He thought about Rhea's comment about how the vampire world would crush her spirit. He knew she was right; Pixie's heart was as pure as the woman to whom she belonged. He took his sweet time saddling the white mare. He was in no hurry to get to Jeremy. It was dark outside when he and Pixie walked out of the stable. He guided her with the leather reins; both held their heads high.

She watched them walk tall and proud. Though the gods had finally made it clear that they were not to be together, she could not let him ride into vampire hell without saying goodbye. She could tell herself a hundred times over that she was over him, and she knew in time she would be, but she was of the heart, and hostility was not in her veins. He did not see her but sensed her. The dark was casting shadows all about. If he let himself try making one of them her form, he would surely be disappointed. Rhea stood there hoping he would see her, but he refused to look in her direction. Her hair blew in the wind. Pixie neighed at the smell of her mistress. Travis could smell her too. He knew she was there. At that moment, she stepped into the small glow of the moon, hair billowing in the wind, a tangle of copper curls. She looked like a vision. Surely no woman could be that beautiful in the moon. There she stood watching him with those spellbinding eyes, dress of velvet clinging to her body and dancing with the wind. She moved more gracefully than a goddess. She walked to them, never taking her eyes from him. He wasn't sure of her mood or what she wanted, so he put up his guard and was ready for another go-around, if that's what she wanted. She walked up to him, calm and serine. She put her hand on Pixie's head and patted her gently, saying nothing. The horse stood there taking in the love of her human. Pixie would always be loyal to Travis, but she would always belong to Rhea.

She smiled sweetly, still holding her eyes on Travis. What did she want? She sighed, and her smile fell slightly. "Travis, I know things have never been easy or conventional for us and that things will never be as I had once hoped they'd be, but the things I said last night are the truth as I know them to be. You can never be what I need in a romantic partner, and asking you to try would be selfish on my part. It would destroy us both. Travis, the love I have had for you over these many years has waxed and waned. It is not a lie to say that I was in love with you once or that the bond between us is one that is not easily broken. I can never be satisfied with being a passing craze, and that is what I am with you. I know you have loved me deeply and that you will battle Jeremy in the name of that love. I know that you ride off to Hell cloaked in darkness and holding on to that love. I am truly sorry I hurt you last night. I really am. I know that time is short and you must go, but I need you not to hate me. I need to know that the ties that bind us can include being just friends. I will always and forever care for you, but loving you is like dying a slow death by poison. I need you to set me free. Love comes in many shapes and forms. Can you love me as your friend and as your partner?" She looked at him pleadingly.

He searched her eyes, but he knew this was her truth. He admitted to himself that he was surprised it took her this long to come to this conclusion. He was sad but knew it was for the best, especially for her. Her need for happiness was more important than anything he had ever felt. The fact that she was begging for something said that she had truly tried to move on these last few months but was not successful. He respected her and her wishes, even if it had poked holes in his frozen heart. "Rhea, I won't lie, this is not easy for me to hear. Somehow, we have always found a way back to each other, but I understand what you need. Light and dark are not meant to be together. That is why the sun never shares the sky as the moon. You have always been my sun in a moonless sky, and now it is the time for day to be day and night to be night. We started as friends, and we will end as friends. On the day of battle, I will give my life to save you, and that will be my final act of love, but you deserve so much more than I could ever give you. I hate letting you go, but I will not go back on my word—you, Rhea of light, are now free. My heartstrings no longer hold you tight." He offered her a smile; tears were rolling down her cheeks. She smiled back. He pulled his arms around her and pulled her in. The hug was sincere and simple, just as it should be between friends. He let her go and mounted Pixie. He was still a man, and lingering would be detrimental to that moment. "Fare thee well, Rhea. We will meet again."

She waved to him. "Goddess be with you, my friend."

He rode through the dark of night until hunger began to creep in. He had not had a decent meal in more than four days. Travis had vowed never to feed on human blood when in company with Rhea. It was hard to explain why he couldn't when she knew what he was and what he ate, but he just could not bring himself to attack another human being with her near, especially since as of late, he would feed on a female that he had chosen as a plaything. Kill two birds with one stone: the desire to eat and the desire of passion. Most of the women he chose were dull and drab, mindless, and all too eager to spread their legs. He used them as playthings to kill the sexual boredom of eternity and then drained most of their lives. He never drained a human completely; he felt it tacky and cruel. A human could still survive and live a normal life if a vampire stopped sucking long before the heart slowed. He needed their blood to survive but didn't feel it fair to drain them of their own survival. His hunger crawled through him, making it hard to concentrate. Rhea had set him free, but he was not ready to take someone else to bed, not after sharing the last two days with her. He needed human blood, though, so he was going to have to get it another way.

He slowed Pixie and patted the side of her head. The village was small and quaint. There was a tavern with light a glow; the tavern sat in the middle of merchant shops that were long closed at this late hour. He dismounted the white mare and left her to eat the sparse grass heads that grew along the dirt road. He entered the old tavern. It was full of meandering, wayward travelers. Here and there, two or three men would be huddled around a table, slamming pints on the hardwood and grunting and grumbling among themselves. A few serving wenches toyed lazily with some of the men. No one gave Travis much notice. He crossed to a lone table and sat down. He eyed the room, searching for his target.

He wasn't sure who would be the one to quench his thirst when a wench came up alongside him. She was blond and well-endowed. Her face was pretty with rosy cheeks and full pouty lips. Her eyes were blue and silent. Nothing reflected through them. Her skin was weathered from sun and many hours of hard work, and she looked like she had been ridden by her fair share of tavern men. She smiled a crocked smile. Normally, this would have been exactly the kind of woman he would have taken to bed and then feasted upon. Her breasts heaved beneath her bodice, which was a dingy shade of baby pink and a bit on the small side for the woman's assets. Trying to avoid the urge to take her out back and have his way with her, he kept his eyes on the table.

Her voice was sweet and sticky. "What can I do you for, love?"

Travis kept his focus on the table. "Just a pint of ale will do fine, thanks." She lingered and ran her fingers through his hair; he didn't acknowledge her attempts at flirting. She walked away to fetch his pint.

He surveyed the room again; in the corner of the tavern, away from the crowd, he found his prey. He sat alone as Travis did. He was old and tired. His days were numbered. His skin sagged around an ancient sad face; his eyes were white and distant. Drinking his blood would be how the old man would die. It gave Travis a quick, sharp pang in his stomach. He hated taking a life, even one that was barely surviving, but there was no one else in the room that wouldn't cause for complications or make him hate himself for betraying the way he had always felt about Rhea. He knew she loved him, but what she didn't know was how much he loved her. The old man was going to meet his death tonight. Travis thought he was probably going to be doing the old man a favor. He got up quietly not to make a scene. He crossed the room to the old man's table. He eased into the chair, not making a sound. He knew the old man could not see him. Travis let out a breath to let the old man know he was there. The man stirred but didn't speak. The wench brought Travis's ale and lingered briefly, hoping Travis would give her the time of day. When he didn't, she got bored and moved on to someone who would pay her attention. Travis didn't touch the ale.

He spoke to the man with a voice as clear and calm as water as not to frighten the old man. "Sir, may I sit and keep the company of a tired old man this evening? The road is long and lonely."

The old man cocked his head at Travis and let out a heavy sigh. "My son, you are much too young and full of life to keep company with the likes of me. What you need is a pretty lady to keep you company. Don't any of these wenches strike a fancy?"

Travis chuckled. "Old man, I am not as young as I sound, and life is only full of darkness for me. As for the women, well, any other night, I would take their company to yours greatly, but as I have just left the one woman who could make my heart stop beating, it wouldn't be fair to her to hold another in my arms this eve, so if you will, I would very much like your acquaintance."

The man nodded a knowing nod and stared off into nothing. Travis still didn't drink. The old man began talking, and so Travis sat and listened. The old man spoke of love and of life and told Travis many stories. When the time had crept by longer than Travis would have liked, the old man stopped midsentence and stared at Travis with hard, glazed eyes. Travis would not have in a million years known what the man would say next. "Son, I know of what you are. You are of the night and of immortal blood. You have given me much company tonight, more than I have had in many years. I am grateful to you for that. You let me talk of my life and my past. Now, I must ask you for a favor in return. Please end my life. Take away my hurt and my pain. End my suffering and my longing to die. You will not be condemned for doing so as it is my wish. I long to be with the woman who made my heart stop so many years ago, and I wish for death every day. Please."

Travis was in utmost shock. How could this man know what he was, and how could anyone ask for death this way? The old man's request did make it a bit easier to go through with it. "Old man, I will not ask how you know of what I am. I won't lie to you, when I sought out your company, it was for the purpose of, forgive me, but my dinner. If it is your wish to die this way, I will grant it. I promise to be quick and efficient so there will be no pain and no chance of lingering life. But, before I do, I must be absolutely certain this is how you want to die."

The old man sat back in his chair and folded his arms across his chest. His clothes were torn and ragged, and he was dirty. "I want nothing more than to die. If you can give me that and refresh yourself as well, then there is nothing more to discuss. I want to be dead by morning, and you have a long way to travel. I will not fight you or struggle, but there is one thing I must know before you take my life. The woman you spoke of before that could stop your heart beating, is she what you are?"

Travis sighed. "No. She is the opposite of me. She is good and pure. Her heart knows no evil except me. She is an angel of mercy, and she loved a monster because she knew him as a boy and saw the glimpse of the man I would be before I crossed over. She is the woman of young men's dreams and old men's thoughts. She is the one good thing I have ever known."

The old man nodded again in knowing. "Would you die for her?"

"I would cut off my own head with my own sword if it meant saving her. I would give my immortality to know she lives. Sometimes I think I already have died for her."

The old man smiled and leaned onto the table. "Travis, I don't believe Jeremy is going to like that very much, do you?"

Travis gasped. There was no way the old man could know of such things. Travis breathed heavily. What was he going to do? Was this old man a spy?

The old man answered his thoughts. "Travis, do not fear me or even worry. Jeremy will never know we spoke as you are going to end my life when this is done. I was a prisoner in Jeremy's lair of Hell for the past ten years. Before he took my sight, he made me watch as he took first my wife and then my daughter to his bed for mere pleasure before draining them completely. I know of the evil plans he must end the world. I knew who you were the instant you sat down. I have seen you in hell many times, and I have heard your voice. I have heard your protests of this maddening war. I was set free when you finally agreed to join him as second-in-command. He said I was useless to him now that he had you. He was going to use me as a spy since I can't see, no one would suspect me. But you were more valuable. I begged him to kill me, but he said it would be more insufferable to keep me alive to live with my memories. I hate that worthless pig who calls himself a king. I hope he rots in the hell he put me in, and I hope you do what is right by your lady and turn your back on this war as soon as you get the chance. This war is a fool's errand, and you know it as well as I. Travis, you kept company with an old man this evening for the simple purpose of a meal and not wanting to betray the woman you love. I believe she sees the good in you, as do I. I know there is a heart of good under all that darkness. Please don't let my life be in vain. Please remember all I have shared with you and remember that love conquers all. Now, Travis, the road is long and the night fades away. Please walk me out to your horse and end my misery." He pushed himself to standing and flipped a silver piece on the table to pay for Travis's drink. Travis stood up as well. He took the old man by the arm and led him out front of the tavern.

The wind had picked up and was much cooler than when he came in. Pixie was grazing lazily at the small grass patches. The road was dark, and not a soul was about. Travis walked the old man to the side of the tavern. No windows made it an easy place to drain the man's life without being seen. He let go of the old man's arm for a moment. "Old man, I don't know your name, and at this point, it doesn't much matter. But I thank you for your company and your wisdom. I also thank you for offering me what is left of your life. I hope your wife and daughter are waiting for you on the other side, and before the end comes for you, I want you to know I fight with Jeremy because I fight for good. I believe that right will prevail in this war and that this world will know love and compassion and goodness. I believe that I will die saving the love of my life and that she will triumph over Jeremy and bring him to his own death. Therefore, old man, your life is not in vain."

With that, he pulled the man into him gently and let his fangs protrude into his neck. The old man kept his promise and didn't struggle. He stood there as Travis drained life from his veins; the blood was hot and moist. It had a bit of staleness to it, but it was human blood, and Travis hadn't realized how famished he had been. The man fell limp in Travis's arms as the blood slowed. He wanted to make sure he kept his end of the deal and drained him completely. When the man was truly dead, Travis found a shovel and dug a shallow grave for the old man's body. It was not fair that the old man should be left to rot, and as for his soul, it needed to be laid to rest properly. A spark of humanity still lingered within Travis.

Chapter 6

Travis stood staring across the craggy bay into the gates of Hell. It was always sort of amusing to Travis that the world's most dangerous vampire named his lair Hell. Hell was set in the depths of nowhere. Four days' ride from the little village where Rhea stayed, Hell was perfectly positioned in such a location that any of the world's major cities could be reached quite easily in a few days' time, especially with the supernatural speed vampires possessed. Even with that speed, Travis preferred the company of the white mare to the onslaught of whatever internal demons lurked in the corners of his mind. The fog never seemed to lift here, and it was bitterly cold. The irony for Travis was that if there was a true hell in the biblical sense, Hell would have been fiery hot versus frigid. The only way to the monstrous cave was by boat, not really a boat at all, but a small flat-bottomed wooden dinghy with room for only three adults where standing was the only option. Water splashed over the sides, and your feet always got wet. The boat had no oars as to detour curious travelers from a shallow, rocky death. The boat only sailed by being pulled by a rope that was tethered from the bay to the other side to a rock at the base of the enormous cave that held inhuman creatures of the darkest sort. The rope could not be seen through the fog, making it virtually impossible to get across, unless one knew the rope was there. The wind howled relentlessly, sending a shiver down Travis's spine. Of all the places he had been in this world, he hated this place the most. It was not natural that the sun never shone here or that the wind never stopped or that the fog never lifted. It was eerie how the temperature never changed so much as five degrees in one direction or the other. Travis knew all this made it the most perfect hideout for the king of the dark, but he couldn't help the fact that the hairs on the back of his neck stood erect every time he arrived here.

He dismounted Pixie and stood stroking her head, wishing he didn't have to cross the rough, uncharted waters alone. The salt from the water stung his face as the wind pelted his skin. What a terrible place. He sighed a long, heavy breath; Jeremy was waiting. He patted Pixie. This was where he and the perfect white mare parted ways. The weight of her would sink the wooden flat, and if he could get her across the murky bay, she surely would wind up the meal for some new vampire that had no self-control. As much as he feared what Jeremy was capable of, he knew the wrath of Rhea would be ten times greater if her horse became a snack to the undead. A slow, evil smile crossed his face at the thought of her rage. Jeremy wasn't going to know what hit him. He took one last look at Pixie. "Okay, girl, this is where we say goodbye. Rhea will be looking for you, and I need you to make sure she doesn't go wandering off." The mare whinnied as if she understood everything he said to her. Sometimes he almost felt like she did. He stepped down into the misty fog and disappeared. Pixie turned and walked away slowly. The place made her uneasy too. As soon as the world was once again night, she set off toward the direction in which she and Travis had come. He watched her go until she was out of sight.

The water was freezing as it splashed over the edge of the flat while Travis pulled his way across the bay. This was not going to be a fun visit as it never was. There were four months till the battle was set, and there was much to be done. Travis docked the boat at the entrance of Hell. There was a lone guard standing watch. He was taller than Travis, but smaller in frame. His blond hair blew in the wind. Travis knew the guard's name was Liam. Travis didn't much care for Liam as he was dumb as a post. He had been a vampire for one hundred years and still didn't have a clue. He had fallen prey to daylight sickness more times than Travis could count on one hand. He was not high on Jeremy's enlisted soldiers, but standing guard, even Liam couldn't screw that up. Travis shook his head in pure pity and walked right past Liam into the cave.

Jeremy had many hundreds of years to perfect the place. It was like a castle made of rock. It had many rooms most lavishly furnished in the latest trends of the times. There were turrets and large gathering rooms, banquet halls, and even a dungeon. There were torches lining the rocky walls. It truly was the perfect lair for the king of the vampires, spacious and comfortable. It was just a bit outlandish for Travis. He liked simple pleasures. He wandered on through the cave, seeing few vamps lurking here and there. He knew Jeremy was going to be ideally toying with some female in his private chambers or yelling at someone from his throne in the throne room.

He didn't much care to interrupt the horrible tyrant in his sexual endeavors, so he decided to check the throne room first. There he sat, tall and regal and completely full of himself, chest puffed out like a peacock. His hair was blacker the Travis's, and he kept it short. He didn't wear a crown, but he was high and mighty, his eyes dark matching his heart. The deepest shade of brown, his eyes could burn through a person's soul, and worse, they could melt a person's heart. He was strong, featured, tall with sharp lines. He was built with rock-hard muscle and had more confidence in himself than anyone Travis had ever met. He was shrewd and cocky and arrogant to boot. His face was hard but handsome. Travis didn't think a smile had ever crossed his stern mouth. His skin was a bit darker than the perfect olive complexion that was Rhea's. Vampires cowered in his presence. He could kill a mortal just by flashing his fangs. Those that survived would cry tears of utmost horror. He truly was a force to be reckoned with. Travis stood in the entrance, watching him yell at some poor sucker who had not followed Jeremy's exact orders. Travis knew the poor guy would be dust before the sun came up. When the young vampire was dismissed, Travis made his way through the magnificent throne room. The gold encrusted floor sparkled as if freshly polished. Travis knew, one of the many things Jeremy was the most brutal about was cleanliness. His cave had to always be spotless; if not, the wrath was deadly. Even after fresh blood had been spilled in Hell, it had to be washed clean.

Jeremy stood as Travis approached. It was well-known that these two demons of the dark didn't much care for each other but shared a certain air of respect for the other. Jeremy held Travis as the only vampire worth a damn, and Travis held to the regal violence that made Jeremy rule the other vampires. Travis bowed to keep the peace but hid the grimace as he did. Travis didn't answer to anyone, let alone an egocentric centuries-old vampire who planned to destroy the balance of things for a pastime.

Travis stood. There was instant tension. Travis bit back his irritation and greeted Jeremy as a trained soldier should greet his commanding officer, though he refused to address him as anything other than Jeremy. "Jeremy, you sent for me. How can I be of use to you?"

Jeremy stood there searching for any telltale signs that Travis had betrayed him in the time Travis had been gone from hell. Jeremy could read anyone, mortal or otherwise. He never could get a good read on Travis, and that always unnerved Jeremy just a little. Travis didn't seem to be hiding anything; he looked of having eaten recently and had the certain gleam only a woman can cause a vampire to obtain. There were no signs of treachery. Jeremy, by nature, didn't trust anyone or anything. The fact he decided Travis could be trusted was a good thing, and that trust had earned Travis the title of second-in-command. Jeremy nodded in approval and began to speak. "I wish to move forward with my war plans. I have let too much time pass without action. I need you, and a group of vampires, to go and scope out the battlefield. I need to know the layout at night, as well as during the day. The mortals will soon hear of my war before the Yule is out. I am planning small-scale attacks that will show them that vampires not only walk the earth but plan to rule it. They can bend to my whims, or they can die. I believe they will be more inclined to my whims. Don't you agree?"

Jeremy didn't give Travis time to answer but continued with his orders. "After you investigate the battlefield for the spring equinox, you will lead these small but vital attacks on the mortal world. You will take what prisoners you can and kill the rest. You will scream my name to all and make them fear the words *Jeremy* and *vampire* as if they were one and the same. These battles will be one they won't see coming. I want it ringing across the mountains and valleys, though, that on the day of equinox, the world, as they know it, will be mine.

Of course, there will be those who stand against us, but they are no matter. My armies will crush them where they stand. If the gods and goddesses are watching, let it be known that the only deity that will be forever worshipped will be that of the vampire king." He laughed at this, his laughter ringing through the walls of the cave. His laugh was melodic and the essence of pure, utter evil.

Chapter 7

Rhea sat on the bank of the small brook with her toes in the water. She had once again managed to sneak out of the inn without her would-be protector. She liked Blake; he had been good company since Travis left, and they had become friends, but Rhea liked her solitude as well. She was bored, and when she was bored, she tended to wander. She was having a hard time staying at the little inn. She really wanted to keep her promise to Travis, but she was restless; plus, she was close to home, and that made her even more fidgety. She wondered if she could convince Blake to take a trip for a day or two to her home village. She could see her family and Selene. She could start putting together an army. There was so much that she could accomplish in two days.

The sun was warm on her skin, and the stream was cool on her feet. She hadn't been able to bathe in almost a week. She stood and pulled the black velvet dress over her head, tossing it upon the bank. She didn't wear anything beneath her dress for she loved the feel of the material against her skin. She stood there nude and let the sun streak her skin. Her hair fell around her shoulders as she pulled out the ribbon that bound her braid. Toes first, she stepped into the brook. It was not very deep, but it came up to her knees. It was colder than she anticipated, but it felt good. Rhea let herself drop slowly into the water, letting it cover her waist and stomach. The chill made her lovely nipples go hard, but she still dropped until she was submerged in the stream to her neck. The brook rolled over her body as she soaked. It was a feeling of pure release, like the rolling of the brook took her troubles right downstream with it. She longed for a hot bath but was content to just be. The water caught her hair, and she leaned her head back so that her curls would fully get wet.

Her eyes closed in a peaceful way as her body floated just below the surface. Her mind was full of things, and she didn't even know she was being watched.

Blake sat in awe as he watched Rhea bathe. He never would have stood there while a naked woman was unaware of his presence, but he couldn't take his eyes off her. He had seen many women without clothes, but this one was truly a sight. It was as if her light not only illuminated her naked skin but reflected off the crystal-clear water, making her all but glow. From the looks of it, the lady Rae seemed to be flawless, and her lovely round breasts were hard and firm from the water. He felt ashamed that he watched her with lustful eyes without her knowledge. He cleared his throat to get her attention. She did not look up, so he tried again, this time a bit louder.

Her eyes opened; they scanned the bank until he was in her sights. He was standing modestly with his back to her. She knew he had seen her naked and was trying to be the gentleman about it. For Rhea, the body was nothing to be ashamed of or hide. If he was going to travel with her, he'd have to get over that quickly. She loved being naked. "Blake, it's quite all right to look. There is no harm in admiring a woman's body, especially in the nude. If you care for the cold, you are welcome to join me, but please don't turn and act like you have not seen me, here in all my glory. It's outright rude."

He slowly turned back to face her. She was smiling a smile that was coy, flirtatious, and sincere all at once. He felt his manhood skip a beat. He knew he was in trouble; nothing in the world could contain the urge he had to touch her. He stood there for a moment, not sure of what to do next.

She could see the wheels in his head turning, and it made her laugh. "Oh, Blake, quit being all cordial and prudish. I am not going to blush for the sake of your pride. Get undressed and come play in the water—that is, unless you're afraid of a little cold water…" It was teasing and playful, like they were teenagers, and she was daring him.

He didn't think about it any longer, and he stripped down, setting his clothes in a heap next to her dress. She didn't look away when he stood there with nothing on but carefully took in the details of his body. He was muscular and fit, obviously from hard work on the farm and hammering away at the anvil. She had imagined, at first meeting, what he would look like without his clothes, but he had given her imagination a bit of a run. His pecks were chiseled mounds on his bare chest, and his arms were rock hard from shoulder to wrist. His stomach was washboard down to the hips where it made a perfect *V*; his thighs were as big around as her waist, and she could see the line of muscle in his quads. She tried not to look too conspicuously at his manhood, though she did let her eyes glance in that direction. She said a silent "Oh my" and let her gaze wander elsewhere on his body. He watched her look upon him and said nothing for he had already taken in her near-perfect body, and it was only fair that she inspected him. He stepped into the water prepared for the shock of the cold to hit him, but it didn't. The water was cool but pleasant. He had told himself that even if the water was frigid, it wouldn't keep him from enjoying a naked swim with one of the most spectacular women he had ever met. He submerged himself into the water, careful not to touch her. He let the water run over him, and there was no denying it felt good.

She went back to her float, letting the small current take hold of her hair again. He couldn't help but notice that when her cedar hair was wet, it was really the color of molten metal hot from a flame. He had liked the color cedar when it was dry but found this new shade of what he described as blazing copper to be even more lovely. It made her eyes the shade of fresh ferns. He felt his pulse quicken and his groin grow tight with desire. He let himself slip totally under the water, hoping the coolness would help clear his head. When he surfaced, she was lying on her back, eyes closed, breasts toward the sky, round and perfect; her abdominals were a flat, hard line of feminine muscle, with the slightest curves just before her hips, giving her that hourglass shape. He gazed down her waist to the spot that made her a woman and stopped there for a moment to take in the lovely sight of her exposed. His groin grew tighter, and warmth spilled through his veins; she was breathtaking.

She opened her eyes and saw him watching her. She knew he was hungry for her. She saw it in his eyes. His hard body glistened from the water and sunlight. He was nice to look upon. They were friends; there was no reason why they couldn't enjoy each other's flesh. She was a woman with needs, and it had been a long time since they had been met. With Travis gone and their new agreement of what their relationship looked like, she was free to be with another man. It did make her feel ever so guilty, but she knew that was the way of it. Travis would never hold her in his arms again, and celibacy was not an option she was interested in. She looked at him the way he was looking at her. He caught her looking at him and turned away. Okay, so she was going to have to make the first move. She waded toward him, slowly, letting the water move steadily around her, as did her desire. She touched him gently on the shoulder, forcing him to look at her. He faced her, looking into her green eyes, and knew that he was not going to be able to say no to her even if he had wanted to. He started to speak, and she put her fingers to his lips.

"Hush, words are not needed now. I am a woman, and you are a man. Wanting of the flesh is natural, and if we are going to be traveling companions, we might as well enjoy the simple things of life while we can. There is no guarantee that we will survive this war. The touching of two bodies is something worth dying for." With that, she reached her head up to his and kissed him.

He stood there dazed for a moment, letting her lips press against his before he relaxed into it and parting his lips for her. He pulled her into him, letting his hands run down her back. She wrapped her arms around his neck and drove the kiss deeper, playing with his mouth and tongue. His mouth moved with hers, and it was warm and sweet. She tasted of lavender and honey, and he was going to get drunk on her flavor. He pulled her to him, and she wrapped her legs around him. She felt his heartbeat quicken as their bodies meshed. He wanted to explore her glorious body with his hands, and he could not do that standing in a brook. He opened his eyes, trying not to break the kiss, and walked them back to the bank. He laid her down, still kissing her. He pulled back for air and to look at her fully. She gasped for breath and blinked foggily at him. Her eyes were clouded; it had been a long time since she'd been kissed like that, tender and passionate and hot and hungry all at once and completely different from Travis's. Blake knelt above her on hands and knees. She ran her fingers gently over his chest and smiled at him. He moved to just his knees and memorized her body. He traced a finger along her cheek in a sweet gesture, to her jawline, and down the nape of neck. He lingered at her collarbone then slid down the centerline of her body, tracing a line along one breast and then the other. He stopped there and cupped a breast in each hand, squeezing them tenderly, massaging the nipples with his thumbs. They were already hard from the water, but they stiffened at his touch just a bit more. He bent his head down and kissed her softly and then kissed her throat before he put the whole of one of her prefect breasts into his mouth, licking and sucking a little deeper and harder each time. He moved to the other breast, taking it in and sucking, as if trying to get the air he breathed from her lovely mounds. He let his hands play upon the breast that he wasn't suckling. Pleasure was building up inside her, and she writhed under his touch. He watched her face as he drank in her bosom.

She closed her eyes and let the light of pleasure run over her. The light she bore was as splendid as the woman it encompassed. He was lost in the dazzling glow of her. It wasn't the blinding glow he had heard comes along with a faerie when having sex, but it was the soft glow of a candle in a windowsill or the faint glow of the moon when it's full. He slid a hand from her breast and slid it down to her stomach and played for a moment at her belly button, finding a tiny jeweled stud. He glanced down at it for a second, noticing the tiny silver ball with the head of a garnet. It was odd but strangely beautiful. He moved his mouth from her chest and began kissing down to her stomach, his tongue flicking playfully at the small silver ball in her navel. It caused her to purr from deep in her throat. He gazed back up into her eyes to watch the waves of hunger roll into those green pools. He trailed his fingers down the line of her hip to her thigh, moving slowly as it seemed to increase her gasps. As he inched down the side of her inner thigh to her bare womanhood, she sighed and arched with enjoyment. He grazed along the outer part of her womanly flesh, for a heartbeat, before finding the center of it. Blake touched her clit and rubbed it, causing it to swell. He could tell it was wet and hot before he stuck his fingers inside her. She opened to him, and he plunged deeper, letting her moist lips wrap around his fingers. She moaned and pulled him up from his licking to her mouth, where she matched his finger plunges with her tongue. He had her pulsating with pleasure, and it surged its way through his own body. He had been hard with desire since seeing her in the water, but now the blood pulsed hard into his shaft. He brought her to a peak with his fingers then pushed the length of him inside her. She arched her back and let out a gentle scream as he stretched her tightness. He was thick, hard, and the tip hit in just the right places. She raked her fingers down his back, pulling him desperately tight to her. He began to thrust down with his hips, and she moved her hips up to meet his with the same drive. It was raw passion and need that drew her to peak after peak. He rode on her desire, pushing his own to a craggy cliff, pulling her body close to his, pushing hard inside her one last time before their passion shattered like glass around them. He collapsed atop her, breathless and drained. Her own breath was ragged and shallow. Sweat gleamed off their bodies as they lay there trying not to move.

*****

The air had chilled, and a light breeze flittered through the trees. Rhea looked to the sky and saw the dark clouds rolling in. If she was going to beat the storm, she would have to leave soon. She decided to invite Blake to go with her; it would make his charge a bit easier if he didn't have to chase her down again, and he was good company.

"I am leaving here for a couple of days to go to my home. We are not far, and I am not sure when I will be able to travel there again, especially now that we are heading into battle in a few short months. I need to see my family and try to explain to them why I must go charging into war against a demon. Plus, there are a lot of good people who would be willing to fight with me, and I need to start getting my army together. You are welcome to go with me. We would find good food, incredible company, and warmth unlike any. You are also welcome to stay here if you'd rather." With that, she turned her head to look at her new friend.

He lay there watching the clouds roll in with a contented look on his face. He was the essence of day versus the eminence of the darkest night that was Travis. He was good-natured, mild tempered, had a big heart, was sincere and loyal to a fault. He was also a gentleman through and through, and she knew this would be the first and only time she and Blake would ever lie together. He was not for her. The thought was not sad, for she knew already he belonged to another, someone whom he would meet because of her, and maybe even soon, if he journeyed to her home with her that day. He was now looking at her with those soft sky-blue eyes. So lovable was Blake; she wanted to hold him like a stuffed bear. He spoke, interrupting her thoughts and making her remember she had just invited him to her village.

"Rhea, I know I shouldn't say anything as it is not my place, but didn't Travis give you strict instructions not to go wandering off and to stay here?"

So, he had heard her conversation before Travis had left for Hell. Travis would hate that, but oh well, no harm in him knowing. He was now part of the team no matter what Travis said. "Blake, you will find that Travis and I are very similar in one aspect, and that is, we can't stay in one place for very long. Besides, he doesn't own me, and he would never try to do so. Birds aren't meant to be caged, and he sees me as a bird. He gave me guidelines of a sort: I should not go wandering very far, but as I have said, my village isn't far, and I will make arrangements with the sweet old Mrs. Duff for keeping our lodgings here readily available as we come and go. We will keep this inn as our base for the time. Travis can reach me here by letter or anywhere by thought. You see, that's part of the bond that was created between us years ago."

She could tell he looked a bit confused, so she continued before he could say anything. "You see, because of what Travis is, and because of what I am, when Travis and I joined in love, the magic of light and dark allowed us to communicate telepathically. We can have entire conversations without being in the same country. I am hoping, as time goes by, that this connection will fade. It's rather exhausting having someone in your head all the time."

"Rhea, I know you have a history with him and you loved him, but he doesn't deserve you. I don't think there are many men in this world who deserve a creature of such goodness. I have no reason to stay here if you aren't here, and I would love nothing more than to irritate that bloodsucking leech that plays games with your heart. I say we ride to your village and go build an army to kick some major vampire ass."

*****

Upon returning to the inn, they departed ways to their own rooms so that they could ready themselves to leave. Rhea gathered her things in her saddlebag and changed her gown. Instead of the easy, over-the-head riding dresses she usually wore, this one was a rich mixture of velvet and satin. The bodice was black satin trimmed in black lace, cutting low on her chest; the long sleeves fell off her shoulders and belled out like fairy wings from her hands. It laced up in a crisscross pattern with crimson ribbon. The skirt was crimson velvet with the same black lace trim. It fell in neat pleats to the floor around her legs. The dress itself was incredibly elaborate and beautiful, but it made Rhea look undeniably like a princess out of one of her books. She stood there looking at herself in the looking glass in her room. She herself had to admit that she looked wonderful, all except for one thing. She pulled the ribbon out of her hair. It came cascading over her bare shoulders in a mass of copper curls. She smiled at her reflection; she might have been modest in the way of her looks, but she felt a little braver looking a little more feminine. She gathered her things and left the little room.

She found the kind old woman and explained that she and Mr. Larson would be needing their accommodations left as they were for the time and would hence be back in a few days. The old innkeeper didn't ask questions but assured Rhea that their rooms would not be filled in their absence. She graciously took the silver piece Rhea had given her for her troubles, but before she went back to her business, she looked at Rhea and simply said, "Angels should always ride in such dignity and beauty, my child. This look suits you better than those silly riding dresses you've been wearing." With that, before Rhea could say anything, the old woman was gone. Rhea pondered for a moment how the old lady Nell had guessed what she truly was but figured this would be something she would learn another time. She tied her cloak round her neck and walked out of the inn.

Funny how a little inn could feel more like home than the place where she would ride to. Blake had insisted upon readying the horses, as he didn't have many belongings or the trials of being a woman, so she took her time making her way to the stable yard. She noticed the rosebushes had bloomed their last winter bloom since she first arrived. They were full and deliciously fragrant and would not last long with the encroaching storm. There was one lone white rose that called to her. It was whiter than her mare and as soft and delicate as snow. She decided it would be a nice contrast to the red and black of her dress. She picked the rose, watching the thorns, tucked it behind her ear, and continued walking to the stables.

Blake was busy brushing an already-saddled Pixie, who had returned two days earlier, and didn't notice her walk up. She stood there, not making any noise, watching the man who would stand by her in battle but lose his heart very soon to another. She sent up a silent prayer that he would live through this war, have a family and a life to call his own. It was then that Pixie noticed her mistress and neighed happily. Blake looked up from the mare; Rhea stood there, breathtaking and beautiful. He hadn't expected to see her looking like royalty, but there she was, very much a queen in her own right. He dropped the grooming brush and stepped around Pixie, walking over to his travel companion, never taking his eyes off her. When he reached her, Blake grabbed her by the arms, not hurting her, and kissed her. The kiss was hot with fire and passion, and she opened her mouth eagerly to his. He found her tongue with his own; her taste filled him to his soul. He knew not what lay ahead of them, but he would be a fool if he didn't savor how incredible she looked. She melted into him and deepened the kiss. She'd be damned if she didn't leave a bit of her in his memory since he was destined for another. Knowing this would be their last kiss, why not make it great? He eased his grip on her arms and pulled her more into an embrace. The intensity of the kiss left them both breathless when they pulled away from each other. They stood there, looking at each other, panting for air, and glassy-eyed. She'd give the man credit where it was due; he sure could knock a woman for a loop when he kissed.

She shook her head, clearing away the haze. Looking at him, she smiled. "Blake, what on earth was that for?"

He blinked and looked at her again, seeing her as he had before the kiss, looking regal and stunning. He smiled at her in return and replied, "Rhea, where I come from, when a woman looks as good as you do now, there is nothing a man can do but try and make an impression on her and do his best to get her to notice him as everyone notices her." He bowed slightly to her with his head. He won the chivalry award. Before she could say anything else, he took her hand in his, kissed it sweetly, and said, "Lady Rhea, the stars in the heavens aren't even as beautiful as you are right now. The rose you wear in your hair blushes with envy, for you put its true beauty to shame."

She felt her cheeks getting warm. She didn't blush easily, but with a compliment like that, it was hard not to. He was truly sincere, and that was rare in a man. She bowed her head to him in thanks and gave him the full weight of her smile. Her nerves were lessening, and that was a good thing. She looked back at him and asked, still smiling, "Blake, are you always this charming?" Then she laughed, sending music into the afternoon air.

He laughed with her—he couldn't help it; it was contagious when she laughed. "I didn't know I was charming. You must bring out the worst in me," he said and winked at her.

They laughed again. Even with war and mass destruction lingering in the air, they could still find joy and laughter. They had to hold dear to that, for if they ever stopped laughing, being joyful, Jeremy would surely prevail. She let these thoughts enter her mind but didn't let them consume her.

After their laughter had subsided, she moved into his space again and put her arms around him in a friendly hug. "Blake, I am very glad that I have you as company. The road I have traveled is often lonely. It is very nice to have a companion and to be able to laugh out loud with another." She hugged him tight and then let him go, walking over to her snow-white mare. As she reached Pixie, she heard Travis in her head. He hadn't tried to contact her since he left. She closed her eyes. She couldn't see him unless she was asleep and he entered her dreams but could focus in on his words more if she went inside herself. This was one of the harder parts of being bound to him; her thoughts were never truly her own if he didn't wish it. She sighed and focused on the sound of his voice. It was far away, but still rich, thick, and very seductive. Silently in her mind, she said, "I am here."

She heard him as if he were standing next to her. "Rhea, where are you going? I thought we agreed that you wouldn't go wandering about?"

Even in her own mind, her defenses went up; he was not her keeper. She eased up on the defenses just a bit so that she wasn't mad when she answered him. Her words were calm and collected even if she wasn't speaking them. "Travis, I ride this day to my parents' home, to the village where we met. I have not been there in a very long time and have much to do before this war. I will not go into battle without an army at my back and my family knowing what is to come. I will not be there long—two, three days tops."

She felt him sigh, and it caused her a slight shudder. She knew, though he would not argue with her in her subconscious. She felt his hand on her own, and she smiled. "Rhea, if you must go, please be of great care. It is madness here. I will come to you again when you are alone and tell what's going on. I know I don't care for him much, but please take Blake with you. I need to know you are as safe as possible, and if he is with you, at least you are not alone. Hurry back here, time is not our kindest friend."

"Travis, time has never been our kindest friend. That is why my heart breaks each time I see you. Blake rides with me and will stay with me. Even if I tried to evade him, he would catch up to me. Plus, the company is a nice change. I promise to keep safe. Please promise to do the same. I cannot fight a war I know nothing about without you by my side. If you are to be Jeremy's second-in-command, then I need you to be my commanding officer. That does not give you the right to order me about in a day-to-day basis, but it does mean that when it comes to war and strategy, your word is the one I follow. Now please give me credit where credit is due, and know that I will be on guard at all times and will not speak unless I know for sure they be on our side."

He sighed again. She knew—he knew—she was right. "Rae, you are, without a doubt, the most stubborn woman I have ever met." He smiled. "Okay, Rae, go do what you must. I will talk to you soon. Oh, and one more thing before I let you go, you make it extremely difficult to concentrate when you look as you do. Red always was your color, and that dress, well, it does much for you in all the right places. You look exquisite, and I hate the fact that Blake gets to be the one at your side. Oh, and just so you know, the kiss didn't do the way you look justice." With that, she felt him kiss her forehead and fade away.

She hated when he did that. It made her nuts that he got the last word in, but she opened her eyes, and it were as if time had stood still, for she was still standing in front of Pixie and Blake hadn't seemed to notice anything different. *Good*, she thought. She didn't need more than one man inside her head right now. She patted the side of her mare's head. *Homeward bound*, she thought. Blake moved up alongside her, helping her into her saddle. She smiled at him, and he mounted his own horse. She clicked her heels to Pixie's side, and they were off. They rode for a while in silence—not an awkward or uncomfortable silence, just the silence of two people who shared a journey and where talk wasn't necessary.

They passed through villages and towns through meadows and valleys. She knew this area well; she had traveled it many times, and it was a surreal sense of comfort to her. They would reach her parents' homestead just after dark. Her thoughts drifted in and out of home and people she knew. The sun had slowly started to sink down into the sky before either of them spoke.

It was Blake who broke the silence first. "Rhea, are you looking forward to being home with your family?"

She rode on looking forward but answered him with the only answer she could. "Blake, I love my family more than anything else in this world, but my family doesn't understand me. They don't understand the need I have to be a wayward wanderer as they call me. For as many generations as I can count, the Edwards have lived in Hearts Prairie, have raised families there, have been very content to be the town healers, never go anywhere else or do anything else, and I was the first to break that pattern of life. My family loves me and knows I do great things on my travels, but they wonder when I will tire of the life I have chosen and come home for good. They also tend to believe that my choices are usually wrong and that I need them to plan my life for me. This is something that we have disagreed on since I was old enough to think for myself. I don't know, maybe someday I will go home, raise a family, and be a good little housewife, but I just can't see me setting up shop in one place for the remainder of my life."

He studied her for a moment before saying anything. She didn't look sad or hurt or disappointed; instead, she looked thoughtful. "Will they support you in this war?" The question was one she had been asking herself since the moment she agreed to fight at Travis's side. She wasn't entirely sure they would back her.

"Blake, I do not know the answer to that question. I know they won't be pleased, especially when I tell them Travis is involved. Funny, they never much cared for him even before he was a vampire. I do know that they will beg and plead with me to reconsider, and I know it will be in vain that they do. I will fight, and they will either stand beside me or stand behind me and pray to every goddess they can for my safety." She shook her head and heaved a sigh.

Blake hated the fact that he couldn't help but watch her perfect breasts rise and fall in her time of uncertainty, but he was a man, and they were ever so nice to look at in red silk, black lace, and he figured if she hadn't wanted them to be looked upon, she would have chosen other than the bodice.

The sky started to change colors, and the sun sank lower down the horizon. The air had cooled further, yet she didn't feel cold. She was almost home. Despite their differences in opinion, she would be glad to see her family. She had missed them so much. The scenery changed and became vastly familiar. She was only about thirty minutes from home. She knew every building, from here till her parents' door; it was a comfort to know nothing had changed. The tavern was up on the left-hand side of the road. She could use a bit of encouragement.

"Hey, Blake, how do you feel about having a drink or two before we get to my parents' house?"

He didn't have much choice, and he, too, could use a drink. It was never easy meeting a woman's family. He shrugged and said, "Why not?"

Oh good, she thought, *liquid courage.*

She moved her mare in the direction of the tavern. She had many memories of this old bar. She was not going to let her mind wander as to who could be inside, so she dismounted Pixie and led her to the stables. Sometimes she preferred self-serve stables versus those with a stable hand. The old barn smelled of hay and pine and looked much like it smelled; so far, nothing had changed. It tugged at her heart. She was starting to remember why she had wanted to leave this place; everything stayed the same. They tethered their horses and walked toward the door. Blake held the solid wooden door open for her. As she stepped in, she let the hood of her cloak fall off her head. Her copper curls spilled around her shoulders. She stood just inside the door, taking in a place she knew well. Again, nothing had changed. She saw John, the tavern owner, behind the counter pouring drinks and sharing in the latest gossip. The bar wasn't long or crowded. A few select regulars mulled around it, while everyone else shared the few tables that occupied the space inside the little tavern. Sometimes she thought there was more room outside in the stables than inside, but that's what made it so comfortable and welcome.

Drew sat at the bar throwing back beers, when he felt a shift in the air, a presence he hadn't felt since she left this little town. He knew the earth angel had returned and had walked into the tavern. Not many would notice the change until they saw her, but for him, it was different; it was as if when she was near, the earth shook. He knew it didn't, just the air around her. Drew sucked in breath and held to it as he turned on his stool. Sure enough, there she was, a woman worthy of so much more than he could ever offer her, yet he had been secretly in love with her for a very long time. Hair like silken copper coils, eyes greener than a ponderosa, lips meant for kissing, and skin as soft as feathers, but more than that was her ability to melt the snow with her smile. Her smile was one of the things he had loved most about her as it is for many who meet her. He had heard that she had been back to Hearts Prairie, but it had been years since he had seen her. He had wanted nothing more, at one point in time, than to marry her and settle down, but that wasn't for either of them at that time. They were young and wild and were not ready to settle down as it were. He sat there watching her, wondering why he hadn't gone with her on her travels like she had asked. He knew the answer; he couldn't leave with her when he didn't have a penny to his name. He couldn't help but notice she had a male traveling companion. Had he lost his chance with her? Jealousy washed over him; he knew it was foolish but couldn't help it. He stood up and walked toward her, eyes only for her and her male escort.

She saw him long before he even moved off the stool in her direction. Some things, she was glad, never changed, like the fact that Drew was sitting on his usual stool, drinking beer. She had to admit part of her wanted him to be there, to be the first person to welcome her home, but at the same time, she hadn't been prepared for the sight of him to knock the wind out of her. She couldn't breathe, nor did she want to. The few times she had come home, she had avoided the tavern, knowing he would be there. Travis had won her heart, had shown her passion beyond compare, and had given her romance, fantasy, and she had loved him hopelessly for it. Drew had shown her friendship, laughter, fun, honest, sincere love and affection. He had shown her, her dreams. They had been young, though, and he was too shy to ever pursue her; plus, he hadn't wanted to hurt his friend, and that she found honorable and respected him for it.

He stopped a few feet from her and Blake, and she saw the jealousy in his eyes. She smiled at this; some things really didn't change. She stepped forward, knowing she needed to put some space between Blake and Drew, or poor Blake would wind up with a fist in his face before he even had a chance. She gave Drew her attention; she willed him with a bit of feminine magic to look at only her. She gave him the weight of her smile. He looked at her. She was more incredible than he remembered. She had become a woman, elegant, radiant, confident. He had remembered her as a girl, sultry, seductive, sexy, and coy, and though he could still see those things in her persona, he liked the woman he saw before him better than the girl. He was awestruck and fell speechless. The jealousy that surged through his veins was quickly replaced with feelings he hadn't felt for anyone in a very long time.

She stepped forward again, closing the distance between them. Time had passed and changed them both, so she hoped that what she saw in his soft-brown eyes was of welcoming. "Drew." Her voice was like warm honey, sweet and sincere and very much the sound of the music he had heard in his dreams so often since she left.

"Rhea, I… You… I mean, oh hell, it's been way too long." She giggled at how cute it was that he stumbled over his words. Then she smiled at him again and threw her arms around his neck and hugged him. He wrapped his arms around her and held her as close to him as he could. Taking in everything from the warmth of her skin to the smell of her hair, he rested his head on hers and whispered in her ear, "God, I've missed you."

She kissed him on the cheek ever so gently and whispered back, "I know what you mean." She saw the boy she once knew in the man before her, and though he held a place in her heart, as all those she helped to find their paths do, she no longer saw herself settled down and married to him. She wanted more, and part of her knew she deserved more. With that, she pulled away from his embrace. "So, are you going to buy me a welcome-home drink, or did the gentleman I knew so long ago disappear in the man I see before me?" She winked at him and smiled.

He laughed; she always did have a way about her that got her what she wanted, but he then remembered the man who had helped her with her cloak. "Rhea, as good as it is to see you, I am not sure your gentleman friend over there would appreciate me buying his gal a drink?" He raised his eyebrows at her in questioning.

She chuckled to herself and shook her head. "Drew, this is Blake Larson of Elden Springs. He is a friend of mine and will be my travel companion for a while. If you would stop being a silly jealous boy and buy us a drink, there is much to tell you, and I only have a few days' time before I have to set out again." She hated that she was scolding him, but she hated nothing more than jealousy; plus, as far as she was concerned, he hadn't the right to be jealous after so many years, but that was for another time. She stood there waiting to see what he would do.

He heaved a sigh and let his shoulders fall. He offered Blake his hand. "Mr. Larson, it's a pleasure to make your acquaintance, for any friend of Rae's is welcome amongst us here in Hearts Prairie. The lady Rhea does not greet this little place often, but she is widely loved throughout the whole of the village." Blake reached forward and took Drew's hand. It was a much nicer welcome than what he had received from Travis. They shook hands, and then Drew turned back to his angel. He offered her his arm, and she accepted it without hesitation. "Well, kiddo, welcome home," he said and led her to the bar.

The people in the tavern were already whispering among themselves about the sudden return of Rhea, her new escort, and many other speculations of the like. Drew led her to the bar and offered her his stool. Blake stood to her left, Drew to her right, and all around her were the same faces she had known her whole life. She knew each person—not only by first name, but by last. That was the way of her home. Small town and everyone knew everything about everyone else. In fact, she would put money on it that her family would know of her whereabouts before she left the tavern.

Finally, old John made everyone shoo away from his bar to give her and the men at her sides some room; they would hound her all night had he not. He stood there looking at her. She sure had grown to be a fine woman, and her dad would be proud. He had known her since the day she was born and was, in turn, her godfather. He smiled at her then said, "Well, I'll be damned if my beautiful god-daughter has finally come home again." With that, he held out his arms, and as she had since she was a child, she climbed onto the bar and gently jumped into his embrace. John hugged her tightly as if she were his own daughter. In a way, she sort of was, as he had never had kids of his own. He loved Rhea with all the pride a man could hold in his heart for a child. Then he stepped back so he could look her over more carefully, held her hand, and twirled her around.

She laughed and humored the old man who was her father's dearest friend. Finally, he let go of her hand and shook his head; tears welled in his soft gray eyes. "You are even more lovely than the very rose in your hair. Welcome home, child." With that, he hugged her again.

She smiled and kissed his forehead. She had known John when he wore a younger man's clothes, and she had always found him handsome. Now there was more salt than pepper in his long beard, and his once-black hair was now white. Wrinkles rested around his eyes and cheeks, but he was still handsome. "John, it's good to be home." With that, she climbed back over the wooden slab that was better known as the bar and sat back down in the stool, adjusting her corset and skirt. She introduced Blake to John and ordered up a round of whiskey for her and her friends. John grabbed a bottle of whiskey he kept just for her and poured three glasses full of sweet amber-colored whiskey. He then winked at her and went to tend the patrons. She raised her glass and toasted the man sworn to protect her and the man she hoped would fight beside her the day of battle. "Salute to being home, good friends, both old and new, and to whatever this way comes. May peace and love prevail." They raised their glasses to hers, and both said, "Salute." She drank her drink in one long swallow and poured another. This one she sipped delicately and ladylike.

Drew felt his desire for her stir low in his belly. There was something enticing about a woman that threw back whiskey, and this one was the flame that sparked all his fires. "Rhea, where have you been all these years?" He smiled, wanting to encourage her to share with him.

She laughed. "Drew, the question should be more like, where haven't I been. The world has opened its doors to me, and where the wind called, I followed."

He nodded and sipped his drink. Was she ever going to share with him the way she once had, or had too much time gone by? Just as these thoughts were forming in his mind, she locked her fingers in his and forced him to look down at her. He saw the spark that was his, still there in her green eyes, and it made his heart leap. "Drew, I cannot tell you of my travels right now for there is much to tell and I need to reach my parents' house before they send a search party looking for me, as no one here can keep a secret and my family is sure to know of my return. If you would call on me tomorrow, I would very much like to tell you of some of my travels and journeys. As I said, there is much to say."

He looked at her and could see how full of hope she was and could not resist her. "As the lady wishes, so shall it be." With that, he slammed his own glass of whiskey and poured another. Talk was small from then on.

After her third glass, she knew it was time to go. Any more whiskey and her willpower would not sustain, and she didn't have it in her to go back to being the girl she once was and make out with Drew. Plus, she had already given herself to Blake that day, and one man was more than enough for her in one day. She waved to John, and he returned to her. "What do I owe you for the delicious bottle of whiskey this evening?"

He frowned. "Has really that much time gone by that my goddaughter doesn't remember that she pays not for drinks in my bar?"

She looked at him, humbled; she knew he would not allow her to pay for drinks, and she had insulted him by asking. "John, I am sorry I did not intend to be rude or ungrateful. I just meant that since I was not the only one drinking this eve, I might be able to render for Drew and Blake?"

She smiled, hoping to win him over. It worked, but he still scolded her. "Hear this now," and he raised his voice for the whole tavern to hear. "My goddaughter has always drunk for free, and so it is clear to all if she drinks alone or with a companion, she still drinks for free, as does her companions." He then lowered his voice so only their little group could hear. "Mr. Larson, you will do well to make sure this young woman gets to her family's stead and that she is well tended. Drew, you will do well to remember that the lady has invited you to call upon her on the morrow. Any man with any sense would make haste in such an invitation from such a woman, and you, young lady, will remember that drinks here are always on the house. Next time you come home, you should visit your parents' house before you visit my old bar. I know you and your parents disagree, but home it will always be, and thus whiskey can wait." Then he smiled and hugged her again.

She stood from her stool. She looked at Drew and then to Blake. She needed a minute with Drew. "Blake, will you give us a minute, please?"

He looked at her like "Yeah, right, I'm going to leave you alone."

"Blake, please, I promise I will be all right. These are my people."

He sighed and said, "I'll just go and fetch the horses as my lady requests." He nodded to Drew and then bowed to Rhea. With that, he turned and walked out the door. He knew she was not his, but they had shared their bodies with each other, and that gave him a tinge of the jealousy he had seen in Drew earlier.

Rhea watched him go then turned back to Drew. He had boyish good looks but was not handsome in the way of Blake or the heart-stopping, immortal, dangerous way Travis was, but there was no denying he was good-looking. He stood tall just about six foot. He had strong, muscled arms, but not in the way of Blake's, and he was small in frame. He was lean, skinny, and kind of awkward with his limbs. He was never sure what to do with his arms, so he crossed them over his chest a lot. He had a nice oval face, soft cheekbones and jawline, big round eyes the color of raw honey, which were topped by long, fluttery, soft-brown eyelashes that curled and touched his brow, a nose that fit his face perfectly, and soft pink heart-shaped lips. His face was finished off by a round chin, with the cutest little cleft in the center of it. He wore a thin goatee and mustache that framed his cleft, light-brown hair he kept short, but when it was long, it was as curly as Rhea's. She did have a special place for the man standing in front of her.

Without wanting the whole town to hear what she had to say, she took him by the hand and led him outside the tavern, grabbing her cloak off the wooden hook by the door. The air was colder than it had been in days, and the wind played with her curls. She put on her cloak and fastened it, then she stepped into his space and looked up at him. He brushed a stray curl from her face with his finger and let it linger on her skin. Warmth tingled where he touched her face. She started to speak, and he stopped her, putting his finger over her lips. "Shh!" he said, looking at her. "There is no need for words right now. There is much to say between you and I, and there will be time for it on the morrow when I call on you at your parents' house, but tonight, there is no need for them." With that, he bent his head, and he kissed her cheek. She was grateful the kiss fell on her cheek and not on her lips; she was not about to give him any sense of false hope. For so long she had chased a man who could ignite every desire she had ever had and turn it into her fantasies come true, but he was incapable of exchanging energy of life with her. There was no current of pulse when he touched her. With Drew, she could feel that energy running the course of her veins, his mixed with hers and switching places as it went. She had to be honest with herself that he was not the man for her, but she did need him, so she had to weigh things carefully. She was about to embark on a war she was not sure she could win, and she needed him at her side, but how could she ask the man who clearly hoped she would stay for the long haul to give up his life for her when she could offer him nothing more than a smile or a friendly hug? She pulled away from him and stepped back out of arm's reach. He looked hurt, and she hated that, but she would hate herself more if he got killed fighting at her side.

"Drew, I'm sorry, but I need to go and see my family." She could see his heart sink. She knew she shouldn't, but she stepped back up to him and took his hand in hers. "Drew, please don't look at me like that. I have my reasons as to why I pulled away. I have missed you so much, and I need to believe that you are still the man I could not bring myself to say goodbye to all those years ago. I need you to still believe in me and trust me when I say that this is how it has to be for now." There was longing in her eyes, and it washed over him in waves.

He raised their entwined hands and turned them over so hers was on top. He brushed her knuckles with his soft pale-pink lips and kissed her hand, then he let it go and stepped back. "My angel, I will always believe and trust in you. If this is the way it must be this night, so be it. I promise I will come for answers on the morrow, and I promise whatever you need to say will not change my mind about you. I have waited for your return for a long time, and I won't go quietly into the distance of your mind again. I thought my heart stopped the day you left this town and blew a passing kiss in my direction, but I lived, and as I live and breathe, I will wait for you as long as I need to." With that, he turned on his heels and walked back into the tavern, leaving her alone in cold night air.

She heard his voice a second time that day; he was in her head again, and so she obeyed his call. "Travis, don't you have anything better to do than raid my thoughts and spy on me?" She knew she sounded a little annoyed but didn't care she had a lot on her mind.

"Rae, I'm not spying on you, nor am I raiding your thoughts. You have your work cut out for you with that one. He is still the boy in a man's form. He has never grown up, and he never will. His childish ways will cost him your affection and his life if he is not careful. You know very well that he is not the man for you. You're too good for him, and he knows it."

"Travis, it is very hard to concentrate with you in my head all the time, but you are right, he is not for me. Maybe I am not meant to settle down."

"No, don't say things like that. You are meant for great love. The thought of you being with any man other than me drives me mad, but we both know how this war will end for me, and the thought of you being alone for the rest of your known life doesn't bode well either."

"So why don't you defy the fates and live, and then you could have me my whole life through?" She knew she was taunting him with a dare he could not fill. Even if he did live, she knew that he could never be just hers, and she was okay with that.

"Rhea, you don't need me. I am no good for you. You know as well as I do that I could never be faithful to you, and it would wear too much on that pretty face of yours to let me go out and be selfish. I want you to *live*, and a life with me would be pumping death into your veins every day. I won't do that to you. Plus, I know I die saving you, and I could think of nothing nobler than ending my life so that your light can shine."

"Travis, what am I going to do? He'll stand at my side, just as you will, but if he does, it is because he thinks he loves me. If he falls, he loses his life for love that was never meant to be, and that is not the reason why I charge into battle. If I have to watch those I love die around me, why should I fight at all?"

"Rhea, no one is forcing you to fight, and no one is forcing any of them to follow you. You will fight because it's in your heart to do what's right and you know Jeremy will destroy all mankind if you don't. They will all follow you because of who you are and what you stand for. Drew does not have to stand and fight with you, no one does, but he will because he loves you and he's not a coward. Rhea, I am counting on you to shine brightly the day of the war and bring evil to its knees even if it means losing some of the ones whom you love. Now go, Blake is ready with the horses, and your family is waiting." With that, he was gone from her mind as quickly as he entered it.

She turned around to find Blake watching her, a horse in each hand. She smiled at him and let her troubles crawl back into the shadows for another time. Her family's house came into view. He was etched in her thoughts as he always was after he entered her mind, but Rhea had bigger things to deal with than the way Travis wanted her to find true love. Drew would be there on the morrow; she would set the record straight, and that was that. Right now, she had to build up her courage to face her family after being gone for so long and bearing news that she was going into battle against pure, utmost evil.

The Edwards had lived on this piece of land for over three generations. The house was large for the time, but not in great splendor. Each generation added or changed what they needed to for their family. The only thing that had stayed the same over time were the gardens; they were lush and rich and full of life. From late March to early November, roses of all colors and sizes roamed the property, some climbing the walls of the old house, some in trees and bushes that went in all directions. Her mother prided herself on the roses, for they were truly a work of art and the smell was utterly intoxicating. Reds and pinks, whites, yellows, even purples—sometimes the plants would cross-pollinate and the colors would mix, giving new shades of roses. Rhea loved the roses more than any other part of the property. If she thought about it hard enough, she could smell them through the frost and winter that had them dormant.

Muttering under her breath about home and hearth, she pulled Pixie to a stop and dismounted; Blake did the same. They still hadn't spoken much since they had left the tavern. She felt she owed him an explanation, but for what, she was not sure. Still, she needed to say something to him. She walked her mare to the stables; her family was of good means but refused to have hired help. They loved working the family property on their own. She unsaddled her horse and brushed her out. Blake did the same to his own horse.

"Blake, I need you to understand something. After you and I had our little romp down by the creek, I saw a vision of you with someone I hold very dear. I am not yet sure who that person may be, but I know she is close and that once you two cross paths, she will be the only woman in your heart. I know you will do your duty to protect me through this war, but you will no longer be fighting for me but for her. I have seen you making a life with her, and I will not come in the way of that. Please know that from here out, we shall be just friends and this afternoon was amazing but shall not happen again." She looked at him, hoping she was not sounding horrible or hurting him, but he seemed to look on her knowing her to be right.

With a smile, he nodded. "Rhea, I know what you say to be true. I have felt it just as you have seen it. I would have been hurt by this before I had met you and had visions of my own. I have come to accept things to be sometimes strange around you, no offense, but they tend to be strange more than they are normal. I think that is what makes you so special. Weird, wonderful, and unusual things happen in your presence." He smiled again and continued, "This morning by the creek was, as you say, amazing, and I will treasure the fact that I got to be in your arms for a time. Not many men can say they've gotten to make love to an angel." With that, he winked at her and went back to brushing his stead. After a moment, he looked back at her and said something that took her off guard. "Rhea, I know it is none of my business, and you can tell me to mind my mouth if you'd like, but I think Drew is much better suited for you than Travis, but I don't think he is right for you. You have too much spirit for Drew. He would try and tame you, and that would not suit you at all." With that, he was again busying himself with his horse.

She was at a loss for words. Not only had Travis declared Drew not to be her match, but so did her new travel companion who had barely known her but seemed to know her like a lost friend. She brushed Pixie, not really paying attention to what she was doing. She was lost in thought. She had always liked Drew but, deep down inside, knew it was just because she couldn't help but love him, because she loved anyone that she spent time with. Numb from the day she put the brush aside. She had more pressing matters to deal with, and that required her to snap out of it. She shook her head and heaved a sigh. Straightening her clothing, she stood up straight and tall, bringing her awareness back to her family. Blake saw her shift gears and did the same. He was on her terms now, and this was her home. She looked at him and gave a little shake of her head and shrug of her shoulders. "Well, here goes nothing, I hope your skills of protecting me are in full force, because none can hurt me more than those who reside within that house, and this will be the first of many battles we are sure to fight on our journey." With that, she gathered all her strength and courage and became the cool, confident woman he had met but a few days earlier, the woman who had held her own against a rude stranger, the woman who had cut a vampire down to size, the woman who was destined to save the world, and all he had to do was keep her alive.

Chapter 8

She stood there on the front stoop, pondering whether she should knock or just go in. The time was long between visits, but this was her home, the place of her birth, the place of her childhood. She was just about to push open the old door when it flew open and Rosa, her baby sister, breezed out along with light and sounds of some of her strongest memories. It was warm and welcoming and filled her with an exhilarated sense of joy. She and her family might not always agree, but she was home. Rosa was a little taken aback by seeing Rhea standing there, and it briefly showed in her brown eyes, but she recovered quickly. "Well, if it's not my lovely older sister." She smiled and threw her arms around Rhea's neck. Rhea returned the hug. She had missed her sister. Pride filled her heart as she stepped back and looked at Rosa. Rosa had always been pretty, but last time Rhea saw her, she was still growing from teenager to woman, but now she was all woman. She had their mother's height and stood three, maybe four inches, above her older sister. The height was just a small similarity to their mother compared to the rest of her. It was as if time had been flipped and Rhea stood before her mother at the age of twenty-one. Rosa had the same long straight brown hair that fell down her back in a solid sheet instead of ringlets and waves like her own. Her sister's eyes were as brown as her hair, and every feature of her face was chiseled in exact replica of Rene's. Rhea had always thought Rene was the most beautiful of women, classy and eloquent, like the roses she prided herself on, and now her younger sister was the spitting image of her. Rhea gained control of her emotions before they began to show on her face. She hugged her younger sister one more time.

Rosa, being of nature to speak her mind, spoke first. "Rhea. Damn sister, where the hell have you been, and why has it taken you so long to come home?" With that, she tossed her long brown hair over her shoulder and laughed. "It's so good to see you. Welcome home, sis." Without further conversation, she threw her arm around her older sister, turned, and went back in through the door which she had opened just a few minutes before. Rhea followed without much resistance. She did turn back to look over her shoulder at Blake and beckon him to follow, which he did silently.

The house was filled with noises and smells, most of which flooded through her senses, bringing back more memories than she had realized she had suppressed, all of them carrying their own weight upon her. No amount of time or distance could change the fact that this was her home and in these walls were the people who had raised her. They loved her in their own way, she supposed, or at least in the best way they knew how. Tears began to well in her green eyes when she heard the voices of her parents. Seeing them, the tears fell down her cheeks. Richard and Rene were sitting by the fire, side by side, as they always had, holding hands and a glass of wine. Their focus was held softly on the fire glow and each other. Richard and Rene were the idea of the perfect couple. They disagreed, bickered, and bantered as if they had been together since the beginning of time, like just any old married couple. They also loved each other with an undying affection that was stronger than any other force Rhea had ever seen. Their love for each other was Rhea's original reason for setting out into the world... *Move out into the world and find true love, love that withstands the sands of time.* Now as she watched her parents converse, she realized her mission had become so much more than that. Her heart did a small, little flop and settled back into her chest. So much love was going to be overshadowed by so much death and destruction. She had to prevail so that love like her mother and father's would be in the making of stories years to come.

The room was as it had been the day she was last there: simple pieces of furniture, two oversize stuffed chairs made of wood and leather that Richard and Rene occupied, an elegant old writing desk of dark wood, a matching sideboard, bare wood floors that she knew her mother had spent countless hours sweeping, and a very simple woven rug in front of the fire. The fireplace itself was beautifully handmade with rocks from all over the area that reached to the top of the tall vaulted ceilings and all the way back down to the floor, where there was a long shelf of rock coming out three feet. As a younger girl, she used to curl up on that shelf and lay there reading and feeling the full warmth of the fire. The rock looked odd and out of place against the wooden wall panels, but Rhea loved it for its uniqueness.

Rosa interrupted her tranquil outline of the room. "Mom, Dad, you will never guess who I found lurking in the doorway." Her parents turned and stared in wonderment then both scrambled up out of their chairs and threw loving arms around their daughter. She didn't even try to hide her tears at this point but, instead, let them wash down her cheeks. It had been a very long time indeed since she had been home and in her parents' embrace. The last time she had been there, she left in haste after yet another argument about how she was living her life incorrectly. After a long hug, she stepped back out of their arms. Her mother and father both had tears in their eyes. It was truly a welcoming reunion.

Rene spoke first, in her soft, easygoing, classic way. It had always reminded Rhea of a lullaby when her mother spoke, a lullaby that was cold and condescending. "Rhea, my darling, is it really you? It's been so very long." Rhea nodded. Her mother's tears sprang forth from her dark-brown eyes.

Richard had always had a soft spot for his daughters, but he and Rhea always had a bond no one could quite explain; maybe it was because they were so much alike, but his eldest daughter held a very special place in his heart. He opened his arms, and she fell into them as if she were a child of six who had fallen and scraped her knee. Rhea, in turn, threw her arms around his neck. He smoothed her hair and let her cry. In his wise way, he spoke words that had more power and meaning than what was said. "Welcome home, my beautiful daughter."

With that, there were no other words needed. She was home, with her family. Distance and time didn't change that in the least, even if it would surely end with, once again, their disapproval. Blake stood back and watched the scene of homecoming and watched as the most confident woman to ever cross his path let all her guard down and became this beautifully vulnerable creature. He stayed in the shadows, giving the family time to reunite, and listened to the idle chitchat of "It's been too long," "Where have you been?" and "So much to tell you." Rhea had been right; these would be the people who could harm her the most. He was not sure how the news of mass destruction was going to go over with this family, but he knew that love would always triumph over evil and there was enough love in the open room to smother even the strongest vampire.

He drifted into thoughts of war, battle, and love. Was Rhea right about him finding his love? Was she near at hand, and would he know who she was when he saw her? As if in answer to some inner question, he looked up, and there she was standing next to him, watching the same reuniting scene he had been watching. Her hair was the color of sunshine and skin like ivory. She was slightly taller than Rhea, but not by much. His heart broke as he saw his future in her soft-green eyes. She smiled shyly at him and looked back to the family. "They are always like this when Rhea comes home. You learn to get used it." Her voice was soft and sweet like a summer breeze.

He came out of the fog that clouded his brain and realized she was talking to him. "Oh, do you know the family then?" He was very pleased that his voice was his own.

She smiled at him again, innocent and sweet. "You could say that. I am Kayla. Rosa and I have been friends since before we were born. I am Rhea's youngest sister. And who might you be? It is not often that the earth angel returns home, let alone with a gentleman in tow."

He couldn't help but smile. She might have looked as pure and innocent as the stars in the heavens, but she had a bit of an attitude that gave her sweetness a bit of an edge. He was hooked! "My name is Blake Larson. I travel with your sister on a mission which she shall soon reveal to you and the rest of the family. It is my greatest pleasure to make your acquaintance." With that, he took her hand and kissed it softly.

A soft-pink blush rose to her delicate cheeks, and she turned her eyes away from his, bringing her awareness back to her family. She watched them reunite for a few moments before she stepped away from Blake. He watched her intently. She moved cautiously, knowing he was watching her, making her very self-conscious. She stepped into the center of the great room, paused briefly, before getting closer to the family. "May I join in?" Her interruption took all four family members aback. They all looked up as if they had forgotten anyone else even existed. Kayla moved toward them. She might not be of blood, but they were her family. Richard opened his arms to let the youngest of his daughters into the embrace. Kayla fell in the arms of those she held dear. "Welcome home, Rae! We've missed you around here!"

Rhea's heart tore as she hugged her family. How was she going to keep them all safe, and how were they ever going to forgive her for embarking on this mission? Her thoughts were heavy and weighing her down. She wanted to curl up in her bed and sleep, but there was much to be done and much to be said. Rest would just have to wait. Rene broke the circle. "Well now, since I am blessed to have all three of my daughters home, I think we shall have dinner in the hall this evening. Daughters, if you would be so good as to set the table, I will go pull the stew." With that, she turned on her heels and swept away into the kitchen.

Richard looked at his daughters, his heart swelling with pride. "Rosa, take Kayla and do what your mother asked. Rhea and I will be along shortly." The two younger girls didn't protest but turned and followed Rene into the kitchen. Richard looked at his oldest daughter and saw the woman she had become and the unique beauty that made her stand apart from the other two women, but he also saw his Rae of light struggling internally. He could always tell when she needed a confidant, and he saw storms in her eyes he didn't understand. She was the only one of them to ever venture out beyond the village and into the world, so he knew she had seen things the others probably never dreamed of. He didn't much care for the heaviness of the air that hung around his girl. "Daughter, let us sit and talk. It will be a while before your mother has dinner ready, and I would much like to hear of your travels. It has been a long time since we sat and talked." He sat in his chair and motioned for her to do the same.

With a heavy sigh, Rhea sat in her mother's chair. She knew her father could tell something was wrong; he always could. He watched her wage her internal battle, but what she was battling, he could not tell. She knew there was no way out this conversation, but she didn't want to have it more than once. It would be easier just to tell her father everything now and let him tell the others later, but that was unfair to all parties. The family deserved to hear of the nightmare that was about to take place on mankind all at once. There would be questions, and she would be the source of answers. It plagued her to bring dark news and even darker times to the ones she loved. With that, she let the storm clouds fade away from her eyes and pushed war and hatred from her mind. She formed her thoughts clearly before she finally spoke. "Father, I have much to tell you of my travels and of the world. I have seen things that are so wondrous that they could bring tears to your eyes, but for now I want nothing more than to be here in this place. It has been so long since I have been home. Please let us just set everything else aside for another time."

He eyed her with great suspicion but did not push. He knew his eldest daughter would come around soon enough and share her troubles, and since he was just happy to have her home, the issue was dropped. "Well, my Rhea, it seems as if we are having Christmas early this year, for it surely is a gift having you home. The room seems a little brighter for it."

She smiled at him in a form of thanks for dropping the prior topic. "Thanks, Dad. It's nice to be home."

"Well, just remember, Rae of light, the next time you come home to this little village, you stop here first before the old tavern, ye hear!" She knew he was scolding her. She pretended it didn't bother her and chalked it up to jest since he laughed after he said it. Richard had a great laugh, and Rhea had always loved the sound of low rumble that came from his very core. "Rhea, I was made aware that not only were you visiting old John before you came home, but you were traveling with a male companion. I do not like the idea of my girl in company alone with men." His tone had a sense of seriousness to it.

Rhea gasped for, as she was so busy reuniting with her family, she had all but forgotten poor Blake. Oh, she had been so rude upon her arrival home. She sat up in the old chair and looked around the room. She finally found him against a wall in the back of the room looking a little annoyed and a little overwhelmed. She jumped up and went to him. Her father watched with curiosity, wondering the nature of their relationship. Was he friend? Was he lover? What did this stranger hold in store for his family? Rhea stood before him. "Oh, Blake, I am so, so sorry. I did not mean to neglect you. Returning home overtook me." She smiled at him, tearstained cheeks and eyes bright and shining.

He couldn't be mad even if he had wanted to. "Rae, it is really all right. I understand what it means to be home." She knew he would not see his home for a very long time, and she hoped that he would return to see it one day.

She took him by the arm and walked him into the room to meet her father. Richard stood there waiting for this introduction. He hated that his daughter traveled alone, but he wasn't thrilled about the idea of her traveling with a man whom he did not know. "Dad, this is Mr. Blake Larson of Elden Springs. He joined my travels recently and makes a wonderful escort. Blake, this is my father, Richard."

Blake held out his hand to Richard. Richard, who befriended everyone, took Blake's hand and his daughter's word and pulled Blake into a hug. He traveled with his Rhea, and that made him family. Blake accepted the embrace and returned it in the manly way men hug each other. "It is a pleasure to meet you, Mr. Larson. I hope that your travels have been smooth and uneventful?"

"Please, it is Blake or Bull, and the pleasure is all mine. As for my travels, well, they have been interesting, as I am sure you can imagine, having your daughter as a traveling companion."

Richard laughed a full belly laugh, and it echoed through the house. "He knows you well, huh, Rhea. Keeping things exciting as always?" He laughed again, and she rolled her eyes. Blake was now one of them, and he fit right in. Just what she needed, another brother. She shook her head and laughed.

Rosa reappeared. "Sister, do I get to meet your new beau?"

Rhea looked at her like she was crazy. "You mean Blake? He is not my new beau but my very dear friend and traveling companion. Blake, this is my sister Rosa. Rosa, Blake."

"Oh, I see, I just thought since you were bringing him home that maybe you had finally met the man of your dreams." She shook Blake's hand. "It is nice to meet you, Blake."

He bowed slightly to her in customary gentleman fashion. "Ms. Rosa, it is nice to make your acquaintance." He smiled at her.

"Rose, go tell your mother there will be one more for dinner— that is, unless Derick will be joining us as well?" Rosa blushed and set off back toward the dining room.

Rhea turned and looked at Blake; he was watching everything around him. "You see, Rosa has been spoken for since she was barely a teenager. Derick has been in love with my sister for more years than I can count. I keep waiting for the letter saying they are getting married. Derick is the brother I never had, and you two will get along splendidly."

They all retired to the dining room, where the smell of Rene's stew was wafting through the entire room. Its smell was enticing. It had been ages since she ate anything but inn or tavern food, and her mother was a great cook. Her mouth watered slightly. Blake was chatting with Richard and getting along just fine. This was the way things should be: food and family, home and hearth. She knew there was nothing else on this earth more valuable than all that surrounded her in that moment, even if she didn't fit in. She silently sent a prayer to the goddess, asking her to let love, laughter, and joy prevail; let this be the reason she saves humanity. Just as she finished her prayer, her mother put the stew on the table. They all gathered 'round the table, sitting together the way that families should, enjoying one another's company, talking and laughing. She wondered if dinners were always this bright and cheery in the Edwards household. She watched her family and listened to the chatter. It was here where she was never alone but always out of place. She didn't belong, but where she did belong, she didn't know. She knew her heart would have the answers when she was ready for them, but for now, it was nice just to be there.

Richard raised his glass, and everyone followed. "A toast to having all my girls in one place and to new friends. I hope this is the first of many nights to come that we are all together." Resounding cheers filled the room. Her heart sank. So much good cheer was going to come to a crashing stop, and she was going to be blamed, just the way she had always been blamed for something that didn't go right. How could she have possibly thought coming home was a good idea? Blake saw the pain in her eyes. He reached for her hand under the table. He squeezed gently, not in the way of a man seeking the affection of a woman, but in the way of a friend consoling another friend. She looked at him. He was so sweet and kind. In his eyes, there was comfort. It was like he was telling her, without words, that everything was going to be okay. She wanted to believe that with everything she had. She sighed; now was not the time.

As the evening passed, her troubles fell back to the corners of her mind. She let herself be present and enjoy the time with her family and new friend. Hours later, she finally lay in the bed of her childhood, a large four-poster of the darkest wood. With blankets worn and warm, she snuggled in as if she were seven years old. Her eyes heavy and her mind full, sleep overcame her. It was a sleep full of wicked dreams and happily ever afters. She tossed and turned. She dreamed of vampires and weddings, of death and birth, none of which made any sense to her. Somewhere between midnight and sunrise, she awoke in tears. She stifled her sobs as not to disturb anyone. The moon shone through her window, and she crawled out of bed to look upon the sliver orb. The moon, in all its inconsistencies, was always the only thing that was consistent in her life. It guided her travels, heard her troubles, and never deserted her. Tonight, it shone big and bright, gray clouds lurking on the edges, threatening to dim its celestial glow. She took one deep breath then another, calming her mind.

She heard his voice, sultry and alluring. She sighed. No matter how alone she felt, she never truly was alone. "What's wrong, beautiful?"

"I can't sleep."

"I know, but why? What troubles you so? You only look to the moon like that when your troubles are great."

She knew he was right. "There is much that troubles me. You know me better than any other person in the world besides Feeorin. I am sure my troubles are not hard to figure out." She looked sad, tired, and weary. It was not a look she wore well.

He tried not to balk at the mention of Rhea's dearest friend. "Rhea, it is all going be okay. Good always wins, and evil always falls. You know this to be true."

"Travis, what if I fail? What if I lead them all to their deaths? What if Jeremey wins? I can't bear to lose all that I love and hold dear. There would be nothing left for me to fight for, and then I would fall, and darkness would shroud the earth."

"Go back to bed, my sweet, rest."

"I can't."

She felt him run his fingers through her hair as if he were standing beside her. "I will stay with you till you fall asleep."

"I can't. All I see when I close my eyes is a sea of blood and slain bodies at my feet. Then, I roll over and see those same bodies uniting in marriage and love. I can't tell which shall come to pass first, death or life."

"Rhea, do you remember the night you found out I had been changed?"

She wrapped her arms tight around herself as if protecting herself. "You know I do. You were ravenous and hungry. There was blood in your eyes, and for a moment, I was afraid, not of you, but of what would become of you."

"Yes, and you held me tight and let me cry or, rather, roar. You told me nothing in this world would change the way you looked at me, that you would always see the man and not the monster."

"I remember, you begged me to end the darkness."

"That's right. Now crawl into bed and let me try to end your darkness this night."

She looked to the moon one last time and then returned to her bed. She slept naked, and she pulled the covers up around her, sinking into her pillow. She let another round of tear spill down her cheeks.

"Rae, you know I think you are the most beautiful woman in this world even when you cry."

She gave a weak smile. "Travis, what am I going to do without you? The thought of not having you in my life is still, by far, one of the hardest pills for me to swallow. I don't want to lose you." They both knew it was inevitable, and neither had wanted to broach the topic, but they both knew it had to be discussed. It was easier to voice when it wasn't out loud, when she couldn't stare into his eyes, when he couldn't touch her.

"Rhea, I don't want you to think about that right now. You have so many other things to worry about."

"Travis, I have spent more than half my life loving you in some form or another. I have followed you here and there. A girl never truly loses sight of her first love. It destroyed me when you walked away from me this last summer, but at least I knew you were alive. How can I go into this knowing you will not survive?" Her body shuddered a sob, and she felt him touch her cheek. "Angel of light and mercy who hath loved a demon, fear not for the future as it is only dark and gray for a little while. I will not survive, this is true, but you will. I give my life for you, I always have. You are the only person in my life worth dying for. You stood by me when no one else would, and you gave your love freely. Because of those things, my death will not be in vain. It will be honorable, and my soul will not perish. Nothing is truly immortal except for love. You taught me that, and my love for you will circle eternity. Let me be your champion." His fingers found their way once again to her hair, tracing her curls.

"My prince of darkness, I wish I didn't know your fate, and I wish that I could change it. I know all you say to be true, and I will never be able to express to you how honored I am to have you as my champion or how sorry I am that it will have to come to that. Love is worth fighting for, but I never thought it would mean death. I don't know how to let you go."

"'Tis for another time, my darling, for now it is time for you to rest. You have much to do over the next few days, and I have much to tell you. Just know this before I go, I have seen your future, and there will be a man who is your match in every way, and he will ride at your side. The love we have shared will pale in comparison to what is in store for you. Now sleep, sweet angel. I must go." With that, he was gone. She lay there hurting for the love she would lose but hopeful that what Travis had said was true. This time, when sleep found her, it was soundly.

Chapter 9

Daylight broke, and the roosters crowed. Sunshine streaked its way through her window. She groaned and put the pillow over her head. She was not ready to face the day or all that it held for her. She wanted to stay in bed with the covers overhead. She wanted to be a child and pout instead of being an adult and saving the world. The rapping at her door was soft. She ignored it, hoping whoever it was would go away. The rapping continued and got a little louder. She sighed. Round one. "Who is it?"

"Rae, it's Blake. Are you awake?"

"If I say no, will you go away?"

"No." She hmphed and grumbled. "Blake, the door is open. Come in." She adjusted the blankets so that she was covered. She knew she was a mess but figured at this point it didn't much matter. Blake opened the door and stepped inside. He looked well rested and ready for anything. She really wanted to hate him for that, but she couldn't. She was not going to allow her bad mood to plague everyone around her, so she had to put on a happy face. She forced a smile; she was used to pretending that everything was okay. "Blake, what brings you in this morning?"

He looked at her, still in bed, hair rumpled, and shadows under eyes. She looked worn-out. He was guessing she didn't get much sleep and figured she was probably a bit grumpy. "Good morning. Rough night?" His tone was even and steady. He was not mocking her or trying to jest.

She shrugged her shoulders. "Let's just say that I need about four more hours of sleep in order to even comprehend all that has to be done today."

He sat on the foot of her bed. "Rhea, I know we have not been friends long, and I don't have the right to say I know you, but I can see something troubles you. Let me be your confidant. If we are going to travel down this dark and dangerous path together, there is no need for you to have to carry burdens alone."

She studied him. He was sent here to guard her, and they had agreed to be friends. Maybe she didn't have to be a martyr. She had carried on alone for so long she had forgotten what it was like to need someone's companionship. She made her decision. He had a right to know of all things; it was only fair. Another perspective could only aid her cause. "Blake, my mind is heavy, and my dreams didn't help. I see so many things, yet I don't know what is real or what is stress-induced. I know not of what things will come to pass, so I can't plan accordingly. I have much to do on this visit home, and none of it is going to be easy or pleasant. There was so much love and happiness last night I was reminded what we will be fighting for, but today I will darken those feelings with a thunderous cloud none are going to understand. I fear time is not going to be on our side, and all this rests on my shoulders. I already know of one death, and it hurts me to the core, especially knowing that this death will be to save my own life."

His features shifted, and the color drained from his face. "Is it my death that you know of?" His words were strangled. He would die saving her if that is what it took, but he wasn't ready to know of this so soon.

She shook her head. "No, my friend, your future has yet to come to me clearly, for now I trust that you will live. The death of which I speak is that of Travis. He and I both know he does not survive this battle. We have both seen it foretold. Travis will die defending me for the sake of light and love. He will die so that I can rise above evil. The only problem is, I don't know if I will rise above." She paused, searching her thoughts. "Should it arise, do you want me to tell you your fate?"

He sat there listening to all that she said. He started breathing again and felt his heart rate slow. For now, he lived. How did he convince this incredible creature that exuded love that he was glad her demon lover would die saving her? She deserved so much more. She needed him to be her friend and shove aside his disdain for Travis. She was looking at him both full of hope and hopeless. "Rae, you have to trust that it is for the greater good that Travis will sacrifice his life. I don't think he would be so easy to sway in giving up his immortality if he didn't think you were going to succeed. Good always triumphs over evil. It is the balance of nature. I know there is much to do while we are here, and I know that none of it is going to be easy, but I promise, though I don't know much, I will be there with you every step of the way. I will sit with you when you tell your family. I will do whatever it is you need me to do. I believe in you, and I believe it will be you who leads us into victory. As for my fate, I don't think I want to know if it is all the same to you."

She sighed. She needed more people in her life like Mr. Blake Larson. Jeremy and all the forces of hell were going to have their hands full with this man as their opposing soldier, strong and steadfast. She sighed one more time. She needed to stop wallowing and start planning. "Blake, thank you for being my voice of reason this morning. I appreciate that you let me confide in you. You are indeed a good friend. I think the time has come for me to ready myself for the day. We must have breakfast and let our task commence. I value your strength and wisdom this morn as I seem to be without my own."

He got up off the bed and bowed, turning to leave. Before he stepped out of the door, he looked at her. "My lady, sometimes it is in the strength of others we find the ability to muster our own courage. I will protect you with my life and sword, but it will be the strength in our hearts that allows us move forward." With that, he closed her door. She couldn't have said it better herself. With that, she got up and got dressed, ready to face round two.

*****

Somewhere else across the land in Hell, surrounded by an everlasting darkness, Travis lay in the most luxurious oversize bed he had ever seen. It was six feet high and could hold up to six people easily. The bedding was black velvet and should have been the most comfortable place he had ever slept, but it was tainted. He knew that this room had held many a blood orgy for Jeremy and his men, and yes, the linens had been replaced, but it still made him queasy thinking about it. He never understood what it was like to lust for human blood for the mere sake of watching it run red down the victim's body or pool on the floor. For Travis, human blood was a means of necessity; for Jeremy, it was a means of pure entertainment. Sure, he needed it to survive, but why not play with your food in the process? Travis shook his head, finding the entire thing revolting. He was waging his own war internally. He would be summoned today to give a strategy layout for the first attack on the human world, which, to him, seemed like a waste of time and energy, but he would deal with that as it came.

He also couldn't shake off the weight of his conversation with Rhea. He knew it had to be breached, but he wished so much he could have been there to hold her and dry her tears. It was no longer his place to be by her side. She had wasted so many years loving him already. The man to whom she belonged was not far away, and he would be the one to mend her broken heart and, with any luck, keep her eyes from crying. He didn't like that she carried so much weight on her slender shoulders, and he liked it even less that he had caused such a weight. He had never been able to do right by her, and God knew she deserved more. Did he really have the strength to let her go? Maybe he should try to defy the fates. He shook his head again; he knew the answer was no. He knew their time had passed, and he would sacrifice all of eternity to save her. He would die defending the woman he loved so she could save the lives of all those who had ever loved. Jeremy might have armies and brute strength, but nothing was stronger than the forces of love. He had to rely on that come the day of battle. How many more would stand with her under the invisible flag that waved proudly for matters of the heart? He hoped, for the sake of all things good and for her, that she would have an army at her back.

He needed to clear his mind. The last thing he needed was to have the most intrusive, mind-probing leech of a man (if you could call him that) reading his thoughts. If Jeremy knew that Travis would betray him, especially for the love of a woman, Travis's head would roll, and Rhea would not stand a chance. He needed to start thinking like a vampire and quickly; night approached rapidly. Less than two hours before his summons would commence. Less than two hours before he would have to convince the one being he truly loathed that he needed to wait to strike humanity. He got up and wandered around the windowless room. No matter how rich or how lush the space was decorated, it still felt like a prison. Travis needed to be out in the open and free, not caged like a little bird. He knew deep down that he had kept Rhea's heart in a cage all these years, but he needed her in ways he could never explain even to himself. He kicked an antique end table that looked to be mahogany or some other expensive wood from some king in which Jeremy had drained of all their earthly possessions and, he was sure, said king's life. Damn it, he needed her out of his head. Jeremy read minds and could manipulate minds to do his bidding.

Travis was the only known being whose mind Jeremy could not breach, which is partly why he had offered Travis the position of second-in-command. The position came with unlimited power and more wealth than one could ever dream. Jeremy paid well, in pounds and pounds of gold; Travis would be able to live like a god for the whole of eternity. He wondered briefly what it would be like to squander money as if it were nothing. What would he do with all that gold? It didn't matter; he was not going to live long enough to see it, let alone spend any of it. Then it struck him what he needed to do; he would make sure Rhea got all his promised gold. He would get his payments in installments from Jeremy, and he would send them back to her at the little inn. She would refuse, of course, but he would be able to send her enough gold to fund her army and still enough for her to live rather comfortably for the remainder of her life. She would never want for anything again. He knew she would use it to help others if she could get past the fact that most of it was blood money. He would leave her everything in hopes that she would be able to rebuild her life with a good man who would love her in ways he never could, a man that would hold her in his arms every night and could see her worth was more than any amount of gold. It didn't matter what happened to him so long as she lived and found true happiness. With that one final thought, he pushed her out of his mind and got to work on a strategy.

*****

Her day was long. She sat in the old juniper tree that grew at the edge of her family's property. The tree was as old as the earth, or so she had always thought. She had spent many hours tangled in the branches of the old tree, climbing and swinging, playing hide-and-seek with Rosa and Kayla, or merely sitting in one of the outstretched arms reading a book. Today, she leaned against the gnarly gray bark, sitting on the longest, thickest branch closest to the ground. The tree had heard her thoughts many times before; today was no different; her soft sobs absorbed in the wind, tears fell down her cheeks. With knees pulled up to her chest, her head was resting on her knees. Drew had acted like a child and had stormed out. She knew it was only his pride that was wounded and that he would recover, but it was still hard to watch a grown man pout over nothing more than a fleeting crush. Drew was the easiest part of her day. Her family had not taken the news of war very well and taken it even worse when they learned that she would fight in this war alongside the one man whom they could never understand what her attraction to him was. Her father was angry, and her mother cried. They were a peaceful lot and had raised their daughters to be the same, and now their headstrong eldest would go charging into a battle that was not hers to fight. Once again, her decisions were ridiculed; she could not make them see that this was what was right for her.

The weather shifted, and the winds got colder. She heard footsteps but didn't look to see who was coming her way. She had worked so hard so that her family would be proud, and now she was letting them down as usual. There would be no swaying them to get them to understand, and there was no changing her mind about fighting. Maybe coming home was not a good idea. The only good thing that seemed to be coming out of her visit was that Blake seemed to have found his heart's desire in Kayla. Her visitor was getting closer. She didn't have to look up to know that it was Selene. Selene was the only person, besides Travis, that Rhea knew who could be both soft and deadly. Selene had the best heart of any person Rhea knew even though she had had her fair share of heartache and despair. She had been dealt every wrong hand imaginable, but she still came through, hoping for a rainbow. Rhea loved her as much as she loved anybody. They understood each other in ways that no one could explain. They were connected on levels deeper than the ocean. Rhea considered her family, and Selene returned the sentiments. Selene stepped around the tree and sat down before her friend. Her bloodred hair billowed behind her in the wind. Her porcelain skin shone in the setting sun. Rhea always thought she was beautiful.

"Sounds like you have had a rough day."

Rhea smiled; she knew Selene had heard all about the events that transpired that day. "You could say that."

She laughed; Selene joined her. Their laughter echoed through the tree branches. Moments passed by, and for that brief time, life was sweet and simple. Their laughter passed, and they just sat. One of the best things about their friendship was, words were not always needed. The sun sank lower into the sky, and the wind died down. Rhea knew Selene would not push for details, and Selene knew Rae would tell her all when she was ready. Rhea looked off toward the setting sun.

Selene brought her attention back. "So, I hear Old John has some traveling musicians playing at the old tavern tonight. Do you want to escape for a while and go check it out?" Music and fun were something she hadn't experienced in a long time. The perfect way to end to a bad day.

"You know, that sounds perfect. I could use a little distraction. Besides, how long has it been since we shared a drink and a night just for us girls?" She remembered Blake. Maybe she could convince him to stay put this evening. Selene smiled and had a wicked twinkle in her eyes that meant mischief. Heaven knows she could use a little mischief.

After what seemed like it was going to be a losing battle, she finally convinced Blake that she didn't require an escort for the evening; she made her way through the village to Selene's house. It was a nice cottage, one that would be the perfect nest for children someday. Her four cats meandered around the living room; it was cozy and homey. Rhea knew Selene longed for a family of her own, children and a loving husband. Rhea also knew Selene's luck with men was as bad as her own. Selene had found a nice man a couple of years back, but he still had not asked her to marry him. It was only a matter of time. Something in her pinged with sadness. Maybe Rhea had been wrong to think that home and hearth were not for her. She had spent so much time traveling she had never really given it any thought.

Selene saw the sadness cross her face. "Rae, what's the matter?"

She wanted to cry but refrained from letting her tears fall. She was not a silly girl, and she would not let these thoughts overcome her. "I don't even know where to start. I think part of me is homesick, but not homesick for my parents' home. I see what you and Bryce have. I see the love Derick has for Rose, the way my dad still looks at my mom, and I wonder if I have it all wrong. I went in search of life beyond this place, and I have discovered so many wonderful things and met some wonderful people. I have had my fair share of men and relationships, though most of them not lasting long. I have endeared a broken heart more than once, but none of it seemed to call to me. I march into battle fighting for love, but whose love am I fighting for? I don't fight for Travis's love, nor Drew's, nor any other man. I fight for love because that is what I know to be true, but what about my own love? Don't I deserve the same happiness that you all have? Maybe I should settle down. Maybe I am not meant to walk this earth alone."

It was not the first time Selene had heard her friend spout these sentiments, and she knew it was the one desire in the earth angel's heart that she longed for the most. She also knew that she loved her life out in the world and that this little village would never be her home. Selene also knew that the right man was out there for this unique and wonderful creature; they just had to keep looking. "Rae, maybe after this war is done, you can come back, be here, and find some roots again. We all miss you, and there is bound to be a good man within the vicinity that would be a good match for you."

Rhea didn't want roots; she wanted freedom and a life that was her own. She wanted passion, and that was not something the village held. Rhea nodded, not really agreeing with this. She had searched villages and towns, near and far in search of the right man. No matter how hard she looked, he never seemed to appear, and Travis always seemed to get in the way.

"Come on, Rae, let's change and go listen to some music. A night away from everything might be what we both need." With that, both women made their way to Selene's room to raid the wardrobe. Selene always had a selection of dresses, gowns, and bodices to rival any royal; it was a mere matter of picking a fabric and then picking a color, for Selene had it all. It would be nice to adorn something other than her simple riding dresses. The outfit she wore home the day before was only for special occasions, and since she moved around so much, there wasn't room for feminine clothes in her life. Selene, on the other hand, made dressing a ritual, one in which Rhea envied. Selene had a sense of style that was all her own, even for the times. Rhea shuffled through the wardrobe, looking for just the right thing to catch her eye. Selene watched her dearest friend fondle different materials. Selene knew exactly what Rhea was looking for, something that would make all her insecurities hide in the shadows for one night, something that will remind her how truly beautiful she can be, something to remind her that she was the earth angel and that, for one night, there were no demons or monsters wreaking havoc on the world or her heart. She pulled out a dress of the purest silk and as black as night; it was trimmed with ribbons on the sheer sleeves. The bodice laced up in corset fashion up the back with emerald green, and the neckline was low and cut to a full *V*. The dress was tapered in all the right places and flared out just past the hips and fell to the floor. It was the most exquisite dress Rhea had ever seen.

A small purr escaped her lips. "Sel, I could not possibly wear this. It is much too beautiful for tonight."

"Rae, you are entitled to wear something beautiful. You are one of most incredible women I have ever met, but you don't know your own worth. You have spent far too long on the road, taking care of others. You need to remember what it is like to be a woman and not just a healer. Your light will shine brighter if you allow yourself little feminine indulgences. You care so much for those around you, let me care for you this evening, let me show you what everyone else sees when they look at you."

Rhea dropped her head knowing Selene to be right. "Maybe you are right, but I would not do justice to that dress, not when I am so long out of practice."

"Being so long out of practice is the perfect reason to wear a dress like this. Come on, Rae, put it on. It is screaming to be worn. I might be able to tame those curls of yours as well." She knew protesting would accomplish nothing. Selene was as stubborn as she was, and she would not relent.

Rhea removed the simple gray riding dress she wore that day. Trying not think about all that had transpired that day or all that she needed to do, she stepped into the gown of silk, the material sliding over her skin in the most innocent but intimate ways. She worked it up over her curves, and the feel was intoxicating. She, in all her travels, had never come across something so decadent. Once the dress was on, Selene cinched up the ribbon in the back; the contrast of the green against the black was striking. The dress fit Rhea as if it were meant for her; no other dress would ever hold her as enchanted as this one did. She turned and faced her friend. The look on Selene's face said all the same things that she was feeling inside. She had needed this more than she had realized.

Selene took Rhea by the hand and led her to the washbasin. Careful not to get water on the gown, Selene washed the copper hair, as Rhea relaxed into Selene. After the mass of curls had been wet and washed, Selene pulled out a set of combs and brushes. Rhea didn't wear her hair straight hardly ever, and it was a rather in-depth process to get the curls to surrender, but Selene worked through Rhea's mane with ease and a practiced hand. The curls faded with each brushstroke, and after a time, the hair that was once unruly and untamable was smooth and soft. Now, her hair, straight, cascaded like a waterfall down her back and over her shoulders. Selene used some rouges and paints on the face to accentuate Rhea's features. Rhea really was beautiful, and Selene would be damned if she left her feeling anything but.

Once done, Selene let Rhea investigate the full-length looking glass. Rhea was beyond speechless. She had never looked more radiant; she almost didn't recognize herself. She hugged Selene tightly. Selene put on a lovely dress the shade of red wine. The contrast of her porcelain skin and her bloodred hair with red-wine dress made her look gorgeous. The two women left looking alluring and spectacular, feeling confident and a little bold.

They entered the tavern upon the hour of 9:00 p.m. A handful of people were scattered throughout. The tavern was not large; it had the old bar along the back where John was tending to the liquid desires of the patrons. There was a small fireplace in the right-hand corner; the fire was blaze orange and red. The rest of the place was slightly dark except a few candles that sat in the middle of select tables. John had not changed anything in all the years that he had owned the bar. They approached the bar, and John gleamed when he saw his goddaughter and her dearest friend. Rhea was not accompanied by the gentleman who had been her escort the night before, and he felt like that was a good thing. He didn't feel that stranger was the right man for her but would not voice this. She had always cleaned up nicely. He worried that there would be a scene caused if Drew showed up as he did most nights. For now, though, he would not worry. She was safe in his place. "Well, it is not often that my goddaughter pays me a visit upon her returns, but two nights in a row. The stars really must be aligned."

She laughed. She really did love this old man for he was like an uncle to her. "Sometimes even the lost need to find familiar ground, John. It has been a rough go. Can a lady beg for a drink while in search of her place in the world?"

He smiled at her. "Ladies don't beg, and you know in your heart where you belong. With that, however, I wouldn't refuse two of my favorite girls a drink, especially when they look as lovely as you do. What be thy poison, my dears?" They all laughed. It was going to be a good night. He poured both ladies whiskey on ice.

They took them graciously and wandered over to one of the few tables lining the edge of the worn, splintered dance floor. The musicians were setting up their instruments; there was not really a lot going on. It was nice to be away from everything. Selene and Rhea chatted and caught up. Selene told her how she felt that Bryce would propose to her soon and how things had changed around the village, and Rhea told Selene of war, of Travis, and of her travels. The unspoken words between them were truly those of the best of friends. Rhea didn't have to say that all this darkness was hurting her, and Selene didn't have to say that she was disappointed by the lack of marriage in her life. They were friends of the heart, and they knew each other's deepest secrets. It was amazing being with someone who knew her completely and didn't question her every move. It was the first time since her arrival to Hearts Prairie that she truly felt at home.

Before they knew it, the musicians were playing a sweet melody that drifted throughout the tavern. It was easy to forget when the music spoke softly to the soul, the company was the best around, and the whiskey hit just right. She was always on alert and always aware of her surroundings, but somehow, she missed him entering the tavern. So, when he approached her and asked her to dance, she was caught off guard. It had been many years since she had been asked to dance, three years to be exact. She had not let herself dance since the last time her heart had been broken by someone other than Travis. She had spent the last three years blocking out Keaton and how he had left her curled up on the floor broken and shattered. Enough time had passed though. Maybe this was what she needed, to let go of all things she couldn't control or change. Maybe it was good for her to finally put herself out there again, and he was handsome; she did long to dance again. It was the sweetest form of human courtship. One leads, and the other must follow. She looked to Selene for encouragement, and Selene was already nodding. This was her chance to do something she hadn't done in a while, her chance to be brave and try again. She took his outstretched hand and let him lead her to the floor.

He was tall, very tall, at least nine to ten inches taller than her, if not a full foot. The boots she wore with her dress had a small heel, but not enough to really give her any extra height. He had a strong build and frame. He looked like he was built for battle. He had thick strong arms, like Blake's, that gently pushed her through the steps effortlessly. He had a kind, sweet smile and honest eyes. He wore spectacles, and in the dim light of the tavern, it was hard to make out the color of his eyes, but she was sure they were brown. He wore facial hair, neat and trimmed, in the mustache and goatee fashion. His hair was brown, like the color of tree bark. His voice was deep but soft, and just like that, she had forgotten what she had come there to forget. He swept her around the floor in turns and spins. He kept time with the music. She found herself, for the first time in forever, having fun. It was one song after another before she realized that they had danced through three to four songs. His name was Ronan, and he had moved to the village shortly after she had initially left. He was a knight in the queen's army; he also constructed buildings and houses. He was a widower. Rhea found this man easy to talk to and was enjoying his company.

They sat down to catch their breath and to rest their feet. He joined the two ladies at their table, and his group of friends pulled chairs up alongside them. The conversation flowed, and there was never an awkward silence or moments that were uncomfortable. He spoke intelligently, but light, and made them laugh. His laughter was full and echoed. He stepped over to the bar to get everyone refills.

Rhea looked at Selene and asked, "When do we need to head out? Will Bryce be looking for you soon?"

Selene shook her head. She had been waiting for this moment to come for a long time. "We can leave whenever you are ready to leave. This is good for you, and he seems like a good man. Let's face it, good guys and you don't cross paths often." She smiled her wicked smile, and Rhea knew this was dangerous territory. Selene didn't like anyone, especially when Rhea was involved, and she liked this guy.

Ronan returned with their drinks. The music filled the air, and he once again led her to the dance floor. He kept close to her side and looked her in the eyes. The musicians shifted the tune, and the melody got softer and slower as he pulled her into his arms, holding her tight. She did not resist, just relaxed into him. He felt like he would never let her fall. He held her tenderly in that moment.

In the same moment, trapped in Hell, Travis felt his cold, unbeating heart break. He felt strong arms holding his Rhea tight. He felt their connection instant and undeniable. He felt her give in to this stranger's embrace. He felt her light shimmer, and he could feel her letting go. There was a very good chance this guy could be the man that she falls to when this war was done and over. He could be the man that could make all her dreams come true. He could be the man that would be able to give her everything that Travis could not. He might be the man who would fall asleep next to her every night for the remainder of her life. Whether this was that man or not, he knew she had finally put the steps in motion to find her heart's desire. He was of her past, and someone new was of her future. Travis was not a jealous man, but for the moment that this stranger held his girl, he let jealousy wash over him. Travis knew that this was where her story really began. Travis let the tears roll down his cheek. He had not shed tears since he was mortal. These tears were for the love of his life, for the woman who saw past all the darkness and whose heart was too big to shut out a vampire. They were not tears of sadness. Yes, his heart was breaking, but his tears were for her. No other person on this godforsaken earth deserved true happiness more than Rhea did. He had known of her many suitors in the past, but he had also known they wouldn't last. The earth angel would not be tamed, and men were often selfish and controlling. Somehow, through the bond that he and Rhea shared, he knew this man would never try to change her. He knew this man would not be able to resist her charms, but was he strong enough to stay? Would he be the one she had waited her whole life to find even though she would never admit to it? He might not be her soul mate, but Travis knew he was out there, and it made him overwhelmingly relieved to know that she would never be alone again. He knew she would be taken care of, and that caused a wave of empowerment to surge through his veins. He would give up immortality and bring down Jeremy, no matter the cost, and she would live happily ever after. With that, he locked the door to his room and began to plot the demise of the king of the vampires.

Chapter 10

Somewhere around midnight, Rhea and Selene left John's old tavern. She was tired but happy. She had forgotten how much she needed fun in her life and how much she loved to dance. Selene, Ronan, and his band of friends showed her how much she had been missing. She had been merely living, but that night, she knew what it was to once again feel alive. She would scold herself for neglecting this aspect of her life later, but for now she was content floating on air. Ronan had said he would call upon her in a day or two; she hoped he would. She saw Selene safely home and meandered through the village to her parents' homestead. She wouldn't let herself wonder if Ronan was the right man for her; no, this time, she would just let things happen as they were meant to. In her heart, though, she secretly hoped that this time would be different and that he would be the one brave enough to stay.

As she walked toward home, she felt a burst of cold air, and it chilled her to the bones. It was unfriendly after the warmth she just left. She wasn't sure what was wrong, but she knew something wasn't right. Rhea quickened her pace. The sky was dark; a storm was on the horizon, but there was more to the frigid cold than just the lurking storm. She sent up a silent prayer to the goddess, asking for safe passage home. The wind swirled around her feet. She was not far from home, but still she was uneasy and a little scared. Her heart raced, and her hands were cold and clammy.

As she reached the edge of her family's property, she heard him before she saw his shadow. Blake was waiting for her. He, too, seemed to be affected by the strange and terrible cold. "Rae, what is going on?"

"I am not entirely sure, but it feels dark and evil. Come, let us hurry to the house, where we can try and make more sense of what is going on." Together, they ran through the field.

She stopped at the barn. She could hear the unnerving neighs of Pixie and Blake's stead, Zeus. She waved for him to follow. They stepped into the barn, which was the oldest building on the property. It had truly withstood the sands of time. It was rock and wood, very much like that of the main house; there was straw and wood chips lining the floor. Five stalls lined the west wall, and a small tack room was along the east wall. It was designed for practicality and everyday use. All the horses were in a tizzy. Something was amiss. "Blake, we need to calm the horses. There is evil on the wind this night."

Blake nodded and turned toward the first stall. The yearling was the newest member of the Edwards' equine family. He stood fifteen hands high and would grow another ten to fifteen before the summer. He was reddish brown and had white markings on his hooves and muzzle. His mother was Rene's mare, whom she prided as much as her roses. Rhea knew he was of good breeding and would be strong for the harvest. His name was Tucker. Tucker stomped the ground nervously. Blake gently inched toward him. Tucker snorted. Blake stood there, letting the yearling adjust to his presence. Tucker sensed the danger, but not from Blake. He lifted his muzzle, searching for Blake's hand. Blake touched the young colt and rubbed his nose. Blake was good with animals. He had a calming aura about him.

Rhea tended Pixie; it was rare that the sweet white mare got spooked. She had spent so much time with Travis and on the brinks of Hell that she was immune to darkness, but even she was unsettled tonight. Rhea hugged her muzzle and whispered in her ear, "Shhh, my pretty girl. It's okay. Whatever it is will pass."

The air stirred, and the hair on her arms stood on end. She closed her eyes and focused all her attention on her surroundings. It had been a long time since she had to invoke what magic she possessed. Her powers were rusty, but she could feel them emerging from her being. She felt sparks of light, she concentrated, she drew her focus over the entire homestead. Her light shimmered and flickered. She drew in a breath, let it out slowly, and as she did, a brilliant lavender light emitted from her entire being. She encompassed all that she loved. She wasn't sure how long she could hold her light in place, but she would protect her family if she possibly could. Blake stared at her in pure amazement; he had never seen anything like it. He could feel the warmth emanating from the radiance of the soft glow of light that poured from his new friend. The horses seemed to instantly calm as her light force shrouded them. She could still feel the presence of evil, and she pushed her power as far as she could. She would not falter, not now. Her tiny body trembled and shook, but she never wavered. She stood strong, knowing that all she held dear was literally in her hands.

She heard his voice and knew who it was. It was dark, seductive, and coiled around the earth like a snake. Jeremy's voice echoed out through the land. He didn't sound angry, but his tone was malicious. He was arguing with someone. Rhea guessed it was Travis, for Blake didn't seem to hear anything except the wind and the horses.

"I don't care if you think it is a bad idea. I want to execute a small-scale attack." Travis had risked leaving his mind open to her so that she could hear Jeremy's plans. "Jeremy, listen to me. The humans are unsuspecting of this war. You have the advantage right now. Send some of the younger vampires out into the larger cities. Let them cause a little havoc so that your presence is known throughout. They will start to notice that people are going missing and that there is a danger they need to fear. Let this play out for a bit, one month or two, then let me instill a fear of mass destruction of the world for those who do not concede to your every command." Rhea felt the tension surmount between Jeremy and Travis. It was a power struggle, and Rhea needed this to go in Travis's favor. She needed an army and more time. She concentrated on her powers. She would not let her guard down. She listened intently for the evil king to reply. He pondered Travis's words. She wished she could see what was going on, not just hear this discussion. She was growing tired and weak, but still she held her force field in place.

"Hmmm, you make an interesting suggestion. Let the world know of our existence before I dominate. That isn't half bad. Give them a taste of our blood before we drain them of theirs. Let kings and queens come at me with all they have before I squash them like the insects they are. You know, I like it."

She sighed, thank goddess. Travis had succeeded this time. "I will give orders upon the morrow for the newly turned to set out on this mission. Their hunger is insatiable. It won't be hard to get them to obey."

"Good, I knew I hired you for a reason. Now what do you say we go enjoy the pleasures of the flesh and feast ourselves on whatever tasty morsels are waiting for me in my room tonight?" Rhea's stomach lurched. She heard Travis grumble before he closed off their connection. She was grateful for this. She wasn't sure she could endure listening to Jeremy slaughter some pretty maid with Travis at his side.

She felt a shift in the air, and the wind died down as if Jeremy controlled it with his mood. It wouldn't surprise her if he did. The horses were instantly calmer. She couldn't hold on any longer, and she drew her powers back to her being. The force of the light returning was too much for her, pushed into her. Blake watched the beam explode into her chest before she fell to the floor unconscious and bleeding from the nose. He rushed to her and knelt beside her. He lifted her head into his lap. Her family was sure to be asleep, and he dared not wake them for the day that they all had. He checked her chest for breathing. Her breasts rose and fell in a shallow motion. She was still alive. He felt her head to make sure she wasn't bleeding. She seemed to be unharmed, less the bloody nose and being unconscious. He sat with her, not moving her. "Rhea, Rhea. Are you okay?" His voice was thick with concern and so quiet it was barely a whisper. She didn't respond. She was in a gown of the blackest silk, and she looked spectacular. He hoped her night hadn't been all bad. He whispered again, a little louder this time.

She groaned in agony. The punch of light through her chest hurt like hell; she didn't want to move. She didn't want to open her eyes; she just wanted to lie there as still as possible. Her body would be stiff and sore in the morning light. How could her night have taken such an awful turn? She remembered her night in detail; it was full of laughter and enjoyment. She had even let herself be entertained by a handsome new stranger. He had been so sweet and charming.

Then the cold wind followed by fear and terror. She would thank Travis later for changing the vampire king's mind. He had bought her some time, but not much. She had so much work to do. She needed an army, and she needed one fast. She wondered if she could convince Ronan and the other knights to gather in the name of love. She would have to weigh that conversation carefully and in due time. She groaned again.

She heard Blake calling to her. He must be beside himself at what he just saw. She still didn't want to move, and her body was protesting everything. It even hurt to breathe. She had never had to use that much power before; she was surprised her body hadn't shattered completely. She would have to practice controlling her powers more in the coming weeks. She could use that in battle, though she was not sure if it was only a shield mechanism or if it could be used as a weapon. She never wanted to use her gifts in such a way, but it could come to that. She would ponder this further. Blake gently shook her; she needed to come to. Her friend was worried about her. She willed her mind to concentrate on opening her eyes. The movement was small and took a long time for her brain to connect with her body. Her eyes opened, a little glassy and glazed over. Everything was out of focus. Blake heaved a sigh of relief. His sweet blue eyes looked at her. "Are you okay? What was that?"

She wasn't sure if she could speak, but she tried nonetheless. Her voice was weak. "I am not sure yet if I am okay. I can't seem to move. As for what that was, I will explain after I get some rest and maybe some feeling back in my limbs. Do you think you could carry me inside?" She hated that she had to ask him for help and that she was not in control. She was not accustomed to needing anything from anyone. Her night had taken a strange turn for the worst.

"Rae, are you sure you're okay? You were just blasted to the ground by a shimmering ball of light."

She tried to shift and grunted in pain. "Blake, I'm fine. Can you please take me inside?"

He moved her head off his lap and rested it on the floor. He scooped her up in his arms, and she heaved a groan as he gathered her up. "Am I hurting you?" He was concerned; she adored him for it, but at the same time, it was making her crazy that he thought her fragile. She remembered her night, what it was like to feel feminine and pretty, what it was like to dance with a nice man. She was a woman; she was of the softer gender. That wasn't a bad thing. She spent so much time having to be strong, sturdy, independent she didn't know how to let someone help her; she didn't know what it was like to have someone take care of her. She had no idea what it was like not to have to do things on her own. Maybe that was why all her relationships failed. She would sort through this later. Coming home had brought to light things she didn't know were hiding in the depths of her mind and her heart.

"Blake, you are not hurting me. Thank you for helping me this evening. I appreciate you waiting for me to come home and for tending the horses. I am just a little sore and very tired. I will be better after some sleep."

He adjusted her in his arms, a little more tenderly as if she were a small child who fell and scraped her knee. They didn't say anything else. He carried her into her parents' house. Luckily, everyone was sound asleep. He carried her into her room. It had been a very long twenty-four hours. She was not going to risk ruining Selene's stunning dress; she was going to have to once again ask for help. "Blake, I am sorry to keep asking you to help me this evening, but do you think you might be able to help me get this dress off?" He arched his eyebrows quizzically. She rolled her eyes. "Blake, first, I lack the strength to even stand, let alone have a good romp. Second, as much fun as it was to share that with you, it was a onetime thing. You lost your heart the moment you saw Kayla. You won't lay with another woman this night or any other. I don't want to ruin Selene's dress. It does not deserve to be slept in no matter how I can't move."

He knew she was right, especially about Kayla. He set her down gently on the edge of her bed. She found her balance and righted herself. Sitting up was hard; it caused her pain when she breathed. She grimaced. He saw her face scrunch in pain. "Rae, are you okay?" She nodded. He gently untied the ribbons, loosening the corset. The dress slipped off her shoulders. He tried to be gentlemanly and look past her as he continued to slip the material off her body. She grimaced again in pain as he adjusted her to remove the last little bit of the dress. He lifted her legs up onto the bed and helped her under the coverlet. He eased her head to the pillow.

She smiled at him. He would protect her with all his might; she was grateful for the companionship. "Blake, my friend, I am glad you are here, and I am very grateful for the aid you have given this night. I shall not forget your kindness."

He looked at her in all her feminine beauty. She was not your typical woman, and he loved that about her, but tonight she had to let herself be cared for by another, and he could see how that pained her. "Rhea, I gave my word to protect you in any way that I could. I will stand by that no matter what we are up against. I am glad you let me help you tonight. We will make a good team when it comes time to fight. Just so you know, there is no shame in asking for assistance every now and again. I know you are used to fending for yourself, but you don't have to do that any longer. I am here for you, and we are in this together." She nodded and gave him a tired smile. He turned to go and thought better of it. He bent down and kissed her forehead sweetly and brushed the hair from her face. "One more thing—and I say this as a man, not as your friend and protector—you looked absolutely ravishing in that dress tonight. I have never seen a woman more radiantly beautiful as you were tonight. The man who steals your heart from Travis should consider himself the luckiest man alive. You are such a magnificent creature and have so many wonderful gifts to give. I hope they won't always be wasted on a vampire. You truly deserve a prince. I hope I am around when you find him, because I will give him hell to make sure he is worthy of your hand." He kissed her head again as her eyes fluttered closed. She was pondering all he said. She knew he meant well and that he spoke with the love of a true friend. He would become her brother and not just in arms.

She drifted off to sleep, body sore and aching, mind full of things she had to sort out. Alas, exhaustion took hold, and she fell into a deep, soundless sleep. She didn't move, she didn't dream, she just slept. She did not hear the rooster crow when dawn arose; she simply slept. She knew she could count on Blake to cover for her when her family asked what kept her in bed. She rolled over somewhere around noon, the sun hot and streaking through her window. Her body protested the movement, and she groaned. She was not ready to wake. She let herself drift back to sleep.

A few more hours passed before she stirred. She sensed magic, powerful magic at that. She felt a weight on the edge of her bed that was not there before, and she was warm, almost hot. No one in the house possessed such power, and Travis would never set foot in her parents' home. There was only one other she knew who could wield that much magic: Feeorin. He was the only other man who had ever captivated the earth angel and the only other man who had ever occupied full time space in her heart. She was afraid that if she opened her eyes, he wouldn't be there, that it was just a dream or his distance healing. She needed him to be there. She found her body moved stiffly but without pain; she could breathe easy. Whether there or not, he had removed her pain. She sighed and slowly opened her eyes. There he was; it would be unfair to say he was her favorite person in the entire world, but it was probably true. They had been kids when they met. He was the first boy who had ever loved her. Their relationship had waxed and waned over the years. She adored him completely.

She searched for her voice. "What on earth are you doing here?" The question was tender like she was still fifteen years old, and he had just sneaked into her bedroom window after all lights were off.

He smiled at her. "Word travels fast when the earth angel comes home. Besides, I would know your light anywhere. So, how's my gypsy girl?"

She looked confused. "What do you mean you would know my light anywhere?"

"You are the only light bearer I have ever met whose beams are lavender in color. I have never seen you exude so much power at once, so I figured that meant you were in trouble."

"Wait, you mean to tell me you saw my light over two hundred miles away? I don't understand, and then you mean to tell me you rode the same distance in less than a day? What is going on?" Her head was starting to spin. She was perplexed as it was not possible for her power to travel that far. She looked at him, confused. She searched his face for answers. It was calm. Wisdom and experience had aged him, but not in an old-looking way. He was distinguished in a way. He always had mature features even at twelve.

"Rhea, you lit up half of the western hemisphere. You could see your light from here to the ocean. That is why I thought you were in trouble. I didn't think, I just got on my horse and rode as fast as I could. When I got here, your friend Blake told me what had happened. It's a miracle that the blast didn't shatter your entire body." He rubbed the back of his hand gently across her cheek.

He had loved this woman more than half his life. She stole his heart as an awkward teenager, with her quirks and whimsical ways— the way she should would flit and flutter around in pixie-like fashion, the way she would bat her eyelashes. She wrapped him around her little finger. He had, and always would, do anything for her. The years had changed their relationship in many ways, from childish flirting to tangled passion and emotions. They had tried it together, and they had tried it apart, but nothing seemed to fit or make sense. All they knew was, they needed each other in their lives, and right or wrong, she was his siren and he would always answer her call. She lay there tired; he could tell nothing was making sense for her. He had to dig a little deeper in order to put all the pieces back together.

"Rhea, I need you to tell me what is going on. You are the most together person I know, you are always in control, especially of your powers, you always err on the side of caution, just to be safe. The fact that you have no idea how far out your powers shot last night concerns me greatly. Blake was vague in his details. All I got was, there was something evil in the air, you were tending horses, and then you started to illuminate. After a time, the ball of light crashed into you and you fell to the ground. I know you better than that, and I have a feeling I am not going to like what you are going to say, but give it to me straight so I can help you. I can't stay long. I am going to be in enough trouble as it is when I return."

The woman Feeorin had been in relations with didn't understand his and Rhea's "friendship." It bothered her that he was so close to other women, especially with Rhea, maybe in part because of his undeniable, outspoken love for her. Rhea hated that their relationship always had to be complex. She looked at him; if ever a soul had more than one mate, he was destined to be one of hers. She scooted herself over toward the middle of the bed, and he snuggled up beside her. He put his arm around her, and she laid her head in the space between his shoulder and his chest. They had sat that way more times than she could count, for more hours than she could recall. Her heart was happy.

She sought her words carefully; he was going to be mad and rightfully so. He hated Travis with a vengeance, and he hated how he treated Rhea. "Feeo, why does everything always have to be so complicated?"

He caressed her hair softly. "I don't know, Gypsy. 'Tis the way of it." She loved that he called her Gypsy. She was a gypsy, and he loved that about her. He kissed her head. They sat in silence for a little while before she knew she had to make things more complicated. His hand moved from her hair to her bare shoulder, fingers rubbing her skin idly.

She took a deep breath and then began to retell the events that had transpired over the course of the last few days, which had been a lot. She made sure to leave out the part about her and Blake's romp down by the creek, but otherwise, she let it all out. Feeorin wouldn't settle for surface-level answers; it wasn't in his nature. Besides, he knew her better than any other person in this world or any other. He would know if she was holding back. She talked fast because that is what she did when she was nervous or excited. She was both. He listened intently, in true Feeorin fashion, pulling her in when he felt she needed a little comfort. It was amazing to her that, besides her dad, Feeo was the only other person she ever really sought reassurance from. The only difference was that Feeorin usually gave reassurance, where her dad didn't always. He had a way of putting her mind and heart at ease, and he understood her in ways no one else even could fathom; they were in so many ways one and the same.

His touch grew heavier on her shoulder as she continued to talk. It was hard for him to swallow all she was saying, especially the parts about her charging into battle in the name of love against the known leader of Hell on earth with an army of vampires led by a mere glimpse of a man who had, on more than one occasion, betrayed her. She had always relied on Feeorin. He was her knight in comforting armor; he was the one she turned to when all else failed, the one who helped her pick up all the pieces when everything fell apart. He was her true confidant. He was the voice she heard when she needed reason and the voice she heard when she needed to throw caution to the wind. He was her everything. He was the only real champion she had ever known. His head ached; he couldn't comprehend how he was going to save her this time. No, the earth angel didn't need to be saved; she was more than capable of saving herself. Rescuing her was a better choice of words, but he couldn't see a likely solution that left either of them alive. There would be no talking her out of it; her mind was made up, and there would be no changing it. Her damned big bleeding heart wouldn't allow humanity to fall into the clutches of a monster, and she would always believe that love would prevail. He was not sure he or his magic was strong enough to protect her. His mind was racing with all the possible worst-case scenarios as she came to the end of her account. He had heard all she had said, and most of it was still being absorbed, but he pulled her into him, as close as he could, both arms wrapping her up tight, as she snuggled into him and waited for him to process everything.

She was still exhausted from her power surge, and it felt good being in Feeo's embrace. If she were honest with herself, she didn't want that moment to end, ever. She loved this man on a completely different level than she loved Travis or any of the others. He was her very best friend. He had parts of her heart no other would ever touch. She knew their time had passed and that there was no chance that they would ever wind up together; she also knew that she would say yes in a heartbeat if he ever asked her to. Rhea knew that Feeo expected the worst but hoped for the best and that he was envisioning both their deaths as he processed all she had said.

There was a gentle rapping at the door. She heard Blake's voice calling from the other side. She looked at Feeo and sighed; their moment wouldn't last. He nodded as if reading her thoughts. "Come in, Blake. The door is open."

The doorknob turned, and he opened the door. He saw the two of them cuddled up on the bed, Feeo's arms wrapped around her, her head on his chest. It was an intimate picture, but not that of lovers. He could tell they were very old friends. Blake carried in a wooden tray of food. Goddess love her mother, she was starving. He set the tray down on the bed next to Rhea.

She smiled at him; he was such a good guy. "Thank you, my friend."

He nodded. "Your mom is really worried about you. She says she hasn't seen you stay in bed this long since you had scarlet fever." He sat down on the edge of the bed, careful not to spill the tray of food.

She grabbed a roll and dunked it in the bowl of soup. Her mother made the best chicken and dumpling soup she had ever tasted, and it smelled heavenly. She offered Feeorin the soaked morsel before ripping off another chunk for herself. She again dunked the bread. The broth sopped into every hole of the sourdough bread. She had not eaten in over a day, and she heard the rumble of her stomach. Rhea ate the piece of bread, savoring the flavor. It had been years since she had her mother's dumpling soup, and it was delicious. She and Feeo shared the small loaf of bread and the bowl of soup. Blake watched the pair eat quietly. Her head still rested on his chest. Blake knew their friendship was seated deeply. He hoped that his own friendship with the earth angel would survive this war, let alone the sands of time. She finished eating and set the tray aside and sighed. She was ready to go back to sleep.

"Blake, how has the day treated you? I am sorry that I was not able to be a good hostess. I hope you found something to pass the time."

"Rae, you don't need to be sorry. I had no idea power like that even existed, let alone that someone so little could wield it. I am just glad it didn't kill you. Besides, your family is lovely. I helped your dad around the house today and met Derick. That guy cracks me up. Your mom has made sure that I was not hungry once today. I feel completely at home here. How are you feeling?" He inched his way closer to her open side. He was dressed in brown leather breeches and a gray tunic that he wore untucked. It hung open at the chest. She was surrounded by her oldest friend in the world and her newest. She looked at one man and then the other. Both good men with big hearts and more love than they knew what to do with. Both would stand at her side through thick and thin, and both would charge into a vampiric bloodbath to defend her.

"I am glad that you have had a pleasant day. My family has a way of working their way into your heart." She said it with a smile.

"I am feeling a bit better, still rather tired, but the pain is gone, thanks to Feeo."

Blake looked slightly perplexed, like he was trying to understand. "So, both of you are light bearers?" Rhea shook her head; her hair, something of a disaster, fell into her eyes. She pushed at until it stayed behind her ear.

It was Feeorin who answered Blake. "No, only Gypsy. I mean, Rhea is a light bearer and the only known one who is also an earth angel. It is a very rare and special dual set of gifts that courses through our lady's veins. She is one of a kind. I work more with actual magic, spells and potions, incantations—that kind of thing. My powers come from practice and concentration and are mostly learned. My magic has been handed down through generations. Rhea's powers are gifts from the ancient ones, and she was born with them." He toyed with her curls again, but only 'cause he needed to do something with his hands.

Blake had never encountered magic of any kind until his vision from Clinton. Now he was surrounded by it tenfold. His eyebrows knitted together, and his lips pursed. "I don't really seem to understand all of this. How does it work? Can I learn like you did, Feeorin?"

Feeo shrugged. "Anyone can learn if they have patience and dedication. There are some very simple spells and charms I could teach you. However, our goal for the next few days is to help Rae learn how to control her light orbs so she doesn't have another incident like she did last night. We cannot have the savior of mankind blowing up because her powers obliterated an entire vampire army and she can't control it." He poked at her rib cage playfully.

Her eyes lit up. "You're staying? But what about…" She stopped.

Feeorin's significant other was not a topic they discussed often. He knew why she stopped. "Gypsy, you need me. Who else is going to help you hone your inner powers? She will understand. Eventually. You have more power than you know what to do with. What were you thinking when you were calling your light? Do you remember?"

Of course, she remembered. How could she forget? She might have been knocked out by her power, but she knew exactly what happened. "I was thinking about protecting all those who I love."

He nodded his head, his dark-brown eyes deep in thought behind thick glasses. He had worn glasses for as long as she had known him. They were as much a part of him as her curls were a part of her. He crinkled his face, and worry lines crept onto his forehead. His receding hairline gave him that distinguished look of being wise. He reminded her of an ancient wizard or mage from one of her books. Her adoration for him was deep and thick and completely unbreakable. She knew he was contemplating the source of her powers. He was analytic and precise. "Gypsy, were you thinking about each person you loved individually or just everyone you loved as a whole?"

She thought about it for a minute. "I simply thought about protecting those that I loved the most. So naturally, that included you and Travis. Travis, however, is out of my realm, so I don't think I could protect him. Though that could explain why I was able to hear his and Jeremy's entire conversation. I had to have opened a mind portal of sorts." She said the last part questioningly like she was unsure if that was even possible. She had never used her powers so outwardly before; she was not sure what her magic was capable of.

Blake watched her facial expression change to uncertain. In their short friendship, he had never known her to be anything but cool, confident, and completely in control of everything. He was not sure how he felt about the vulnerable, insecure side of her.

Feeorin, too, was thinking rather intently. He got up and started to pace, shaking his head. "Rhea, Rhea, Rhea. Whatever am I going to do with you? You seem to find yourself in the most precarious situations, not really knowing how you got there." He was not scolding her in a serious manner, his voice light and teasing. He looked at her mockingly and stuck out his tongue.

She just laughed and rolled her eyes. "I can't help it. It is not like they have teachers for earthly celestial beings. You are lucky your powers have been taught to you by at least two generations of women who, in turn, were taught by the women before them. I am flying blind and solo."

He knew she was right, there was no one to show her the way. Her powers never had been truly tested; they were harnessed, having never really been unleashed. She was capable of great healings and had the unfaltering gift of love that she could spread effortlessly, but she was a light bearer, and those powers came from a different realm and had many levels. Light always radiated from her being, and she always shone brightly, but to be able to push that light with an intention was something completely different. Learning how to use her orbs for combative purposes could be tricky and needed to be handled with great care. Feeorin's mind raced; if she was able to learn how to project the light within her, they might all stand a fighting chance at winning this war. He stopped pacing and looked at her. The entire human race depended on the woman before him. All her doubts and insecurities were showing in her eyes. Could she really be destined for such a fate? He hated that the love she held in her heart was the reason she had been dragged into a battle that was not hers to fight, but if she could wield light like it was sword, then she was the only real chance they all had. She was the secret weapon that was needed to win this war. He would never tell her that for he knew she would balk at being referred to in such a way. He had a feeling she was more powerful a weapon than she knew.

"My sweet gypsy, do you think you could call upon your light again? This time on a smaller scale like around Blake and I?" Both men looked at her hoping the answer was yes.

She shrugged her shoulders. "I don't know, Feeo. I called upon the light when there was danger lurking and evil in the air. Even Pixie was afraid. I don't think my powers work like you think they do."

"Will you please try?"

She knew she would not deny him; she never denied him much if she could help it. She sighed; she was not very good at telling Feeo no. She took several deep, steadying breaths and closed her eyes. She called upon her spirit guides and drew her attention inward. She needed to center. She was not sure all her strength had returned, thus far, and feared another power surge might leave her down and out for days. She had work to do; she had wasted enough time already. She rubbed her hands together, feeling the heat warm her palms. She could feel the energy surfacing and circling through her. She loved the feel of flowing energy. It reminded her of a creek or stream and how the water moved over rocks. When she felt the fullness of heat emitting from her hands, she lifted them, palms facing outward, arms outstretched in front of her. She tried to concentrate on Blake with one hand and Feeo with the other. Her arms started to tremble and slightly shake. She heard Blake move but felt Feeorin stop him. Blake made a "humph" sound in protest.

She brought her focus back to her oldest friend and her newest friend. She thought about how she felt last night with the evil wind and how she needed to protect her loved ones. What would she do if she ever lost either of these men? She couldn't bear to think about that; she needed them more than she would ever let either of them know. She would die a thousand deaths before she let them fall to an untimely end. Love coursed through her veins, and she felt herself quiver all over; heat poured out of her. She let little sparks of light shoot from fingertips, but they sputtered out. She took another breath; she could do this. She could surround them with light. She let the tremors move through her vibrating her to the bone. She pictured Blake marrying Kayla in a simple ceremony after the ground stopped bleeding red. She saw Feeo and his beloved holding hands by the ocean. Complicated as Feeorin's relationships were, he was happy. That was all she ever wanted for anyone: happiness, love, joy, laughter. She wanted nothing more than to see everyone around her smiling and happy. The heat rose out of her once again, this time filling every ounce of her. She felt the sparks light from her fingertips and then, seeing it through her closed eyes, the most beautiful lavender glow. She was not sure what her powers looked like, so she opened her eyes. Her bedroom illuminated soft lilac-colored light beams. Feeo and Blake were both engulfed in the light. She was shocked. This caused the light to flicker and fade out. She was disappointed.

Feeorin saw her face drop and the look of failure cross her pretty green eyes. He hated when she was self-conscious and insecure. She was the most confident person he had never known. She could walk into any room and own the entire crowd with just a smile. He was not about to let her mope when so much rested on her. "Rhea, stop being so hard on yourself. You are amazing, and you need to stop doubting your capabilities." He was scolding her this time. He never called her Rhea, and she hated it when he did.

She frowned. "Feeo, I was not able to sustain my power for any length period. It is no use. What happened last night was just a fluke." She curled herself back under the blanket and hunkered down till her head found the pillow. She was pouting. She was a perfectionist and didn't like when things didn't go her way.

Feeorin sat back down on the bed next to her and looked her in the eyes. "Gypsy, this was your first concentrated attempt at this. You just need to practice. If we work very diligently for a couple of days, you could learn to control this. Do you realize the possibilities of what you could do with this type of magic? You would be a force to be reckoned with."

Blake was feeling like he needed to chime in. He, too, moved to the other side of the bed. "Rae, I know we have only known each other a short time, but I have to tell you, what I have seen you do over the last few days is some of the most incredible things I have ever witnessed. You are truly gifted. I think Feeorin is right—if you could learn to control your powers, you could be unstoppable."

Rhea closed her eyes, and her chest fell with a heavy sigh. She knew both men were probably right, but she wasn't ready; her powers had been used only for healing in the past. The occasional parlor trick to coax a scared, unbelieving child. Her powers were a gift, and she respected that gift. She never imagined having to use her gift for anything other than to heal those in need. She needed more time to process all this and to learn how to wield her powers. The only problem was, she didn't have more time. How could she perfect an art that would take a lifetime to master in the little amount of time she had? The Yule and Christmas were rapidly approaching, leaving four short months before spring and war. Feeorin would leave her in a few days, and she would be left with no one of magic background to help her. She was dealing with forces greater than she ever knew existed within her. She was scared and uncertain. So many things she was uncertain of, her insecurities stemming from years of being told she couldn't do this or shouldn't do that, always being told she was wrong or it wasn't good enough. She had spent her entire life being told that she was a failure, a disappointment or, worse, that she was lost.

She felt the air chill around her skin; she felt his ghostly touch, a transparent hand upon her shoulder. She didn't have to look to know Clinton was beside her. She also knew that his presence meant she was about to receive a message from the goddess herself, for it was the only time he visited her in his aspiration form. He was always with her, but his presence was only visible when he did the bidding of his mistress. She had missed him so much since he had died many years ago. He was too young when the goddess had called him up. Their short time together was pure and innocent, nothing more than passing flirtations of adolescent youth. He had been her spirit guide since the moment of his death. She knew he had died before the news reached her. He appeared to her, as he did now in the milky-white wispy figure telling her it would be okay and asking her not to cry. She had managed to keep that silent promise even after all these years. His touch was warm like a living being, but his presence always dropped the surrounding temperature, and she was glad she was nestled beneath her covers. She was not sure if Blake or Feeorin were privy to this visit, but her lady had business with her, and that was all that mattered in the moment.

Clinton spoke, his words low and hollow, but it resonated through her entire being. "Our lady wishes you well. She sends a message both of cheer and distress. I shall give the message of distress first. Jeremy and his army grow stronger every day. Even now as you know, he plans his attack. He will manipulate Travis to do his will, and Travis will try to hold strong, but the day of battle, his loyalties may not be trusted. He will never outwardly betray Jeremy, but as you know, he will die for you. He will play loyal soldier and march under the banner of blood until the moment of his death. Do not let this sway or discourage you. His love for you will not waver, and he really does mean well, but to save you, he will fight as a vampire. You will have to fight against him and may even have to deliver his deadly blow in order to keep up the pretenses. He will die a mortal man, and the goddess will not see him turned to ash. I know this does not make the situation any better, and for that I am sorry." He paused; he had watched her over the years, and she really was lovely.

"The goddess sends word of cheer as well. That is this: you, Lady Rhea, are the key to ending this war. Your army of love will prevail greater than those of kings and queens, their armies will not reach the battlefield, but as long as you hold true to who you are and as long as you believe in yourself, your army will fight proudly beside you in a river of death. Your powers are starting to awaken to their full potential. You need to trust in the light, trust in love, and all will right itself in the end. You are magnificent and meant for greatness. Don't be afraid of that. Also, she wanted me to tell you that your prayers have been heard. The man from the other night will not be your champion, nor will he fight for your cause, for he is a coward and fears commitment, but there is one out there who is coming for you. When he finds you, your resistance will be high, but let him in, for together, there will be no greater match, and he will be your driving force in winning this war. Never will there be another who believes in you more. He is your other half, the mate your soul has sought after your entire life. He will be strong when you are weak, brave when you are scared, and patient when you are unsure. His love will be what pulls you through. You need him, and he needs you. You will understand more clearly very soon. Now rest. Tomorrow Feeorin will start your training. The goddess and I both will be with you." With that, he was gone.

She felt the tears rolling down her cheeks. That was a lot of information to take in, in a very little amount of time. She opened her eyes. Both men were staring at her. Apparently, Clinton's visit was just for her.

Feeorin reached in, wiped away her tears. "Rae, why are you crying? We will get you to where you need to be."

She shook her head, curls falling in her face. She didn't bother to push them away, just let them hang across her forehead and over her left eye. "Feeorin, Clinton was here."

"Oh, I see, and what tidings does the goddess bring?" He knew Clinton only appeared when the goddess, Ariadne, needed the earth angel. Ariadne was the goddess of all things light, the mistress of the labyrinth, and the weaver of dreams. She had chosen Rhea personally when Rhea was but a girl, and Rhea had been her faithful servant since.

Rhea was not sure what she should divulge and what she should hold on to for her own knowledge. She sifted through the bits of information. She decided to keep the parts about Travis to herself for now. Feeorin never trusted Travis, and this new information would not help matters. "Feeo, I need your help. Can you spare me a week's time to see if we can figure out the source of my powers and how to control them? I know it is a lot to ask, but I need you."

He would not desert her, especially when she asked for his help. She didn't ask for help very often, hardly ever. He nodded his head. He would stay if she needed him to, no matter what the consequences are. "Rest now, Gypsy. It has been a long couple of days, and you need your strength. It is going to be a long week. Blake, come, we shall let Rhea retire. You and I can get to know each other better over a glass of whiskey by the fire." Both men rose and bowed their respects to her. "My lady, may you rest well." Feeorin took the food tray as he exited the room.

"Rae, I hope this is wise and that you find the power within. Good night, m'lady." Blake followed Feeorin out of the room and closed the door.

She needed to move around a little as her muscles were sore and stiff from being in bed. She got up and found her feet. The hard floor felt cool beneath her. She walked around her room. She was grateful that her family had left it as it had been. It was a sort of sanctuary. She pulled on a dressing robe and tied it gently around her waist. There was a wash bin in the corner by her vanity mirror. There was fresh water in it, probably put there by her loving mother while she was asleep. It was nice to be home. She washed her face with the soft cloth, the water refreshing on her skin. She ran a brush through her hair, bristles sticking in knots. Maybe she should cut her hair before she went to war; it would be so much easier if it was out of the way.

"Don't cut your hair. It is one of your best features."

Ugh, she thought. She really was never alone for long. "Travis, must you always be in my head?"

He chuckled. "I need someone of substance to talk to. The company I keep here in Hell is dismal and unsatisfying."

She shook her head. "I am sorry you are keeping ill company. I do hope all is going okay, but I just want to be left alone for a little bit. Please, Travis, I have a lot of things to sort out."

"Yes, love, as you wish."

With that, she was left to the sound the of her own thoughts. She sat down in front of the altar space she had created many years ago in honor of Ariadne. She ran her fingers over rocks and tree bark pieces, things of the earth that she had collected on her travels. She had put a smooth new pebble, from the creek where she and Blake had had their afternoon delight, among the many treasures and troves. She lit the candle she kept in the center, for protection and light, and the bundle of sage and lavender to ward off any negativity. She knew what it would mean if she could master her powers; she also knew the risks that went along with that. She needed clarity and to center. She took some calming breaths and closed her eyes. This was the first time in more than a week that she had been able to find some tranquility. Eyes closed, she focused her awareness inward, clearing out all thoughts. She felt her heart rate slow and steady, and her breath was no longer ragged and shallow. She inhaled the aroma of the dried plants as their smoke swirled around her. She needed this time to reconnect to the goddess and to herself. She had always been the one to sacrifice herself for others, to give and give, but it had been a long time since she felt so drained.

From the minute she had encountered Travis at the inn, everything had been altered. The stars had realigned and set her on a different path. That happened a lot for her when Travis was involved, but this time, the course that lay ahead for her was one that she couldn't veer from, and she was exhausted. Though it was a tug on her heart each time she thought about Travis's death, she was glad that she would be able to guide her own course in a direction that suited her and no one else. She let herself drift into a gentle state of meditation. It was soothing and peaceful, and her mind quieted. Her body relaxed. She let the tension leave her shoulders. She felt the goddess energy surround her and encompass her in a loving hug. Ariadne was there with her; she was safe. Time passed by slowly; what seemed longer was only about twenty minutes. She allowed her breath to deepen and her awareness to return to her room. Calmness flowed through her as she opened her eyes. She pinched the candle out but left the sage/lavender sticks smoking. She removed the dress robe, crawled back into bed, and drifted off to a thoughtless sleep.

Chapter 11

She was up with the sun and full of energy. She dressed quickly in black riding breeches and a long gray tunic with a black leather belt wrapped around her waist. She braided her hair back and let it drape over her left shoulder. She wanted to get in a short ride with Pixie before training began. She knew Feeorin would crack the whip and make her focus until she could control the light. It sounded like a ridiculous notion controlling light, but she knew that was going to be her challenge.

She heard sounds coming from the kitchen as she left her room. In search of food, she made her way through the hallway and into the kitchen. It was an amazing place, complete with brick oven. Rhea had spent many hours helping her mother baking and kneading bread. She had always loved the smells that wafted out this room. Rene was putting the kettle on the fire for her morning tea. She heard Rhea before she saw her. Rhea was never very good at being quiet. "Good morning, my daughter. I see you are finally feeling a bit more like yourself." Rene looked at her oldest daughter and sighed; her wayward girl was never still for long, moving constantly like the wind.

Rhea walked into the kitchen and gave her mom a hug. "I am sorry if I have worried you. I am feeling much better."

Rene nodded. "Where are you off to so early? Both your gentleman friends will be worried." She paused, walked toward the wooden counter, and tossed Rhea a freshly baked apple muffin. Winter was approaching, so that meant fruit was scarce, but the orchard had produced plenty of apples, pears, and peaches before the frigid air set in.

Rhea caught the muffin and held it to her nose, the aroma of cinnamon and cloves drifting into her nostrils, and she inhaled deeply. *Yum*, she thought. "I am going for a ride before Blake and

Feeo awake, and then it is off to train. I have to learn to control something that isn't meant to be controlled, and Feeo is going to help me."

Her mother looked up, confused. Rhea had a way of speaking in riddles. "That sounds like it is better if I don't know what you are talking about, but your ride will probably have to wait. The boys are already up and have been out in the stables for close to thirty minutes or so."

Rhea's shoulders dropped, and she sighed. Pixie would have to wait. She took a bite of her muffin; it was delicious. She chewed her food and sulked slightly. "Thanks, Mom. I guess I better get going then. We have a lot of work to do."

"Rhea, whatever it is that you are doing, make sure you are careful, and don't do anything to get yourself into more trouble. A battle of blood and death is no place for a lady."

It was Rhea's turn to nod. "Yes, Mother, I will be careful." With that, she headed out the side door and toward the stables.

The air was cold and crisp, but it felt good on her face. The wind blew as it always did in the prairie. She longed to lie among the tall grass-blades and listen to the wind whistle through them. She walked into stables, and there was Feeo and Blake, Pixie saddled and ready to ride, along with Blake's chestnut stead, Zeus, and Feeorin's gray gelding, Merlin. Pixie neighed and whinnied in excitement at seeing her mistress. She walked over to her snow-white horse and hugged her muzzle. Pixie nuzzled the crook of her arm. Rhea giggled. They really were a perfect pair. Feeo shook his head, he never understood how the demon had wound up with Pixie in the first place, but he was glad when she was handed over to Rhea. As far as he was concerned, the only thing missing from Pixie was the wings of a Pegasus and the two would look like characters straight out of an ancient myth. Rhea looked at her male companions questioningly.

It was Blake who spoke first this morning. "Good morning, Mistress Rhea. You look well rested. We thought you could use a ride before we put you through more exhaustion. The fresh air will do you some good after the last couple of days of being down and out." He bowed to her in his gentlemanly way.

She couldn't help but smile. She returned the gesture and grabbed the reins of her horse and walked Pixie out of the stables. The air was not quite frigid, but it was heading that way. The sky was a soft shade of silver, and there was the smell of weather on the wind. Blake and Feeorin followed her out. Not another word was spoken among the three of them as they mounted their horses. All magnificent creatures, but just like the woman who rode her, there was no comparing Pixie to the other two horses. She was lean, strong, and lithe; her mane soft and flowy like silk; her tail always in the most beautiful, intricate of braids; eyes gray like smoke. She was entirely white except for the very small black star that rested between her ears. The star had not always been there; it had been a gift from the goddess when Travis had given her to Rhea. The star was a mark of honor and to show that Pixie was truly Rhea's familiar, her guardian spirit. Rhea loved the horse; she had been the one source of constant company along the healer's path. They shared magic and secrets.

Rhea had kicked her heels, and the majestic beast soared off into the horizon. The men let her fly for a short while before they urged their horses to pick up the pace. They never fully caught her, but she let them close the gap on her and Pixie. They rode as the sun crested over the hills. It would not be a warm day, but with everything hanging in the precarious balance, any day that the sun still shone was a good day.

Rhea pushed Pixie to a full gallop. She needed to run. Unfortunately, she wasn't allowed to run very far today. Feeorin and Blake would chase her down and bring her back. She wasn't accustomed to being confined to one spot, and it gave her a sense of being trapped, imprisoned. If she couldn't roam and wander, she would settle for the wind in her hair. She leaned her small body over the front of the saddle, her chest almost resting on the nape of Pixie's neck. The land flew by in a rush. She needed to clear her mind before the grueling task of trying to master something that was not likely to be mastered. Trying to tame the light was like trying to tame the wind or the sea. It would be easier to focus, though, without a million distracting thoughts running ramped in her head. The faster Pixie went, the more her thoughts seemed to drift away. She felt the wind bite at her cheeks and felt it lift the weight of her braid off her shoulders as she pressed on. As fast as her horse could run was as fast as she would go. She was an experienced rider and knew how to maneuver the mare with precision and accuracy, never fearing for her safety. She knew with every beat of her heart that Pixie would not misstep or go too fast. The men rode as hard as they could, but she could not be caught, and they backed down. They would not catch her but didn't worry that she would flee. Rhea was completely reliable and always followed through. She would not go far and would face her lessons head-on.

She heard the goddess on the wind and inhaled the sounds. This was her destiny, and it called to her. She would answer the call and do what was required of her. She headed toward the trees. Ponderosa was the tree of her home. They climbed high into the sky, branches dropping down in triangular fashion, long dark-green needles hanging from every branch. They would soon be weighed down by heavy snow. The wind whispered through them and sang to her, so she never slowed Pixie but just kept running right through them.

Feeorin stopped at the edge of the clearing; Blake pulled up the reins and came to a sliding halt next to him. Blake looked confused. "Feeorin, why do we stop when the lady continues?" Blake was tasked with keeping an eye on this headstrong female; he was not about to lose her now.

Feeorin shook his head. Blake had a lot to learn about the gypsy. "Let her go." He said it with conviction and distinction. Blake started to protest but was quickly shut down. "Blake, I promise she will return. Let her have some time to herself. She knows that forest better than she knows her own bedroom. Besides, how would you feel if you were charged with saving the entire world?"

Blake thought about this for a minute. In a way, he was charged with saving the entire world. He had to keep the savior of the world out of harm so she could prevail in her conquest. He sighed. All this was starting to feel like a ton of bricks on his shoulders. "Feeorin, can I ask you something?" Feeorin nodded, watching the trees for his Rhea. "Why is it you and Rhea are not together? Watching the two of you, one would think that you were a match made in heaven, and goddess knows, Travis is no good for her. You two seem to fit together in a way that only soul mates could."

Feeorin took his eyes off the trees and looked at the man who was going to help keep the gypsy girl safe. He liked Blake, there was a decent quality to him that was hard to find. The question, though, was one that had been so tangled up for so long that he wasn't sure he really knew the answer. His chest fell after he released the breath he had been holding. "Blake, the answer to that is unknown, but I often ask myself the same question. What it comes down to is, Rhea is as stubborn as she is beautiful, maybe more so." He chuckled. "Rhea does not want to be doted on, nor does she want to be adored. I don't know how to love her without doing either of those things. She needs someone with a fiery spirit, the patience of a steady oak tree, and a heart of gold. She is a handful and likes to get her way. I would never be able to tell her no, and she would always get her way, which would make her crazy. She is a contradiction. She wants things her way because she likes to be in control, but she doesn't always want to get her way, because she isn't that selfish. She needs someone who will push her and call her out when she is being a brat but will give in to her whimsical ways and let her control as much of the situation as she can. She is strong-willed, and I am too soft. We would butt heads because I would never challenge her. I am what she calls a pushover. It is as simple and as complicated as that." With that, he looked back to the trees. This was the truth to the best that he could explain it.

Blake, too, looked to the trees in search of the infamous woman that captivated everyone around her. He watched the trees. "Feeorin, do you think she can do this? I mean, she is just one woman, and she is going up against mass forces of evil and an army we know not the size." He felt his stomach fall with guilt as soon as he asked the question, but there were a lot of lives at stake, including his.

Feeorin, loyal and true, never missed a beat; his eyes remained fixated on the direction where Rhea and Pixie were last seen. "Blake, it is really not a matter of whether I think she can or not. It is a matter of whether she thinks she can. Rhea is a lot of things, most of which are complex, but her confidence waxes and wanes. She needs to believe in herself or she will fail. As I said a minute ago, though she is stubborn, and the thought of letting mankind fall into the grips of this retched monster won't sit well with her, she will find it in herself to overcome. As her friend, you need to remind her of this frequently, and you need to remind her not to lose sight of who she is or what she can do. You have been charged with a task that is not an easy one, so you will need to look inside yourself and decide if you are up to the task. There will be a lot of tears on her part as she sorts through things, but if you stand by her and allow her to process things in her own way and are brave enough to see this through, then and only then will you know the answer to the questions you seek. The day of battle, you will have your answer."

They sat on their horses in silence. The sun had risen; the birds sang their morning tune. The wind was chilly this morning, but neither men were cold. Their horses nibbled lazily on the dying grass. About an hour or more passed by before they caught sight of Pixie. She was walking next to her rider. It looked as if she was talking to the mare or maybe just to herself. Pixie's reins were loose around her neck. There was no need to worry about her running away; Pixie would never desert her lady. Rhea was making large gestures with her hands as if the horse were human and understood her thoughts, but it made Rhea feel better to talk to someone, and Pixie couldn't argue or try to persuade her otherwise. They crossed over the line between the meadow and the trees.

Blake anxiously hopped down from his horse and went to escort the earth angel the remainder of the way. Rhea was deep in thought and didn't seem to notice her companion moving toward her. Blake stepped into her path, but she gave no notice, just kept walking and talking. Pixie knew her mistress did not see Blake and nudged her arm. Rhea looked at her horse. Pixie stopped forcing Rhea to stop. Rhea looked up and realized she was about to collide with her new friend. She hadn't been aware that she was back to the meadow or that both men had not followed her into the wood. She became very aware that her solitude was once again over. She sighed; not all her thoughts had been sorted yet, but here she was back at the beginning. The sun was up and shining; it was time to work. She saw Feeorin, still mounted in his saddle, and wondered how long they had been there waiting for her and wondered why they hadn't followed her.

Blake walked up to her and took hold of Pixie's reins. The horse whinnied in protest. "Shall we escort you back to the homestead, Rae?"

She shook her head. "Thank you, but no. I think the meadow would be better suited for what we are about to do. Let the horses graze. They won't go far. I need to be away from the house to concentrate, and goddess knows I need the space." She took the reins from Blake and patted Pixie's head. "Go on, girl. I need to practice, and you need to eat. Take the boys' horses with you."

As if the horse understood, she nuzzled her lady and trotted off toward the center of the field. She swatted Blake's stead with her tail as she walked by, and he followed the command. Feeorin dismounted, and his horse trailed behind willingly. Blake was amazed that the horses seemed to follow instructions but didn't bother saying anything. Rhea walked toward Feeo; she was going to need his help above all.

"Did my gypsy girl figure things out?" It was not so much a question as it was the beginning of conversation.

She gave a noncommittal shrug. "It is too soon to tell," she said with a neutral air. "Whether I have or not doesn't change what we are about to embark upon or change the goddess's request. I am the chosen one, and with that comes certain responsibilities. It is time. Feeo, I need you to walk me through the steps you did last night. We will start there." She began to untie her boots.

Blake interjected, "What are you doing?" He was confused by her removing her boots.

"Blake, until I learn how to harness the power of light, I need to be grounded, or I am going to wind up back in bed for days at a time. I need to connect to the power of the earth so the current of the light doesn't drain all my energy, once again knocking me on my backside." He didn't understand but shrugged and stepped back out of the way.

Rhea finished removing her boots and her socks. She felt the cool grass under her feet and allowed herself to ground. She closed her eyes and focused on her breath. She called on the elements of earth, air, fire, and water to help her center. She walked around the area with her eyes closed as she connected her energy to the forces of nature. She was the earth angel, but light was her element of choice, so she needed the others to be in balance when she called on her own powers. The ground calmed her, and her breath eased. She felt stable and balanced. She opened her eyes. Feeorin looked at her. This was the Rhea he knew and loved, calm and peaceful. Her eyes were bright, shining, and she had color in her cheeks. Nothing like a morning ride and brief meditation to bring her back. She was ready to begin. "Feeo, let us begin. Time is short."

Feeorin nodded. "Rhea, close your eyes and concentrate. Call on your powers, allow them to course through you entire being. Feel the warmth that they possess, and let it fill you with love and happiness. That needs to be your focal point. Love is your driving force. Love is what you fight for, so let it be your strength." He paused, letting her power surface. Blake stood off to the side and watched.

Rhea felt her power surge through her. She saw the soft, radiant lavender light behind closed eyes. The warmth was welcoming, embraced her like a hug. Feeorin continued to speak, his instructions clear and specific. "Let your light come into your hands. Now think about protecting Blake. Only focus on Blake. What would you do to keep your new friend safe?"

His words drifted to the background as her body turned to face Blake. She saw him in her mind standing there in the meadow, far from home, and out of his comfort zone on a mission to keep her safe, a mission she wasn't sure he fully understood. As she felt the sparks fly from her fingertips, her eyes opened. She kept her focus on Blake and only on Blake. She felt her power pour out of her hands and envelop her friend in what looked like a bubble of light. It was weak and flickered, but it surrounded him. She held the light for a moment before her hands began to shake and the light diminished. The energy from her power zinged her fingertips. She looked frustrated.

Feeo was by her side before she could say anything, "You did well for your first real attempt." She looked at him as if he had just told her the earth was square. "Rae, it's going to take some practice. You can't expect to master this on the first try. Magic doesn't work like that, and you know it."

"I know," she said with a shake of her head.

"Try it again. This time, call upon Ariadne, let her guide you. She is the one who tasked you with this. Let her help you."

Rhea took a step away from Feeorin, giving herself space. She closed her eyes and took a deep breath. She called the elements and her power before sending up a silent prayer to the goddess of her calling. Ariadne was with her; she had been with her all day. Rhea inhaled the element of air deep into her lungs. She focused on Blake, once again, as Feeorin talked her through the process of pushing light from her hands. Once again, her fingers sparked; lavender light flew from the tips and shot out over Blake. She made sure her magic never actually touched for him, for fear that he would implode. She opened her eyes, and this time, the soft purple orb of light held in place for five minutes before it began to dim and sputter out. Her breath was ragged, and her hands hurt. Magic always came with a price. She looked at Feeorin and nodded.

"Again," he said definitively.

Her heart raced, but once again, she closed her eyes and let her power surface. It took longer this time, but it found its glow and shone brightly, projecting around her travel companion. With each attempt, her powers held a little longer, but each time it was paid in full by the power of three times three and she got weaker and weaker. Hours went by. Her arms ached, her hands trembled, her breath was tight in her chest, and she could feel the fatigue setting into her muscles. She was not going to last much longer, but her orb was still only holding for a short time. She had gotten it to hold for up to fifteen minutes, but that was not good enough for her. *One more try*, she thought. She focused all her heart and soul into the last thrust of light as it shrouded Blake. The brilliance had begun to fade. It had a sense of lackluster to it, but she held it with everything she had and everything she was. She was bound and determined to keep those she loved safe.

Fifteen minutes went by, and the light bubble held. Shudders were running through her entire being, and she could feel it slipping from her control. She pushed the beams with all her might and willed them to stay put. Seconds seemed like hours, and minutes felt like days, but twenty minutes passed. The power she emitted finally wasted away to tiny flecks of light, and the bubble popped. She fell to the ground, her fingertips bleeding, and she could hardly breathe. Her body convulsed, and she was weak. Her vision was cloudy, and she couldn't think straight. That was her lot, and she was spent. Day one of training came to an end, and both men rushed to her side. She lay flat on her back, not moving, much as she did the other night. Both men kneeled beside her one on each side.

It was Feeorin who spoke. "Gypsy, can you hear me?" She nodded her head slightly. He grabbed her hand, searching for a pulse. He gasped when he saw the blood dripping off her fingers. Rene was not going to be happy that her eldest daughter returned bleeding, and Feeorin was sure he would be the one to blame. He put her hand in between his own and called his own magic into play. He had not used his magic for some time, and he was rusty at the craft, but he knew he could heal her fingers just as he had two nights prior with healing her body. He felt a pang of guilt; he shouldn't have pushed her so hard on the first day. Her powers were different from his. He could recite chants and spells, read enchantments, and combine herbs all day long. Was it exhausting? Yes, but her powers were elemental and not easily controlled. He hated that she was injured because of him and his teaching styles.

She looked at him, her green eyes glassy. "Feeo, it is not your fault." Reading minds was not one of her gifts, but the look of pure guilt was written all over her dearest friend's face, and worse, it was written in his dark-brown eyes. Her own vision was skewed, but she knew Feeo well enough to know when he was taking the blame, which was often. "Feeo, you did a great job today, thank you. We will try again tomorrow." Her fingers had stopped bleeding. Rhea linked her fingers with his. She allowed herself to slowly sit up. She was sore, but nothing a hot bath and some herbal tea wouldn't cure. She squeezed Feeorin's hand. "Feeo, I love you. You know that, right?" It tugged at his heart knowing that though their love was timeless, and unlike any other, it would always be platonic in nature.

He sighed. "I love you too, Gypsy. Are you sure you are okay?"

She smiled sarcastically. "No, but I am not going to tell you that." She laughed.

He just shook his head and rolled his eyes at her. "Rhea, I swear you are the most impossible, pigheaded, impetuous woman I have ever met, and I completely adore you. I will make you pay for that snarky comment later." He winked at her. He stood up still holding her hand. He gently pulled her to her feet. She seemed stable enough. She found her balance and stood on her own. She was still holding Feeorin's hand, but it was nothing they hadn't done a thousand times before. Blake didn't say anything; he was not sure he would ever be able to understand the connection between these two, but Rhea was okay, and that was all that he was concerned about. He grabbed her boots and offered them to her. She took them and smiled but made no attempt to put them on her feet.

They walked in silence in the direction of the horses. She moved slowly, fatigued and tired. She reached up and pulled the band from her braid. Some curls had begun to spring from their captivity while she was training, but it was time to set the rest free. They were a tangled, sweaty mess. She shook her head, allowing the unruly mass of copper to fall where it may. The horses were just over the hill, beyond the training grounds, grazing lazily. Three sets of ears perked up when they heard their riders approaching.

Pixie saw Rhea, and, like a puppy, trotted over to her. Rhea hugged her tightly and stroked her neck. Pixie loved on her mistress, all the while checking her for injury or harm. Once Pixie was satisfied that Rhea was as she should be, the horse dropped her head and continued to gnaw on a patch of grass. The men had gathered their horses and were already in saddle. Rhea wanted to walk. She took up Pixie's reins and started toward home. Blake and Feeorin looked at each other slightly confused, but both dismounted and took their horses by the reins.

Walking three across, side by side, Rhea started to hum. They were all tired and hungry. As they came in sight of the Edwards home, they were welcomed by Rosa and Kayla. The two young women carried baskets of flowers. They were lovely. Rosa, whose hair was straight like their mother's, was tied back in a satin ribbon, and she was dressed in her everyday attire, simple dress of black and a white apron tied around her waist. Rosa was cut out for the life of a domestic goddess, and she knew Derick would ask for her hand sometime soon. They would live on the homestead and give her parents grandchildren. Kayla would wed Blake, if he survived the war. Rhea didn't think either Blake or Kayla were aware of this yet, but she knew it to be true with all the power of the goddess. Kayla blushed when she saw Blake. No one noticed except Rhea and Feeorin.

"Well, sister, you look as though you have had a rather trying day. You should have picked a different day to go gallivanting and come back in disarray." Rosa was always direct and to the point when she spoke.

"It is nice to see you too, little sister. Why did I pick the wrong day?"

Rosa had a wicked gleam in her eyes, and a sassy smirk crossed over her face. "Father has a friend for supper."

Rhea didn't understand; her father often had friends over for dinner. "This is nothing out of the ordinary, Rose. Father has a friend for supper a lot, or he used to. Why should it matter if my appearance is in disarray on this particular eve?"

Rosa chuckled, knowing how her older sister would react when she learned who the dinner guest was for the evening. She reached up and tugged at one of Rhea's wayward curls. It was good to have her sister home, and she loved to torment and tease her as often as she could. "Rae, I tell you this out of love, but also because it has been a long time since I have had the privilege of seeing you freak out. This evening's dinner guest is none other than your once-upon-a-time crush. The handsome Drake."

Rhea stopped walking, and Pixie's reins fell from her hand. She was positive that her heart jumped a beat and her stomach did a somersault. Drake had been a friend of her dad's for the better part of thirty years, and Rhea had always had a crush on him. He was sweet and handsome, somewhere between her age and her dad's, making him older, mysterious, and she was drawn to him. She had not seen him for many years. She was not sure why, after such a long time, she was all aflutter. She tried to maintain composure so as not to give too much away in her facial expressions.

She quickly regained herself. "Rose, that was a long time ago, and it was just a crush. I am sure he is married with children by now." She smiled at her sister. Rosa rolled her eyes and shook her head. She and Kayla turned and walked to the house. Blake took Pixie and his own horse to the stables.

Feeorin, who knew Rhea better than anyone, saw the momentary relapse in the Gypsy. "Rae, are you sure you are okay?"

Rhea looked at him; she hated how all-knowing he was. "Feeo, I need you to tell me honestly with as little biased attitude as possible, how do I look?"

He looked at her. He never understood how she doubted his views of her. She was beautiful no matter what she did, and he wasn't the only one who thought this, but for the sake of argument, he looked at her up and down thoroughly. "Gypsy, your hair is unruly, your skin is flushed from sun, wind, and work, your clothes are askew, but you look great. You are a very special mix of chaos and eloquence. That makes you beautiful. I can speak for myself, Travis, and Blake when I say that if this Drake fellow doesn't see the beautiful creature that you are, then he is blind and not deserving of the crush that you hold for him even after years of not seeing him. What is it about this guy anyways?"

She looked at him and shrugged. "I don't honestly know. Feeo, please don't judge me, my life is complicated enough without you judging me for a crush I had on a man almost fifteen years ago. I haven't seen this man in just as many years. He was older and didn't even know I existed. Coming home always brings interesting encounters. This is nothing different."

Feeorin looked at her. He received the freak-out that Rosa had been waiting for. He knew there was some underlying reason why she was reacting the way she was, but he would leave it alone for now. "Rhea, I am not judging you. I am just trying to fit pieces together. I know what it is you want and what you are looking for. Where I truly believe that not one of the men that have been in your life to this point did not, and never could, deserve you or even come close to being good enough for my gypsy angel, I want you to know that I truly hope there will come a day when I look at you and say he is the one. Now, go in there and see what fifteen years has done with your schoolgirl feelings."

Rhea hugged him. She loved his brutal honesty. He always had a way of giving her advice and shutting her up without making her cry or feel badly. He would always be her most trusted confidant and her dearest friend. He hugged her tightly, sighing into her hair. It didn't matter where she went; the gypsy angel always had suitors and admirers. Unless this Drake was married, Feeorin was sure he would find his way under her spell and be lost to her. With a slight hint of jealousy, he hoped, for once, that this would be the man who would match Rhea step for step and would be strong enough to handle her in her entirety and love her for more than just her wild beauty. Feeorin hated thinking of giving over his gypsy girl to another man, but he was not selfish enough not to want her to be happy. She needed a mate, but someone who wouldn't try to change her. He let her go, and she looked to the house. "Go. Don't be a silly girl. It does not become you." She smiled and blew out a breath. She walked slowly toward the house, head held high. "Gypsy, you might want to put your boots on." Feeorin called after her seeing her riding boots still tucked up under her right arm. She stopped, looked at Feeorin, then looked at her feet. They were still bare. She slapped the palm of her left hand to her forehead. She bent down and pulled her boots on.

Her mother was watching her from the porch. She would never understand her eldest daughter; she was strange and odd, but it worked for her. Rhea looked up to see her mom shaking her head at her. Rhea shrugged. "It looks as though you decided to play in the grass today?" Rene looked at her accusingly.

"Mom, I wasn't playing. I was training, and the meadow just happened to be the most open space. Winding up in the grass was just the result of a day's work."

"Your father has company this evening. Will Blake and Feeorin be joining us as well?"

Rhea nodded her head. "They will be in shortly."

Rene gave her daughter another look of disdain. "Are you going to clean up before dinner?"

Rhea shrugged again. "I wasn't planning on it."

With that, she made her way past her mother into the house. It smelled wonderful as she passed through the kitchen, and she was starving. She had not eaten other than the muffin first thing that morning. She followed the sounds of laughter and good cheer. It was the sound old friends made when they had not seen each other for a long time. She wandered into the living room where her father, Derick, Kayla, Rosa, and Drake were sitting. Richard saw Rhea and looked up, pleased. He was always glad to see her. All eyes followed his, including Drake's. Their eyes met, and she thought her legs would buckle and give way to the floor, but she managed to remain standing.

He was older and had started to gray, but he was just as handsome as she remembered, with sweet, soft eyes that were the color of clear creek water, the palest green. She smiled shyly, dropping her gaze. Fifteen years, and he still struck a nervous chord within her. Apparently, childhood crushes lingered still as an adult.

"Well, if it isn't my Rhea. Have you come to join us, daughter?"

She looked at her father fondly and smiled. "Yes, Papa," she said as she moved into the room. She kissed the top of her father's balding head. She could feel Drake watching her.

"Rae, you remember Drake, don't you? It has been many years, but he still looks the same."

She nodded and turned to Drake. "It is nice to see you again. How have you been?"

He stood up in front of her. She swallowed the lump that was lodged in her throat. He put his arms around her in a hug. She hugged him back; it was in that first embrace that she felt the shift around her, and her world began to tilt. He stepped back and looked her. There was something in his eyes that put her at ease but also caused her to step back slightly. Luckily, no one noticed. He smiled at her, and her knees again went weak. She could feel Rosa watching her, hoping to give something away. Rhea held it together.

"Richard, your daughters have grown up to be quite lovely," Drake said without taking his eyes off Rhea.

"They get that from their mother. Though this one has a wild spirit and she goes where the wind blows. Apparently, today the wind blew her into some grass." Everyone chuckled. Rhea held back the urge to run to her room, change her clothes, and run a brush through her hair. She didn't care what she looked like other than she hoped Drake didn't notice what a mess she was. Instead, she sat down and tried not to be discouraged by her father's playful jab.

Drake watched her. He couldn't recall the last time he had seen her, but Drake knew she had not developed into the exquisite woman he saw before him. He felt something he had never felt before, but he couldn't define it. He knew in that moment his life would never be the same. Her green eyes were observant and aware. She watched him watch her. He thought he saw a glimmer in them, but he wasn't sure.

Richard spoke, bringing his attention back to his surroundings. "Rhea, tell us, what have you been up to today?"

She looked at her father. How could she tell them she was trying to harness the power of light? "Papa, I am training for battle. Feeorin and Blake are helping me. With everything that is coming, I need to be prepared."

Her father nodded. "Yes, well, let us not speak of such dark things this evening. We have company, and that is to be celebrated."

Just then, Rene called; supper was ready. A wave of relief washed over her. They all made their way to the dining room. Drake pulled out a chair and offered it to Rhea. She accepted it with a smile. He took a chair opposite her. Feeorin sat next to her, watching the interaction between this man and his gypsy. Blake helped Kayla into a chair, and Derick and Rosa were sitting side by side, whispering to each other. You could all but see the love they shared. It made Rhea sad to see three happy couples. She was good at everything else in her life that she wanted to be, but the one thing she wanted most was the one thing she could not ever seem to make work. She had not bothered since Keaton, and she wasn't sure she was ready to try again, but it was the only thing missing in her life.

Feeorin put a gentle hand on her thigh, forcing her to look at him. He leaned in and whispered, "Don't give up, Gypsy, not now, not ever. He is out there, you will see."

She smiled at her friend. She hoped he was right, and a part of her, without knowing why, hoped the man sitting across from her was who she was looking for. Dinner was casual and the conversation simple. She was grateful for this. Her head was starting to throb from training, and the number of unnecessary thoughts that was whirling around in her brain. She was tired and no longer wanted to think. Being in close proximities with this many people was making her feel trapped. She needed air. She excused herself from the table and cleared her plate. Feeorin looked at her, questioning if she needed him to go with her. She answered no with a silent shake of her head. He nodded.

She made her way outside to the stables. It was too dark to ride, so she wandered down to the rose garden. The magnificent roses were all dormant, asleep for the long winter ahead. She let her finger brush the leaves. She made her way down to the wooden bench, where she sat down. The air was cold, but she didn't seem to mind. She looked back to the house and could see her loved ones in the window. The sound of their laughter and talking echoed down to her. She looked up to the sky; the stars that were starting to sparkle in the night sky were in her counsel, and she sought comfort in them often. Looking up, she tried to slow her mind. There was too much going on both inside her and around her. It was easier to process internally when she was away from home. She didn't have to deal with being the odd one out or with the prospect of home and hearth or making the wrong decisions. She knew she should settle down with a good man and have children, but the world called to her, and she couldn't imagine staying in one place for the rest of her life.

She heard footsteps but didn't bother to look up. She figured Feeorin came looking for her or Blake was checking to see if she was okay. She watched the stars dancing and twinkling against a black background. He watched her for a moment, trying to read her, but he couldn't. She was, thus far, a mystery. He approached her softly, not wanting to startle her. "It is a nice evening, isn't it?"

She was not expecting her intruder to be Drake. The sound of his voice pulled her away from the sky, from her thoughts, pulling it directly to his gentle face. There were no hard lines or sharp features to this man, just a softness that highlighted his sweet eyes and kind smile. He looked as if he would never hurt a fly—peaceful and docile, but masculine. His hair was brown, and she had noticed hints of red and some gray in it earlier, and his very tidy, nicely groomed facial hair matched. He had aged well, though there were not many signs of wrinkle or sun damage. She let her breath roll in and out, trying to stabilize it, so her voice wasn't shaky when she spoke. She had held on to her crush, without his knowledge, for this long. She would not let him know it now. She gave him a smile. "There is something about this place that makes it nice here most evenings."

He stepped a little closer to the bench. "I am sorry I interrupted your solitude." There was something in in his voice that made her think his words were genuine.

"That is quite all right. Would you like to sit down?"

He accepted her offer and sat down next to her. It was not awkward being next to her, nor was it uncomfortable. It felt like being with an old friend. They sat there for a moment not talking. She went back to staring at the stars. Without shifting her gaze, she began pleasant conversation. "Drake, it has been a long time since I have seen you. Tell me something of where time has taken you."

Her hair was blowing in her face, and he wanted nothing more than to reach up and brush it behind her ear, but he decided he had better keep his hands to himself. He sighed, what was there to tell? His life had not been exciting, nor had it been anything like what he imagined it should be, but he liked being in her presence and prided himself on honesty. "Hmmm, there is not much to tell. I moved from the prairie a few years ago when my parents got ill. They needed help around the house and on the land, so I packed up shop and went to their aid. I have been living there. I find miscellaneous jobs to do here and there to keep busy. It is not a glamorous life, but it keeps food on the table and keeps me out of trouble, I guess." He laughed, hoping that she would not think him lame. "And how does the Lady Rhea fare? The years have been kind to you, if you don't mind me saying."

She looked at him, a man of honest words and sweet praise. She couldn't help but smile. "I don't mind at all, and I thank you. It is kind of you to notice. As for me, I have been here and there. I heard a calling to heal outside the village, and that is where I go. I roam, as my mother calls it. I never get very far from here, no more than a couple days' ride usually. I have seen a little of the world, but I never stay in one place very long either."

He nodded. "What brings you home then?"

She thought about it for a minute. "This time, war brings me home." A deep crease crossed his forehead as he tried to understand. She wasn't sure what to tell Drake at this point, but she felt he could be trusted. "Don't worry about it right now. It is not important." She offered him the full weight of her smile, and his heart nearly leaped from his chest. She inched closer to him. "Let us just talk this evening. It has been so long since we have seen each other we should get to know each other better. After all, I was but a girl the last time I saw you."

He was in favor of getting to know each other. He wanted to know everything he could about this enchanting woman. He wanted to be near her and craved her touch even though he had never known it except the brief hug earlier that evening. She started to tell him of her travels, of her call from the goddess, of her failed attempts at love, of her hopes for the future. He was enthralled by her. Not only had she grown up to be beautiful, but she was intelligent and well-read. She was grounded and calm with a wild side that made her a free spirit. She talked with passion and fire in her eyes that made him wonder if this was what was missing from his life. He asked her questions, and she would answer with more than just a yes or a no but elaborate with detail. She would, in turn, ask him questions and listen intently. She liked hearing him talk.

Before they knew it, the sky had turned to black and night fully crept in. Lost in conversation, they didn't notice Richard heading their way. They were laughing about something and carrying on. Richard watched them from the top of the pathway. His oldest daughter—headstrong, determined, and stubborn to boot—she was exactly like he was; like father, like daughter through and through. He loved her, and he was glad she was home, but he wished she weren't always so conflicted. There she sat, in the dark, with one of his oldest friends, her laughter echoing all around them. He smiled to himself and walked toward them. He cleared his throat to alert them of his presence. They both turned and looked at him.

Drake stood up quickly in sign of respect. He was a gentleman and should not be alone with an unmarried female without a chaperone. "Richard, I apologize, I didn't mean to sit for so long in Rhea's company. We started talking, and well, your daughter is rather captivating."

Richard chuckled. "Drake, you will find that Rhea has a mind of her own. She does not require a chaperone, nor would she accept one. She does as she pleases, and we have been friends long enough that there is no disrespect for talking with my daughter. In fact, I think it is good for the both of you. You both need companionship, and heaven knows, it would do Rae a bit of good to escape from the mess that she has gotten herself into." Drake looked at Richard and then at Rhea, confused. She shook her head, and he left it alone. Richard joined the pair; this would be one of the last pleasant evenings before winter. The three chatted about one thing or another.

Rhea grew tired and stood up. Drake stood up as well and took her hand in his. He brought her knuckle to his lips and gently kissed it. "Ms. Rhea, it has been a pleasure to sit with you this night. I have enjoyed our conversation very much."

She smiled shyly, a slight blush rising into her cheeks. She was grateful for the night to hide her girlish flush. "Drake, thank you for keeping me company tonight. I am glad we got to know each other a little better. I do hope I see you again. I must bid you good night." She offered him a friendly kiss on the cheek before pulling her hand from his and moving to her father. "Good night, Papa. Sleep well."

"Good night, Rae. Rest well. I am sure Feeorin will have you out again training bright and early."

She turned and walked toward the house, looking over her shoulder slightly in Drake's direction. He was going to be a distraction she wasn't sure she needed in her life right now, but she sure hoped to see him again.

When she was out of sight, Drake looked at Richard. "I would like permission to court Rhea, if that is okay with you?"

Richard laughed heartily and slapped Drake on the back. "Drake, you have my permission, though it is really not my permission you need, it is hers. She is going to do what she wants whether I give permission or not. What's meant to be will be. Good luck, she is untamable and wild as the wind." Drake nodded and smiled. He liked a challenge and was feeling very up to the task.

She fell asleep that night softly with little on her mind and a crush in her heart, while in another part of the world, in the darkness of despair, Travis watched in mortification as the twenty newest vampire changelings scored the streets of upscale London for their evening meal. The site made him sick to his stomach. His heart was heavy. What had he done? Silently he whispered a prayer to her goddess. "Please, Ariadne, don't let her fail." With that, he covered himself in his cloak and sulked away. As if Ariadne had heard his payer, Rhea dreamed of her powers and of true love.

Chapter 12

She was up before the sun. Word of the first vampire attack would be spreading around the globe like wildfire. Panic and fear would be in the heart of humans everywhere. She knew what she needed to do. She went to the stables and bridled Pixie. She didn't bother with her saddle but rode Pixie out of the barn and straight to the meadow. The temperature had dropped since yesterday, but she was dressed for it. There was not a living soul to be seen, but it would not be long before Feeorin and Blake staked her out.

She dismounted Pixie at the edge of the meadow and walked toward the middle. She needed space and a lot of it. Her powers were not meant to be used as a shield. There was no way she would be able to stand against a vampire army and shelter those she loved. She was a light bearer, a ray of sunshine; as such, that was how her powers needed to be used. She was to shine. She stood alone in the center of the meadow. The sun had not yet risen higher than the base of the horizon, clouds darkened the sky, and she could feel snow approaching. She closed her eyes, willed her mind to quiet, and stood, just listening to the sounds around her. The birds were quiet; the trees were still. She slowed her breath, summoning Ariadne and the elements. She gathered her strength and her focus. She shook her fingers, letting the energy flow. When she felt like she was ready, she brought her hands together in prayer and brought them to her heart. Her heart was her center and the source of all her love. She thought about all those she loved: her parents, Rosa and Derick, Kayla and Selene, Feeo, Blake, Travis. She allowed herself to feel what it would be like to give her heart to that one special person, the one person who would be her reason to live through this war, the one person who could make her feel like she was finally where she belonged.

She was not sure who this man was yet but knew he was coming for her, and she sensed he was close. She allowed the sense of love to fill her; she felt it move from her toes and spiral its way up to her head. The feeling consumed her; she could feel the light inside her. It was time to shine; she held on to all the love and let her power flow. Her body was engulfed in light. Lavender was the dominating color, but there were hues of blues, yellows, and even red. She spread her arms out wide, and the light spread with her. It was a fascinating sight, even if no one was around to see it. She looked like a phoenix rising from the ashes. She controlled her celestial glow and let it roll off her, breathing steadily.

She opened her eyes, hopeful that her power stayed in place. She needed a target, something not moving or alive. She saw a boulder. It was decent in size, far enough away from anything else that there was no risk of anything else getting blown up. She concentrated. It was difficult to stay aglow and bring the burning power to her hands. It was, as expected, hot in the palms of her hands. She held it there, feeling its heat and energy. She allowed herself to experience the warmth as the flaming ball touched her skin. It was hot but did not burn. She admired the ball of light proudly before pointing her hands in the direction of the boulder. An incantation came to her mind: "Fire burn and fire bright, strike the heart of darkness with all your might. Terror ends with the night. Now go and bring forth the light." She was not sure where the words came from, but as she said them, the balls of fire in her hands shot out toward the boulder. In a flash of lavender, the rock exploded, and shards of rock flew into the air. She watched in horror and excitement as the rock became nothing but ash. She released her power and ran to where the boulder once stood. She knelt to the ground and cried, both for the boulder and for the fact that her magic was now deadly and dangerous. She was not a killer; it was not in her nature, but she knew this was how she was going to stand against the demon army and the evilest being in the world. She wept alone at the edge of the meadow. When she was done weeping, she thanked the boulder for sharing its life and took a rock shard and placed it in her side pouch.

She walked slowly back to the center of the meadow. That was enough training for one day. She would not take the lives of more objects today, either alive or inanimate. She got to the center where she had stood to cast her powers. She drew a circle with her fingers in the grass. Stepping inside, she called upon the elements once more, as well as the goddess. She asked for forgiveness of earth and fire and asked for wind and water to cleanse her. The wind started to swirl around her, and clouds filled the sky. She asked of the goddess to protect her through this journey. She was almost complete with her ritual when she got the strange feeling she was not alone. She did not break her circle, for as long as she was inside the circle and it was open, she was safe. She didn't sense danger or trouble; she felt surprisingly safe, and that was not a normal feeling for her no matter where she was.

Rhea finished her ritual and closed her circle. She looked around, trying to find who was watching her. She saw Pixie lying in the grass with her nose on the lap of a man. She could tell even from a distance that it was Drake. She wasn't sure what feelings rushed her, but it was a mix of fluster, happiness, and slight annoyance. Was he following her? She was not sure, but her horse seemed to have taken a liking to him, and she wasn't particularly fond of men. Pixie liked Blake to an extent; she tolerated Feeo and Travis at best, but there she lay, letting this man rub her nose and in between her ears. Rhea made her way toward them. Pixie didn't even bother to look up, but Drake watched her. He had just witnessed her catch fire and then blow up a boulder. He was not feeling as confident in his abilities to tame her as he was the night before. A thought entered his mind; maybe she was not to be tamed. She moved with grace and carried herself tall. She looked powerful and commanding with a feminine sway of her hips. Her body was cut in all the right places, sending warm, small, little jolts to his manhood. He wondered what it would be like to taste her and to feel her underneath him. He chided himself for thinking that way about her. She was a lady and had yet shown real interest in him. He had to weigh things carefully with this one, though he had no idea why.

She approached, hands on her hips, drawing more of his attention to them than necessary. He discreetly moved his eyes to hers. He would swear on his life they were brown, but he wasn't entirely sure. She stopped, shaking her head. He couldn't tell if she was angry or not. Her voice was like silk when she spoke. "I see you have found his company as enjoyable as I did, huh, Pixie?" She was talking to the horse, and as if the horse understood her, Pixie neighed and whinnied in response but never moved her head from Drake's lap. Rhea looked at Pixie and muttered under her breath, "Traitor," before acknowledging Drake. "Good morning, I see you have met my horse, Pixie. She doesn't usually take to strangers or men."

He looked at Pixie and then back to Rhea. "Good morning, m'lady. How does this fine day find you? Pixie found me. I just merely accommodated her request to be rubbed." He smiled at her, and her annoyance melted away. He was charming; she would give him that. Hands still on her hips, she looked him over. Besides handsome, he had a calmness to him, and that eased her worries some. She would keep her distance though; it was safer for them both.

"Drake, are you following me?" She was direct and to the point. He liked that.

"No, Lady Rhea. I was on my way to your father's house to help him with a project. I was hoping I would have had the pleasure of seeing you there this morning, but as I was passing through the meadow, I happened to notice you standing there, so I stopped to observe. I couldn't help but notice you were concentrating very intently, and then you burst into flames. I had never seen anything like that before. I was not sure if you were hurt or not, but I was mesmerized and couldn't move. Then you obliterated the boulder, so I figured you were okay." He got quiet; he was not sure of what he had seen, and he feared she might think him crazy.

She sighed, sat down cross-legged in front of him and Pixie, and patted Pixie's nose. "Drake, it was wise of you not to move. I am just learning how to control my powers, and I know not what I am capable of." He looked at her, confused. Sometimes she spoke in riddles. He was not sure if she knew this or not. She could see the questions in his eyes. Well, there was one way to find out how much this man could take, if he was going to be a distraction. He should probably know the facts. He would probably turn and run, but that was a risk she would have to take. He needed to be able to make an informed decision about her and had the right to decide if he was brave enough or not to stick around. She had learned the night before that he was not married, nor had he ever thought about taking this step. She needed to tell him all there was to tell. What better place than in a beautiful, open meadow surrounded by trees?

She looked at him. There was something inside her that hoped he was different and that he would listen to her and not pass judgments. She took a breath. "Drake, before things go any further, which I sincerely hope they do, I need to tell you a bit more about me and about what is to come. It will be a lot of information to take in at one time, but time is not something I have a lot of right now. If you are willing to stay awhile, I am willing to open up to you a little more." She sat in silence, waiting for him to respond.

He picked up her hand in his, brought it to his lips, and kissed it gently as he had the night before, but this time, he did not let it go. He found himself locking her fingers into his. He was not sure what possessed him to do such a thing, but it felt right. He looked her in the eyes and spoke only the truth as he knew it in that moment. "Rhea, I can promise you, there is nothing you can say that will change my wanting to spend time with you. You seem to have put me under some sort of spell, for I can't get enough of you. I know that sounds terribly strange, but it is true. I would like very much to court you and to spend time in your presence, if that is okay with you?" He continued to look her in the eyes. There was a lot to be said, in her eyes. They spoke words she couldn't, and he could see years of hurt and sadness in them, but he could also see hope and longing.

She wasn't sure what to say; he was so straightforward, but it was sincere, every word he said. She hoped that she was not again playing the fool, but she left that thought alone for now. "Drake, when I am done, if you still feel the same, then you are worthy of courting me."

He nodded in agreement. He had no idea what she could possibly say to make him change his mind. Still holding her hand, he sat back and let her tell him all there was to tell. She started from the beginning and told him who she was and how she came to be an angel of the earth. She told him about Travis and how he came to be a vampire. She told him more of her travels and her purpose to heal. She paused for a time to allow him to process. He seemed to be putting pieces together wherever they would fit. She continued to tell him of her past, relationships, and other bits of information she felt were important. Before she decided to go into the details about the war and what he had seen of her powers earlier, she needed to know where he stood so far. "Drake, now is the time to walk away if you aren't sure. The rest to tell is a bit dreary and may not have a happy end."

He squeezed her hand almost lovingly, and it filled her with warmth, the warmth she felt when she called her powers earlier. When he spoke, he was surprised at how genuine his words were, and it surprised him even more to be speaking from the heart. Wasn't he done making romantic gestures to women? He realized though that this was more than a romantic gesture; this was an act of love. He loved this woman he hardly knew. He didn't know how or why, but he loved her. "Rae, please continue. I may not fully understand, and it will take me time to come to terms with how special you really are, to appreciate your gifts and grasp your magical abilities, but that doesn't mean I don't believe all you say. I have never encountered an angel before, maybe once, but that is a story for another time. I believe you and I believe in you. You are amazing. Please give me a chance and tell me the rest. I fear it weighs heavy on your heart. You have too beautiful a heart for clouds of darkness to hang around."

She looked at him with tears in her eyes. It was the first time ever in her life that anyone had told her she had a beautiful heart. She knew others felt that way, but that was the first time it had ever actually been expressed in those words. This man was playing a dangerous game, and she didn't know the rules well enough to play back. She was afraid. She did not let the tears fall from her eyes. She was not ready for him to see her cry. Instead, she picked up where she had left off and proceeded to tell him of Jeremy and the demon army, of

Hell, and of war. She paused again, making sure he was still listening, which he was.

"Rhea, what does this war have to do with you? I mean, why are you a part of it?" The question was what she was dreading most; she was hoping she would not have to elaborate, in much detail, her part in the war.

She looked away into the distance as if searching for the answer. She didn't know how to tell him that she was the savior, the one being who could bring down the king of darkness and his minions, that there was a very likely possibility that she would fail, that she may not live to see the world fall.

His voice brought her back. "Rhea, please." He was pleading with her.

It was now or never. There was no reason to sugarcoat it. "Drake," her voice was soft and thick, the words wanting to stick together, but she got them out. "I am the only one who can defeat Jeremy and his army. I am the savior, and as of last night, I learned that I must go against everything I have always stood for and believed in. I will use my powers to kill. That is what you witnessed this morning, me trying to control the power of light and turn it into something deadly and lethal. I will fight in the name of love and all things good, yet I will be a force of mass destruction, and I have no real way of knowing whether I will succeed or not. If I do, the world will continue turning and love will prevail. If I don't, it will be the end of mankind as we know it. I am not sure I am capable of saving the world, and I really am not sure if I am going to be able to control an elemental power to the point of making sure no humans of the living, breathing kind with a heartbeat get caught in the cross fire."

Her mood was as cloudy as the sky, but she pushed it away. "I don't know if I will even survive when all is said and done, but I will march into battle, head held high, and fight with every ounce of my being. What is meant to be will be." He found it ironic that her father had used those very words last night. She was quiet, her breath steady in her chest.

There was no more to tell. What he did with this information was yet to be determined. He sat there rubbing her knuckles with his fingers, watching her eyes. They spoke her truth just as her words did. She was tormented by what was to come. He didn't even have this woman, but he knew he didn't want to lose her either. He would not let her die no matter what it took. Somehow, he knew that he had been waiting for her all his life; he was not about to give up just because a couple of centuries-old vampires decided to try to take over the world and the beautiful angel in front of him was to save the day. He would fight for her till the end of time if that's what it took for her to be in his arms. What was it about her that he found himself willing to go headfirst into battle? He did not know, nor did her care.

"Rhea, I know we don't know each other very well and that you have no real reason to believe me when I say that I would do anything for you, but as I live and breathe, I would do anything for you. If you let me, I will stand by your side and fight along with you. You don't have to face this alone." He reached up and brushed a stray curl from her face. He longed to touch her skin, so he let his fingers trace her cheek. She didn't flinch or pull away. The urge to kiss her full pink pouting lips was taking a hold of him, and his self-control slipped away, his hand resting at the nape of her neck. He pulled her into him and pressed his lips to hers.

Her eyes widened in surprise, but she did not resist. Her lips met his, and an electric current surged through her body, as her lips tingled. It was not a feeling she had ever experienced with any other kiss before. Not even Travis had that effect on her. Her lips softened and parted as his tongue sweetly and tenderly sought hers. Butterflies filled her stomach, and she was completely taken off guard. How could one kiss send her reeling? They melted into each other. Without a question in his mind, he knew that this would be his last first kiss. He had never felt this way about any other woman; no one had ever called to his heart before, let alone his soul. The kiss ended delicately. They smiled shyly at each other. There was an unspoken knowing between them that this was the beginning of something neither had counted on.

She moved away first. *Damn it*, she thought; she didn't have time for romance right now. She had to stay focused, but oh, that kiss; her lips still tingled. She heard a voice from far away telling her to let him in. She wanted to ignore it but knew it was to be that Drake would be a part of her life. She would be guarded and cautious; she would take her time and would not let Drake deter her from that of her destiny, but she would not push him away either. She looked at the man who sat before her. What was to be would sort itself out in time. She would make the most out of it, in the meantime, and the day of battle, she would make sure Drake was nowhere near the battlefield. She would make certain that his life was not in any more danger than it already was. If she survived this, she wanted him to be on the other side waiting for her.

There was no point in wasting the rest of the day. Drake was supposed to be helping her father with something, and she was keeping him from this task. She stood up, his hand still holding hers. "Should we head back to the house? My father will be looking for you, and I have much to discuss with Feeo and Blake."

He paused before getting up. "Rhea, this may be none of my business, and you don't have to answer, but am I going to have to compete with these two other men for your hand and your heart?"

Rhea looked at him; he was very serious about courting her. She was not used to being pursued. She shook her head and gave a half-hearted laugh. "Heavens, no. Feeorin has been my best friend for more years than I can count. We have known each other since we were kids, our history is complicated and messy, but at the end of the day, we will always be just friends. As for Blake, well, he has been given instructions of his own, and he, too, will be a player in this war. He will accompany me on my journey sort of like a chaperone. He, however, is in love with Kayla. He is not of any threat, nor am I attracted to him in that sense." She paused, building up her confidence. "Drake, I have a confession to make."

He stood up, her hand in his. "Lady Rhea, should I be worried about what it is you have to confess?" He looked concerned.

She smiled and shook her head. Her curls had worked themselves out of the knot she had put them in prior to setting out that morning. He liked the way her hair fell. With no rhyme or reason, it suited her; he liked the way it slid through his fingers. He brushed it away from her face, her smile softening the thick stone walls around his heart. He waited for the confession patiently. It was only a moment or two before she spoke again.

"Drake, I have always had a rather large crush on you." She felt her cheeks warm and knew she was turning an embarrassed shade of red. She should not have told him this. It would make her look immature and childish.

His facial expression was both shocked and amazed. His eyes twinkled, and a smile crossed his lips. He wasn't sure what he had been expecting her to say, but it was certainly not that she had had a crush on him. He was stunned and slightly lost for words. He could not believe that the woman of his dreams had had secret feelings for him as well. "You had a crush on me? When?"

She shrugged. "I have had a crush on you every day since I was probably twelve years old. You were always the handsome, good-looking guy that would come hang out with Rosa and I when Mom and Dad had to go to town or a diner or something. I about tripped over my horse last night when Rose told me you were to be father's dinner guest. I hadn't realized that a crush could last over the course of some twenty-plus years until I saw you in the living room. When you hugged me, I thought for sure the loudness of my heart would give me away." She couldn't look at him any longer, so she dropped her gaze to the earth.

He took her chin gently in his hands and lifted her head, forcing her gaze to meet his. "Rhea, I am honored that you had a crush on me. I had no idea. Does this mean you will let me court you?"

She gave a half smile and nodded. "Drake, I am scared. I have been through more hurt than you can even imagine, and I don't know what the future brings for me, but if you are patient with me and can understand all that is at stake, then yes, you can court me. I would like that very much. You should know I am not very good at relationships, and I make a mess of things, but if given the chance, you will never find another who will treat you better than I will."

He did not understand how anyone could ever let her go or how she was so hard on herself; she was perfect. "Rae, I will be patient. We can go slow if that is what you need."

She nodded and took his hand. "Let's go to the house. It is starting to snow." He looked up just as the first glittering white flakes fell from the sky. He wondered if she had the power to control the weather, but that was stupid. Snowflakes floated around them as they walked toward the house. The conversation was light, and he kept making her laugh.

Feeorin saw them approach from the barn and saw the look on her face. She was happy, and he had not seen that in a very long time. He saw their hands swing back and forth together as they walked. This was it, the man he had been waiting for, the one who would turn her world upside down. He would always be slightly jealous, but this was what she needed, a good man who could rope the wildness of her spirit and hold on tight. Her laughter echoed, and Feeorin sighed. The gypsy had finally met her match. He stepped out of the barn and cleared his throat. Rhea turned her head over her shoulder, dropping Drake's hand. She saw Feeo and let out a breath. It was not her father or mother. She was not ready for that conversation yet. Feeorin walked over to them, hands behind his back.

Rhea smiled at him. "Good morning, Feeo. Did you sleep well?"

He shook his head at her and tsked his tongue playfully. "Leave it to you to leave before the rise of the sun and come home with a man in tow." He smiled at her teasing. She stuck her tongue out at him. "You know better than to do that." He said, "But since you have managed to find yourself a new suitor, I will let it slide." He looked at Drake, and they measured each other up and down. They both had a place in their hearts for the same woman, though it was clear which she had chosen. "Drake, we were not properly introduced last eve. I am Feeorin." He held out his hand for Drake.

Drake shook it. "It is nice to meet you. Rhea has told me a little about you. Will you be fighting in this war as well?"

"No, I unfortunately will be of no use to Rhea on the battle-field. I fear my part in this godforsaken war will be better served here and now." Drake nodded. They might not ever be friends, but they would share a common civility for the sake of Rhea. "Rhea, we need to train. We have already lost more than a couple of hours since you disappeared so early this morning."

Rhea squared off to Feeorin. "We do not train today. I have done enough of that on my own. There is much to tell you and Blake. We have been going about things all wrong." Her eyes were troubled; Feeorin didn't bother to argue. He knew she would shed light on the subject soon. "Feeo, please find Blake and meet me at the tree in fifteen minutes. I have a few things to take care of here."

He nodded and started to back away. "Drake, it was a pleasure to meet you. I dare say you have your hands full with this one. She is as complex as they come, but you will never find one more loving and loyal and sweet. I do hope that I make your acquaintance again soon. I also hope there will never be a cause for me to dislike you. The lady is not to be hurt, if you catch what I am saying." He bowed to Drake and turned and walked away.

Rhea looked back to Drake, who was standing there with a look of annoyance. "Drake, please don't mind Feeo, he means well. He has been the one and only to pick up the pieces of what is left of my broken hearts these many years. He is mostly harmless."

Drake took her hands in his, brought them up between them at chest level. She stood taller than he did, but their eyes were at the same level. "Rhea, are you sure I am not going to be in the way of you being with Feeorin or anyone else? There seems to be a lot of loose ends surrounding you."

"Drake, I can assure you there is nothing or no one whom you are in the way. There is a lot going on right now. If you don't want to move forward, I understand. I told you before that I make a mess of things. I can't help it. It is just the way of things. Things are never boring around me, stuff just happens. Usually, it is out of my control. I am sorry." She again dropped her head; she couldn't help feeling a little discouraged. There stood this great man, and he, too, was not sure he could be all in.

"Rhea, look at me, please." It was a request, not a demand. She hesitantly looked at him. "Rhea, there are bound to be things that you can't control. You have gifts unlike any other. That makes you unique and special. It is a wonder you are still not married. If this is to work, I need to accept you for the remarkable creature that you are. Your father and Feeorin both have said something about you being a lot to handle. I can sense a wildness about you. I have yet to experience any of this firsthand other than what I saw briefly of your powers this morning, but what I know is that you are the most inter-esting, intelligent, fascinating woman I have ever met, along with the fact that your beauty is beyond compare. I have never met another woman like you, Rhea Edwards, and I promise you this—I will not walk away so easily."

She couldn't help the tears that fell from her eyes or that her hands trembled in his. Drake was willing to look past her differences and try to embrace them. She put her arms around Drake's neck and kissed his cheek. "I would very much like to see you again this evening. When the work is done, I will meet you at the stables. An evening stroll in the first snow would be a lovely way to end this chaotic day." She kissed the side of his neck. She felt his heartbeat quicken under the gentle pressure of her lips. This man would be her undoing. She turned and walked toward the barn, her hair blowing in the wind, leaving her lavender scent behind.

He touched his neck where she had kissed him; he was certain that the flutter of her lips would stay with him all day through. He was falling hard and quick for the earthen angel, like so many before him, the only difference was, he wasn't planning on leaving her. He realized in that moment that for the first time in his life, he was con-sidering marriage. He wanted to spend the rest of his life with this force of nature, and he would do everything in his power to make that a reality. He walked toward the house in search of Richard.

Rhea went to the stables; she was not going to meet Blake and Feeo with tears in her eyes. The stables were quiet this morning. Rhea walked Pixie to one of the open stalls. Rhea stood by her mare and hugged her nose, rubbing her soft white hair. She allowed herself to cry for just moment before she wiped the tears away with the back of her hand. She muttered under her breath to Pixie about Drake and poor timing, but none of it were complete thoughts, just bits and pieces.

She heard him chuckle inside her head. Travis. She did not need this right now, but there he was, invading her mind. "Why do you always have to make things harder than they have to be, Rae? What is your constant need to control everything?" Not only was he in her head, but now he was lecturing her.

"Travis, why must you insist on eavesdropping on my thoughts at the most inopportune moments? If you are going to stalk the inner sanctum of my brain, could you find a more normal time like when I am brushing my hair or something?" She was frustrated; she hated that he could read her mind and knew her thoughts.

Again, he chuckled. "Rhea, I never mean to pry or to catch you at the wrong moment. Whether I was in your thoughts or in person, I would still know that you are struggling and that you are trying to control things that are not yours to control. I am sorry that this is the only way we can communicate right now, but I am stuck in Hell, and there are more than a handful of men surrounding you right now that would chase me off the property with more than a pitchfork. I am guessing Mr. Drake would be part of that mob. By the way, he is the one."

She looked at him in her mind's eye; he was utterly serious. "You are probably right about being chased from the property. Feeorin alone would see you removed, but you are wrong about Drake. He can't be the one. I may not live long enough to have the one. He needs to know that."

"Rhea, stop thinking the worst. We both know that my life ends to save yours. Drake is the one for you, you must trust me on this. None of this, however, is why I am here. Changelings are on the move. They attacked London two nights past, and they are headed for Paris. I am to oversee these attacks. It makes me sick to watch. They are young, ravenous, and sloppy. Jeremy wants there to be a series of five small attacks. Paris is scheduled for Christmas. It will be larger than London. Rae, you must be ready. You need to gather your army now. Start enlisting people to fight beside you."

"Travis, I am not ready. I haven't been home long enough to gather forces."

"Rhea, listen to me, there isn't time. It is now or never. You are stronger than you know, and you have charms that are hard to resist. Work your magic and gather soldiers. The world needs you." With that, he was gone.

She kicked at a hay bale. Sometimes he was infuriating, but she knew he was right, and that was harder for her to swallow. She had to gather forces. She marched out of the stables and down to the tree. Blake and Feeo were already waiting for her, accompanied by Drake. *Grrrr*, she thought; nothing was ever simple. She was surrounded by masculine energy everywhere she looked, and they all wanted to be the alpha. She would have to take charge of this situation or there was likely to be a pissing match among her male companions. She walked up to the tree. Feeorin was standing to the right and Blake to the left, while Drake took up Rhea's spot on the large outstretched branch. Her hands found their way to her hips. She had hoped there weren't still traces of her tears. She was not in the mood for anything after her internal chat with Travis. She needed more time, and she didn't have it. Feeorin went to speak, but she silenced him with her hand. He muttered something intangible but backed down. She surveyed the three men. They were all so different, yet they all shared one thing in common: their loyalties to her.

She would need to be direct but gentle with her words. She knew Feeorin could withstand her temper, but she was not sure about Blake or Drake. "Okay, so it is like this. We are out of time, and the time we do have is precious and short. Jeremy's changelings made their first attack on London two nights past. The next attack is in Paris on the night of Christmas. My powers are not meant to be a shield, but we will get to that in a minute." She turned toward Drake. "I thought you were helping Father with something?"

He shrugged. "Turns out he didn't need me today after all."

She shook her head. "That may be, but you are in my spot." She said it teasingly.

"Would the lady like to share the branch with me?" He scooted to one side, opening space on the enormous tree branch. She sat down looking slightly agitated.

"Rhea, you need to connect your thoughts for us. What is going on?" Feeorin was the only one of the three who was willing to take her on, maybe because he had known her the longest.

Rhea glared at him, the other two just inched away. "Feeorin, please don't start. This has already been a trying day. I am already tired. I am forced to go against everything I hold dear, and now Travis is in my head telling me I need to hurry up and find an army."

He could see the stress and tears fill her eyes. "Rhea, we want to help. Just tell us what happened."

Rhea took a deep breath, holding back the tears that threatened to fall yet a third time that morning. Rhea told them how she dreamed of her powers and how they are to be used as a weapon and not a shield. She told them of her trial with her powers and how she blew up the boulder. She told them about what Travis had said and how time was short. She left out her interlude with Drake as it didn't pertain to the war and that was for her to sort through, not everyone else. When she was done, she covered her eyes with her hands and shook her head. Drake gently put his arm around her for comfort, and she found herself falling into the simple gesture, resting her head in the crook of his arm.

Feeorin heaved a sigh, and his shoulders dropped. Blake stood silently to the side, arms crossed over his chest. The snowflakes were getting bigger and were starting to stick to the ground. Winter was finally upon them. She felt the snow fall on her eyelashes and nose. Winter was her season; she was at her best this time of year, but there was so much to be done she was not sure she could relish in the snow, and that made her sad. They all sat there in silence for a long time. It was Drake who broke the silence. He was soft-spoken, and she liked the sound of his voice. "Rhea, what do you need us to do? How can we help?"

She shifted on the branch and looked up into his face. There was genuine desire to help. What had brought this man to such an easygoing sense of contentment? Was he always so even-keeled? The more time she spent with him, the more time she wanted to spend with him. "Drake, I am not sure there is anything you can do. I need an army, and I have not been home long enough to acquire one. Thank you, though." She stared off into space, deep in thought.

Again, Drake spoke. "Rhea, how many people do you need?"

Rhea shook her head. "Drake, this is not your war. You don't need to worry about any of this."

He looked at her. There was a slight glare in his eyes. "Rae, this is no more my war than is it yours. I am trying to help you. Are you always this stubborn? I am offering to help you. It would not kill you to accept." He pulled his arm from around her and crossed his arms over his chest, the look on his face daring her to challenge him.

Feeorin looked at Drake with a newfound level of respect. It was not very often that anyone challenged the gypsy. She was used to getting her way most of the time. She really had finally met her match. She needed someone who would push her and challenge her. The question was, would she see that, or would she see it as a form of control?

"Rhea, we can do this the easy way, and you can realize that I am not going anywhere no matter how hard you try and push me away. You can let me be part of this and accept my help, or we can do this the hard way and you can be stubborn, difficult and try to be in control all the time and I am still not going to go anywhere and I am still going to help you. Rhea, give me a fair chance. After our kiss this morning, at least be willing to consider the notion that I could be a part of your life."

She was taken aback by all that he said; not only was he challenging her, pushing her out of her comfort zone, and requiring her to trust another human being, but he was also not going anywhere, and he sincerely wanted to be with her. She sat quietly for a moment, not sure what to say. She fidgeted and shifted uncomfortably. Finally, words found her. "Drake, I am not stubborn or difficult." Blake and Feeorin both scoffed. She looked at them the way a child looks at a bowl of split pea soup but didn't engage them further. "Drake, I am not sure what I can say to you right now. I don't mean to be complex. Yes, I can be a little stubborn. I told you I am not good at relationships. Compromise is not something I have to do often. I appreciate your wanting to help, I really do. I don't know how to let you help." She got quiet again for a moment.

"Drake, the real problem is, if I let you help me, I am knowingly putting your life in danger. I like you a lot, and I don't want anything to happen to you. As it is, I have already put Feeo, Blake, and my entire family in harm's way. I can't put you in danger too. I am not sure I can protect you." Her head hung low and her feet swinging back and forth, she was sulking. Feeorin hated to see her like this, but this was not for him to try to soothe. Was the man next to her truly worthy of her heart?

Drake hopped down from the tree branch and stood in front of her. He lifted her chin for the second time that day and forced her eyes to meet his. Tears again had settled in the well of her bottom eyes. This woman was a multitude of facets, and it would take him a lifetime to figure them all out, but there she sat, world crashing in around her, everything she held dear being threatened, changed, and her only concern was for his safety. He had never had anyone have any kind of regard for his safety or well-being. Finally, her eyes met his, browner than green to him. The depth of emotion she held in those hazel pools was enough to tug at even the toughest heart strings. He kissed her forehead. "Rhea, first and foremost, there is never a need for you to hang your head around me. You are beautiful, confident, and your beauty radiates when you are not sulking. You have nothing to be ashamed of. You have not done anything wrong." His thumb traced her jaw tenderly. "Second, I am fully aware now what dangers lie ahead not just for me but for you. It is my choice as to whether I enter this battle or not, just as it is my choice whether I let you push me away or not. I choose to fight, and I choose you. I would choose you in a hundred different lifetimes. There is something about you that calls to me, Lady Rhea, and that doesn't happen to me every day. If you don't want me, then tell me here and now to my face and I will walk away, never to know true love's calling. Otherwise, I am yours and I will be at your side." He released her chin and waited.

This was her chance to walk away from him. She had already given him the chance to walk away from her twice; now she must decide. Was she going to run away from the connection they shared, or was she going to gather her courage and face this?

Feeorin held his breath but didn't say anything. Finally, there was a man worth the angel's affection. She looked into the eyes of the man who continued to turn her world in a different direction. He showed loyalty and honor and didn't seem to scare easily, but could he really, truly love her the way she needed to be loved? She thought about this; the answer she got was, she wouldn't know for sure unless she gave him the chance he requested, and she couldn't possibly be any worse off than she was right now. The only thing that concerned her was that he might have more power than any of the others before him to hurt her, and that was not something that sat well with her. She couldn't afford to lay her heart on the line right now; she needed her heart whole and intact to take on Jeremy. She rolled all this around in her brain. They all could see the wheels turning. She closed her eyes and sought counsel on an internal level. She listened to her mind, logical and all over the place, but then she heard her heart; they were going to wage their own war. Her heart was emotional and precise. There was something different about him, something worth trusting. Her internal battle raged on, but she knew her answer.

She opened her eyes. He was still standing there, looking at her with hope in his eyes. She kept control of her voice but kept it low and soft. "Drake, please don't go. I want you stay. If you are patient with me, I promise to try and figure out how to let you in. I need to go slowly, and I reserve the right to be guarded, but if you are willing to see this through, I will eventually come around."

He took her hand and kissed it sweetly. "Lady Rhea, patience I have, and you shall have an army by 6:00 p.m. in two days' time. I will have the troops gather in the meadow. There you will give the details of what you need and what is to happen. Until then, beautiful angel who has stolen my heart, you shall not be far from my mind." With that, he turned toward the house and disappeared.

Rhea watched him go. Her heart cheered in victory; her mind grumbled in defeat. They could rage their war; it didn't matter. What was meant to be would always find a way.

"Rae, don't you think we should be working on some sort of strategy or plan?" She looked back to her oldest and dearest friend. She knew deep down that watching what just transpired between her and Drake was killing Feeorin. She knew his love for her was never ending, but they had been down that road, and it was not the fit either of them needed.

"Feeo, I am sorry."

"Don't be, Gypsy. It was nice to see a man stand up to you. Maybe, just maybe, I won't have to hate this one. Yes, it stings, it will always sting, but he has proven that he is at least worth the effort to see where things go. You cannot sabotage this, though. You must be open to the notion that this man could be what you are looking for. He is not your past, but he could be your future. You just have to try."

She nodded. "Thank you, Feeo. You really are the best."

"Anything for my gypsy. Now I want to see how you use your power, please. This could be the piece that has been missing all along."

Blake stepped up. "I, too, am very curious about your powers. Please show us."

She looked at them. She knew she was not going to be able to avoid using her magic the rest of the day; she only hoped she would. "Both of you get behind the tree. I don't know how to control it yet. I don't need either of you to wind up as collateral damage." Blake looked at her skeptically, but both men did as they were told. She moved away from the tree and moved out into the open. She closed her eyes and allowed the beat of her heart to slow and her breath to calm. She willed herself to feel all the things she had earlier. She let love swirl around her and fill her completely. She allowed herself to feel hope and joy and happiness. She willed herself to picture all those she loved and allowed the warmth of those feelings to hug her tightly. She thought of Drake and how he had a way about him that she couldn't help but want to love. She realized that she truly wanted to give her all to the man who had just stood before her unfaltering and very sure of himself. She couldn't help but smile. She had never felt anything like what she was feeling in that moment.

Thoughts of him consumed her, and she opened her eyes. She was radiant and all aglow. Her light was bright and bold, much brighter than it had been first thing that morning. Blake and Feeorin both gasped, but she didn't notice. She remembered what it felt like to have Drake kiss her and how she desperately wanted him to do it again. She wanted to feel his touch and know what it would be like in the safety of his arms. She imagined what her life would be like if he were by her side. The more she thought of him, the more she illuminated. The man that had been her crush for so many years was now the driving force behind her magic. It was not possible to love someone this quickly, was it? She was full of love, and she wanted to shower it over the entire world. She concentrated and brought the flaming balls of fire again to her hand. She focused her energy and searched for a target. She saw a tree stump; there was nothing else in the path. She silently recited the incantation that had come to her earlier "fire burn and fire bright, strike the heart of darkness with all your might. Terror ends with the night. Now go and bring forth the light." She led with her left hand, sending the first burst straight to the center of the stump. The right followed, and in a flash of light, the stump was nothing more than ash.

The power overtook her, and she dropped to her knees both in pain and exhaustion. Tears streamed down her cheeks, and her fingers throbbed. Power always came with a price. Feeorin rushed to her side, and Blake followed. They were beside her in an instant. Small tremors rolled over her. Feeorin took her hands in his. She wouldn't look him in the eyes. "Rhea, talk to me. Are you okay?" He was truly worried about her.

She shook her head. "Feeorin, how can I destroy the life of another being, even an undead one?"

"Rhea, do you really think any member of Jeremy's army is going to care if they rip you apart? You can't look at this with an angelic heart. You have to find the warrior within." She still trembled, and he could feel her shake through his hands. "Rhea, you are going up against monsters who have no regard for anything except blood. They will destroy everything if you don't do this."

She knew he was right. The vampires would not care who was in their path or how much blood was spilled so long as they got to drink most it. Every time Rhea thought about the reality of this war, it tore her apart bit by bit. She looked down at her hands; her fingertips were gray and covered in soot. Fire was a messy thing to play with. She knew that physically each time she used her magic, it would take more and more out of her, but that was not information she needed to share with anyone else at this time. What happened to her at the end of all this was up to the goddess.

She had an idea. She needed to set Feeorin and Blake to another task so that she could focus on saddling the element of fire. She needed them out of her way; it wouldn't take Feeorin long to figure out that her powers drained her, and it would cause more undue stress than she needed right now. "Feeorin, Blake, there is something I need you both to do, please. I need you to go on a mission for me." They looked at each other and then at her.

Blake spoke first this time. "Rhea, I am sworn to protect you. I will not be going on any kind of errand without you."

She counted on this and was ready with a retort. "Blake, what I need you to do will help protect me. I promise I will not leave from my home until you return. Please, I need you." She held his gaze, begging him not to argue further. Their friendship was new, but she hoped it was strong enough to aid her in sending him off for a couple of days.

He didn't know what to do. He was sworn to protect her and not leave her side. His mission was clear, to keep her alive, but he knew she wouldn't send him away, knowing whom he had been sent by, if it wasn't truly important. He pondered the consequences of both options. In the end, though, his compassion and need to help won out. "What does the lady require of me? I am at your service." He bowed. She didn't miss the hint of sarcasm in his words, but it was better left unsaid.

Feeorin was next to speak. "Gypsy, what do you need?" Feeorin knew he needed to be heading home as his own lady would be angry, but he would not leave until Rhea was ready no matter how long it took. He would deal with his own misguided fate when the time was right.

She nodded, pleased that both had agreed to help her. "Feeorin, I need you to take Blake to your land. I need a vial of ocean water. I also need to borrow that magic book you are always telling me about. There is a spell in it that will be of great use to us."

He could tell she was grasping for any means she could find to get rid of them, but he would not question why right now; she had her reasons. The lady was always full of secrets. He would find out what she was up to in time. "A vial of water from the ocean. What good will that do?"

She chuckled. "What is the opposite of fire, my dear, sweet Feeo, but water? The element to balance out the power of fire is that of water. Ocean water is that of the strongest opposing force to a burning ball of fire. Please, Feeo, just do this for me?"

He nodded. The journey to Feeo's home was a three days' ride. He had made it in a day when he came to her a few days ago. He and Blake would make it there in two. "Rhea, how much time do you need?"

She smiled at him; he was always so intuitive. "One week should do. Thank you, Feeo. You are amazing. Remind me, when this is all over, to make this and everything else up to you."

"That is not necessary, as there is no way for you to repay me without it causing either of us more grief. You have possibly found your mate, and mine waits for me at home. No good could come of more than twenty years of favors. Just remember that when you fight in the name of love, mine is among the list of those names to whom your heart holds dear. Blake and I will gather the horses and what supplies we need. We will be on our way shortly." He, too, bowed to her in gentlemanly fashion.

"May your travels be safe, my friends, and may good tidings find you back here in seven days." They turned to go. She waved to them and said a prayer that all should go in their favor. With that, she was finally alone. She would have her magic mastered by the time they returned. There was nothing stopping her now or standing in her way. The men in her life were all on separate missions, ones which she hoped kept them busy for a short time. She was now able to focus on what lay ahead, becoming the warrior the goddess wanted her to be.

Chapter 13

S he saw the pair of horses ride out of the barn and toward the west to the valley that Feeorin called home. Drake would not return for two days, if he truly returned at all, and Travis was babysitting bloodthirsty uncontrollable changelings. The masculine energy that was left around her was that of her father and future brother-in-law. There was always masculine energy around her; it was something she was used to, but now she needed her sisters; she needed Selene. She knew Selene would help her, but she wasn't sure about Rosa or Kayla, but she had to try. The only way she might survive the next few days of practice was to have the protection of all the elements. She was fire, that she already knew, and she knew Selene was earth. She only hoped she could pull water and air out of the other two. She had never cast a full goddess circle with a member of each element keeping its place. She knew she needed the energy of the divine feminine right now; otherwise, she would not be strong enough to withstand her own power. Power was not meant to be used by one sole person. It was evident each time she cast her magic outward that it got harder and harder on her physically. If she didn't find some other resources, she would be destroyed long before she could ever defeat Jeremy. She would surely perish before the day of battle. It would not be weakness or lack of understanding that would be her undoing. If she were to die, it would be standing strong in the name of love face-to-face with a monster. She was not going to put that energy out into the universe, though. She was not going to tempt fate any more than she already had.

She set off toward the house in search of her sisters. Both were to be found covering the rosebushes with old bedclothes. They really were being tucked in for winter. Rosa looked up and scoffed. They were working, and she was doing whatever it was she did. "Well, I see you have sent the men away, or did they tire of you and your magical games? By the way, which one of them are you sharing a bed with, or is it both men?"

Rosa meant her words to be slightly joking and teasing, but they stung Rhea badly. She swallowed them down. She was not going to let either of them see how badly words could hurt her. She had enough to deal with. "Very funny, Rose. You know I am not sharing a bed with either of them."

Her sister looked at her and rolled her eyes. "At least not yet." Rosa and Kayla just laughed.

Kayla looked at Rhea pleadingly. "Could you please not engage in any kind of relations with Mr. Blake? I really like him, and I think he likes me too." Her youngest sister was naive at best. She was not worldly or wise. She was innocent, especially in matters of the heart. She couldn't see that Blake was in love with her and would be hers until the end of time.

"Kayla, that is not something you need to worry about. Blake and I are friends, nothing more. He will help me through this war, and then he will live his life as he sees fit. I am afraid my heart calls to another. We will see if his heart returns the call." She smiled at the thought.

Kayla giggled, and Rosa again rolled her eyes. "You two are going to go mad with all this talk of heart calls and such."

"Well, little sister, we all couldn't be as lucky as you and find love the first time out now, can we? It takes a bit longer for some to find the right one." She pushed Rosa's shoulder playfully with her own. "I need to borrow both of you for a little while this evening if you aren't busy. What do you say?"

Rosa snickered. "Depends on what you need us for." She brushed her long straight brown hair to one side. It lay on her shoulder neatly, no frizz or flyaway hairs. Rhea envied Rosa's hair.

"I need to cast a goddess circle, and I need placeholders for the elements air and water." Kayla looked at her, slightly perplexed.

Rosa looked at her like she had lost her mind. "We aren't witches, you know. We have no power. You seem to be the only one with that curse."

"It is not a curse. It is a gift, and just because I have powers doesn't make me a witch either. If you don't want to help, that's fine. I just needed to be able to call upon all the elements, and that requires feminine energy. Let's face it, I don't know many women, especially back here at home. I just thought maybe you, too, might want to help me with something greater than all of us." She waited, letting her sisters mull over all that she had said. Rosa could be very snarky and selfish but could also be very kind. Kayla would do whatever Rosa said.

"What do we have to do?" Ah, a spark of curiosity. That was what she needed.

"You would need to feel the element you choose. You would stand in a circle holding something to represent either water or air. Once the circle is cast and I call upon the elements one at a time, you would be the vessel in which the power of that force would come through. When all four elements are active at the same time, there is perfect balance and divine energy can flow freely." She told them like it was and hoped it would be enough.

Rosa never understood her older sister. She did things unlike anyone else and marched to the beat of her drum, but that was part of what made her sister so unique. She would never comprehend the oddities her sister possessed, but it didn't change the fact that blood and birth made them sisters. It wasn't often that she asked for help with anything. "Okay, sister, we will help you, but I get to be the water element."

Rhea did a secret internal dance. "Thank you. Meet me in the meadow at nine o'clock. The moon is full this night and will just be on the rise. Gather a jar of water and another jar that is empty."

The girls nodded, and Rhea set off toward town. She needed her earthen sister now. She was walking toward Selene's house when she encountered her friend on the pathway.

Selene was beaming from ear to ear. Her smile was infectious. "Oh, Rae, it finally happened, Bryce has proposed." She held out her hand for her friend to see the perfect little bobble upon her most important finger. Bryce had chosen well, a simple band with a simple but stunning stone. If Rhea were to guess, she'd say it was moonstone. It was a perfect suit for her beloved Selene.

"Sel, I am so happy for you." Tears welled up in her eyes. Selene deserved to be happy. "I won't say it is about time," she said with merriment in her voice.

"Rhea, it has been such a long time. I was not sure this day would ever arrive, but I am so grateful that it has. Please tell me you will be there beside me when I wed?"

Rhea had often wondered if Selene had made the right choice in Bryce; he always seemed a little too mysterious to Rhea, but Selene assured her that he was a good man, and he made Sel happy. Rhea wrapped her arms around Selene and hugged her tight. "Of course, I will be there." She hoped Selene would not make her promise as she was not sure she could fill it, but Selene didn't push any further.

She sensed her friend was troubled about something. "Rae, what is bothering you?"

Rhea loved that Selene knew when there was something wrong, and she also knew she could trust Selene with all that weighed on her shoulders. Rhea proceeded to tell Selene what had happened after they had left the tavern a few nights back, how she woke to Feeorin, and about the first round of training. She told her about Drake and their chance encounter that morning after she discovered how she was to use her powers. She told Selene about the meeting of the males at the tree and how Drake stood his ground and wouldn't give in to her. She filled Selene in on the missions she sent Feeorin and Blake on and all she knew of Travis and the mini attacks on the human world.

Selene took it all in, listening, contemplating. She never understood how Rhea could manage to entangle herself with the most unlikely male company. Though listening to her talk about Drake, she wasn't sure if maybe, just maybe, she had finally met her match. She would not say anything on this matter though, for now. Her advice had failed her friend multiple times in the past. She was worried about her friend. Rhea was playing with fire, literally, and was bound to get burned one way or another. She would offer what help she could. "Rhea, what can I do to help?"

"I need you to help me cast a goddess circle. I need you to stand at the point of earth. Rosa and Kayla have agreed to stand in for water and air, and I will hold the spot of fire. Together, we will invoke the goddess and call upon the elements four as one. With any luck, it will bring in the balance needed to keep me from draining myself completely every time I wield my powers."

Selene nodded. "Have you ever cast a full goddess circle before?"

Rhea shook her head. "No, but there has never been a real need for me to."

"That is true. I will help you cast the circle. Where shall we call upon the goddess?"

"In the meadow upon the hour of nine. The moon will be full this night."

"I will meet you there. What should I bring?"

"Thank you, Sel. I knew I could count on you. Bring a jar full of dirt, if you can find any with all the snow." It was then that she realized it was not snowing in the village or on the path. Selene looked at her, confused. "It has been snowing at my house all morning. I didn't realize it hadn't begun to snow here yet, though I am not sure how it is snowing there and not here." She shrugged. "Anyway, bring dirt and your athame, please." Selene agreed; they parted and went their separate ways.

Rhea headed back toward home. She needed to rest before casting the circle. As soon as she reached the boundary of her family's property, the snow was once again falling. Rhea didn't understand why there was no snow anywhere else. She didn't have the energy though to try to figure it out. It was barely noon, and she was exhausted. She needed to close her eyes. She passed the neatly covered rosebushes. No one was outside. She went in through the kitchen. Her mother was bustling about in typical fashion. There was food on the stove, dishes drying on the rack, and the floors were spotless. Her mother was always one for tidiness. "Hello, daughter, what have you been doing this snowy morning?"

"Hello, Mother, I have been working on my strategy for this war. I have much still to do, but it has been a productive morning."

Rene just looked at her as if she were from another country. "I will never understand you, Rhea, not one bit." With that, she turned and went back to her tidying.

Rhea figured that was her cue and walked through the house to her bedroom. She could see the snow softly fluttering down outside her window. She wondered again why it was only snowing around the homestead, but she was drained and too tired to solve the mystery. She removed her boots and her clothes, leaving them in a heap on the floor. She crawled beneath her covers and allowed her head to fall on the pillow. In all her travels, her bed was still her favorite place to sleep. It was molded to her body and hugged her in. It was not long before her eyelids grew heavy and she started to drift to sleep. She allowed herself to relax and gave in to the tiredness. As she fell asleep, the snow stopped falling, the ground covered in a white blanket of sparkling, glistening powder. The world around her was still and silent.

When she woke, the sun was out and moving toward the west. She felt rested but slightly unsettled. She redressed and ventured out in search of her family. Her mother and father were sitting by the fire; her mother was mending a shirt, while her father read. She loved the familiarities of home, even if she didn't fit into those familiarities. It was good to visit from time to time.

Her father looked up at her tenderly. "Good evening, Rhea. Did you rest well?" Her father was always in the know in some way or another. She nodded and sat down on the floor in front of the fire. The warmth felt good on her back. She tucked up her knees and wrapped her arms around them. Even for just a moment, it was nice not to be focusing on war, battle, and vampires. "Your sister said that all your gentlemen friends have left?"

She shrugged. "They have not left. They are just helping me by running a few errands in Sun Valley. They will return by week's end. I needed to be able to practice without them getting in the way or hurt."

Her father rested his book in his lap. His daughter spoke in riddles, and his job was to try to decipher them. "Tell me, daughter, what is it you practice that might cause them harm? You aren't doing anything illegal or dealing with dark magic, are you?"

She laughed. For being so wise, her father sometimes came to silly conclusions. "No, Papa, I am not doing anything illegal, and the only magic I know is that of the light. I am training to be a warrior so that I can fight among men to defeat an army of the undead."

Her mother ignored the conversation and focused on her mending. Her father tapped his fingers together. She could see that she was once again being misunderstood. She didn't know how to make them see all that she was or all that she was going to be, and she would never be able to explain to them how vital her part in this war was. She let the sigh she had been holding escape her lips, and her shoulders dropped in defeat.

"Rhea, just be careful whatever it is you are doing. Just stay safe." He nodded at her, and she understood the conversation was done. He went back to his book. She got up and wandered back outside.

The air was crisp, and the sun once again had stopped shining. She closed her eyes. She had spent her whole life being misunderstood by everyone around her. It was hard to be different, to have gifts that were constantly being misconstrued and undermined. She had always thought her gifts made her special, but the older she got, the more she wondered if this was the case. She let the tears fall; there was no one there to see them. As she started to cry, the sky, too, began to cry and silvery flakes fell to the earth. The angel born in winter was controlling the weather with her mood. She had yet to realize this.

She found her way to the bench where she and Drake had sat the night before. She allowed her mind to think about him. Would he be able to understand her and appreciate the uniqueness that made her who she was, or would she be too much for him to handle? She thought about the way he kissed her that morning and how he stood before her, declaring to her his loyalties. Either he was the man of her dreams, or he was foolishly confident and not all he seemed. She sincerely hoped it was not the latter of the two options. It didn't matter now; once Feeorin and Blake returned, she would be free to go back to the little inn and not have to be surrounded by people who looked at her like she was a leper. She would not have to try to be normal, and she would not have to explain her every move. It hurt knowing she was not like her family or anyone else, but she was proud of all she had done and all of whom she was able to help. A healer's path was often lonely; she just never realized how lonely until she came home. She sat there alone, watching the snow fall. It was romantic, magical and put her at peace. She found tranquility in the dance of frozen fairies.

Time passed, and she heard her mother call for super. She was not hungry; she didn't think she could handle the silent ridicule that would be directed at her. With her friends gone, there would be just the family and she was the outcast. She went to the barn; she would go for a ride. She had grabbed the necessary tools she needed from the kitchen on her way out of the house, so she didn't need to come back before the casting of the circle. She grabbed her bridle and her saddle. Pixie was happy to see her mistress, as always. Rhea brushed her thoroughly before putting the saddle on her back. A ride would do them both good. She walked Pixie out of the barn before mounting her in an effortless motion. She was an experienced rider, and her movements were swift and graceful.

As soon as her seat was on the saddle, she kicked the muscular flesh of the white mare, and they were off, snow flying up behind them in powdery puffs exploding like dandelion fuzz on a windy spring day. The snow continued to fall as she rode. She flew past the old tree and beyond the boundaries of her family's property. She had no real destination in mind. As she crossed the boundary line, the snow stopped. She looked behind her as the last flake fell to the earth. She did not understand. What magic was holding the snow in place at home?

She pondered this as she rode on. She realized, as Pixie leaped over a small broken-down plank fence, that it was her magic that kept the snow around her family. As hard as it was for her to be home, she still wanted her family to be safe. The snow was an invisible blanket of protection. If she were on the premise of the grounds, the snow would gently fall protecting those within. As soon as she left, the snow would no longer fall but would hold as a shield. She realized that was for her protection as much as it was for theirs. Snow was the perfect counterpart to fire. There was no better way to be sure that her powers were contained than to cover the ground with something that doesn't burn. She was not sure how she was able to manifest snow with her mind or that she was even capable of such a feat, but somehow it felt true and right.

She rode the opposite way from town. She was not in the mood for people. The agile mare never missed a beat and galloped along. Rhea let the horse lead the way; her mind was too full of things she was yet to understand. How was it that in the short seven days that make up a week, she had gotten so far from what she thought she was supposed to be doing? She knew destiny played a hand, that she was meant to enter the Dragon's Cauldron and that her encounter with Travis was prewritten in the stars just as she knew all the other events that had transpired were fateful, but what she didn't understand was how so much could change in such a short time. She was not a big fan of change, especially drastic change. She was a creature of habit, and none of this was on her list of things to do. She knew there was no other way, but it didn't change her wanting to grumble about it slightly. Her hair broke loose from the braid it was in. The wind caught it and blew out that mast of copper sails; waves and ringlets billowed out behind her. The scenery darted by in specks of browns and greens. She felt a sense of peace knowing her family was safe. She was not sure how long the blanket of snow would hold, but she was not concerned with this right now. Pixie's body moved and contracted with every steady hoofbeat. Her lean muscles gripped under the saddle. The sun sank lower on the horizon, but neither horse nor rider cared as they were used to riding at night and could cover a lot of ground.

Minutes turned to hours as the world flew by. She saw the glimmer of the moon stretch along the rim of the sky. The hour of nine was sneaking in. She took hold of the leather reins and steered Pixie toward the meadow. She needed to prep her circle before the others arrived. She knew Sel would not let her down; she only hoped Rosa and Kayla wouldn't disappoint her. She let Pixie stay at full gallop but guided her gently in the direction she needed to go. The mare, with a knowing heart, stopped just at the edge. To anyone else, the meadow didn't hold much wonder, except for in the spring, it was alive with color. Thousands of flowers filled the now-barren piece of land. She hoped she would one day see the meadow in its full glory. She dismounted and hugged Pixie before making her way to the center. She carried her small flameless torch and jar in each hand. She set herself up at the point of south. Selene would be the northern point, and the girls would join in at east and west. Rhea walked the four corners, marking each point as her reference. She was slowly touching grass-blades connecting to the earth; she needed to be fully grounded.

She saw the faint glow of skeptical candlelight in the distance; the girls were coming. Selene, who preferred the dark, moved in like a cat, stealthy and undetected. She moved through the trees without a sound. Rhea saw Selene before she heard her. She was wearing a simple dress of velvet, and she had on a long black cloak; the hood covered her hair. She met Rhea in the circle, and they greeted each other in sisterly fashion with a gentle hug. The essence of her engagement still hung on Selene's aura. Rhea was beyond thrilled for her friend.

The two older women waited in silence for the younger two to join them. They entered the circle full of giggles. Rhea looked at them and shook her head. Youth was not necessarily something she missed. She set about getting everyone set up in their corners. Selene had her jar full of earth perched on a rock. The lid was off, and she was barefoot, feeling the earth. Rosa had her jar of water and stood with her hands on her hips, waiting for instructions. Kayla fidgeted, rocking from her toes to her heels. Rhea put the raven feather she had found in Kayla's empty jar. The younger girls had not learned how to be calm and still yet.

Pushing down her need to be mother hen and scold them, she busied herself with making sure her circle was just right. She had created a smaller circle for her fire on the inside of the large circle. The girls watched, not sure what to expect. Once the fire ring was set, she lit the small torch and laid it in the fire ring. The flame glowed orange and red, and smoke filled the air. It was not a large fire, but it served as light and brought forth extra magic. All was right and ready. She took her place next to her sisters.

"First, thank you all for helping me this night. I am grateful to you. Second, this will be the first goddess circle I have ever casted. I do not know what will happen or what to expect, but I can assure you we are quite safe. To start, Selene, may I see your athame?" With no questions asked, Selene handed it over. Rhea took a breath and ran the blade along the palm of her right hand until it bled. Red liquid pooled there. She picked up her jar and let the drops fall to the bottom. She lit the candle. "By the blood of my blood, let us begin. Let us take a hold of each other's hands. I will then call upon the goddess."

The four women, two of birth and blood and two of choice, formed a link, bringing in the bond of sisterhood. Elements in place, the circle of the flesh was complete. Rhea closed her eyes and concentrated on the elements four of earth, air, fire, and water. When she felt the balance among all four, she called on the goddess. "Goddess Ariadne, hear our prayer. We come forth united in sisterhood, joined by the power of the elements and blood to call upon thee in an hour of need. I, Rhea, chosen by you, earthen angel, healer, and light bearer, request your guidance. I request your presence. Please guide my sisters and I this night."

She let her words fill the wind; the torchlight flickered, but she carried on. "Ariadne, mother of all, please answer my plea. You have gifted me with powers to save mankind, and with all power comes a cost. I ask for protection upon using my powers. It takes a toll on my body, and I am weakened. I need to know how to survive long enough to save those with whom you have entrusted me. Please show me the way to save those who need it and how to conquer evil in a way that does not make me weak. Hear me, Mother."

The girls stood holding hands. The air shifted, and the torch burned out. Water splashed like waves out of the jar before Rosa. Kayla's jar fell to its side and the feather floated on the wind, and Selene's jar exploded and crumbled to the ground. The candle in Rhea's jar burned out. Kayla looked scared.

"Rhea, what is going on?" Rosa demanded.

"I am not sure. Just hold tight and don't let the circle break."

Just then, a bluish light rose out of the center of the circle. It rose from mere ashes, transpiring into the figure of a woman. The aspiration took shape, and the goddess Ariadne was before them. They all gasped. Rhea bowed her head in respect; the other three followed suit. Her hair was the color of Indian paintbrush on a summer day. Long and flowing loose spiral curls swirled around her.

She was dressed in a sheer gown of gossamer threads. Pale porcelain flesh peeked through the gown. She heard the goddess's voice and answered her calls, but Rhea had never seen the goddess before in person. She was truly a sight to behold. She was stunning in beauty, and it was impossible not to stare. Rhea kept her head bowed.

Ariadne lifted her chin just as Drake had done earlier. "Rhea of light, raise your head and meet your goddess. You have called me forth, now I answer. Please meet me with confidence and respect."

Rhea allowed herself to look in the eyes of her beloved goddess. "Mistress Ariadne, thank you for answering my prayer."

Ariadne nodded and looked toward the four women. "Your sister needs your help. Each of you will be given a gift that she will need to save all the human world. These gifts will appear to you. Your job is to keep them safe until she is in need. Rhea is of pure magic. It stems from the heart. Therefore, the gifts may not be of magic but of the elements you represent. You will come by them one way or another, but guard them well. Darkness lurks in all corners of places." Ariadne paused for moment.

"Rhea has chosen all of you to complete her circle. That means she trusts you and trusts your abilities. Don't disappoint her. So much rests in her hands. She needs to know you have her back. She will need each of you in your own unique way, and she will rely on you to help her stand strong when she feels weak. This is what it means to be a sisterhood. As for you, Rhea of the light, I chose you for a reason, but your self-doubt and your insecurities cloud all that you are, all that you are to be. You must find your confidence and believe in yourself or you will fail. Your powers do not weaken you, your lack of faith in yourself does. If I didn't think you would succeed, I would have chosen someone else. Your heart and your mind need to stop battling. Your heart will always find you the right way, but your mind, powerful and brilliant, will always find you confused and unsure. Find it within. You must think like a warrior but rule like a queen. Love will prevail if you let it. Stop your fears and find your inner strength. You have it in you. The past is that, it matters not. What matters is what is in front of you. Your path has been set.

There is no turning back from that. If you try and change, the course all will be lost."

Rhea nodded. "Goddess, what happens if I fail?"

Ariadne beheld her for a moment then leaned in so that only Rhea would hear. "You are not destined to fail. It is not what's meant to be. Let him in and surely you will succeed. He is good for you and will not let you fall. I have chosen well. Just find your voice, Rhea, and all will be as it should." Ariadne kissed the chosen one on the forehead and backed away, opening her arms wide. "Hold true as a bond unbreakable by the elements four and the link that joins you as sisters. Go forth and remember to keep your sister safe when she needs it the most. I will answer your call if you should need me, but it is within all of you to find the way. Take care, children, and I will see thee soon." Her words were no sooner out of her mouth and she was gone. There was not a trace of her anywhere. The torchlight was again aglow. The girls looked at one another and then at Rhea.

Rhea closed out the circle. "Thank you, goddess, for hearing our prayer. Thank you for the gift of your presence and for that of your wisdom. We honor you. Thank you, elements earth, air, fire, and water, for your balance. Thank you, sisters, for being of mind, body, and spirit. We close out this circle with much knowledge and love. Keep us safe as we go our separate ways. By the powers of three times three, blessed be." She dropped hands and walked the four corners one more time. The others followed, moving in a clockwise motion. They ended back at their original spots. All were a little awestruck and not sure what to say. They parted ways, returning the way they came.

Rhea stood in the meadow alone, looked up to the heavens, feeling alive and free. "Thank you, Goddess Ariadne. With all my heart, thank you."

Chapter 14

The next two days were spent in the meadow alone practicing her magic. Snow was now following her farther past the boundaries of home. She sat on the earth as evening crept in, snowflakes suspended in the air around her but not yet reaching the ground. She had been trying to hone into what Ariadne had told her but was weak, tired, and frustrated. She sat in the meadow alone. She got up off the ground and stood. There she couldn't understand what Ariadne meant by "Rule like a queen."

She was muttering under her breath, snow swirling in downward spirals, when she heard footsteps behind her. She looked over her shoulder; her heart skipped a beat, and the suspended snow flurries fell to the ground. Drake was nearly skipping toward her. He was not tall, but he carried himself in a manner that not only made him seem tall but also gave him incredible agility. He moved like a mountain goat and had a certain bounce to his step. He wore green riding trousers and a brown tunic. His cloak was strung haphazardly across one shoulder and was clasped with a brooch of garnet and onyx. It was a simple brooch, but it held an ounce of beauty.

She turned around but did not move. She let him come to her. She was not sure what emotions were swimming around inside her, but the snow flurries around her were as chaotic as her emotions. She liked the way she felt in his presence.

He approached her, tucked his right arm at his waist, and bent in a full bow. "Good evening, Lady Rhea. You are looking lovely this eve."

She returned his bow with a lady like curtsy and a slight blush. "Thank you, kind sir. How do you fare this evening?"

He took her hand and kissed it. He noticed the snow falling around her but didn't say anything about it. He wasn't sure he would comprehend the response if he asked. He had spent the last two days trying to make sense of all that she had shared with him. He didn't quite understand it all, but he believed her every word. "Lady Rhea, I am much better now that I am sharing this space with you. I have kept good on my promise, I have returned in the time of two days with an army. They will follow you into battle with a bit of conviction from you. Does this please my lady?"

Her heart melted away from her internal frozen cave of past hurts and lack of trust. She allowed him the full weight of her smile, and her eyes sparkled in a way which he had never seen in hers or any other eyes sparkle. "Drake, I know not what to say. Where is this army you speak of?" She looked around the meadow but didn't see anyone.

"Rhea, they await just beyond, over the hill. I will call them forth if that is what you wish." He took both her hands in his and held them. His pulse kept in time with hers. "They are good men and women, and they are willing to fight for a good cause. Are you ready to give them such a cause?"

She looked at him; he had kept his word. The question was, would she be able to convince these people to fight a war that was not theirs to fight? They would be farmers and merchants with families and homes. She would be asking them to give their lives. How could she lead them knowing what they would be sacrificing? She thought about this for a moment. She knew she could not go into battle alone, so there was no choice. "Drake, please call down the people whom you have gathered. It will be for them to decide what path to choose."

He nodded and let go of her hands. "I shall return shortly." He turned the way he came; she watched him go. What on earth was she going to say to convince a crowd of strangers to give their life? She pondered this as the only man who had ever kept his word moved from sight. He believed in her, and that was a lot, considering their brief encounters over the last few days.

Rhea stood looking at the horizon as it filled with silhouettes of people of all different shapes and sizes. Now was her chance to be heard; all she needed was to find the right words. As the crowd gathered in, she looked to the heavens. "Ariadne, give me strength," she prayed. Some of the people she recognized from her travels. She saw faces of those she had healed. It gave her a sense of familiarity. Her heart filled with wonderment, strangers coming together to stand for something that was bigger than any of them knew.

Drake was back at her side. He put his arm around her waist and pulled her to him. She could feel his body heat radiate. It was a warmth she had never known, safe and comforting. She looked at him; in that moment, she knew her heart's desire. She knew that she loved this man. She smiled at him as her army finished filling in. When the meadow was full of husbands and wives, brothers and sisters, friends, moms and dads, she turned and faced them. She was not sure what she was going to say, but she hoped this was the moment that she was meant to find her voice. Without knowing why, she grabbed Drake's hand and locked her fingers with his. His eyes widened in surprise, but his smile let her know he was pleased by her gesture.

She looked at the faces of those around her. She could feel love radiate from them all. This was her purpose, to fight in the name of love. She smiled at them. She searched for the right words. She heard Ariadne's voice in her head telling her to rule like a queen and find her confidence. This was as good a time as any to try. She took a deep breath. "Thank you all for coming this evening. I see many faces I know, and many faces I hope to get to know in the coming future. For those of you who don't know me, I am Rhea Edwards. I am from this very village. My parents live in the home that has belonged to our family for generations. We are a long line of healers. I, however, am the only one who has ever ventured out beyond the village. I have seen many lands and met many people, of all walks of life, but something much greater and much more meaningful has brought me home again. You see, there is, as we speak, an army of the undead gathering in, ironically, a place called Hell. There is a centuries-old vampire by the name of Jeremy who has decided to wage war on all mankind."

She could hear the gasps escaping lips of scared, innocent people. "I know that sounds terrifying. It terrifies me down to the very core. I have been called upon by the goddess Ariadne herself to fight for what is right and good. I stand here gathered in a meadow in the name of love and all things pure and light. I am not a warrior. My hands are used only to heal, but I believe with all my being that we can win this war if we have the right intentions. I know there is a lot at stake and that there is no reason for any of you to pick up a sword and march into battle, but I am asking you in the name of the goddess and in the name of love to hear me."

She paused, looking at her audience. She saw fear and skepticism in a lot of the eyes looking back at her. She looked at the man next to her for encouragement. There was love in his eyes, and she felt a new wave of hope wash over her. She dug deep within herself and found courage, found her voice. "Gentle people from near and far, our lives are being threatened by a dangerous force. The world as we know it will not be as it is if something is not done and we will all perish. We have a chance to defend our world and rid it of the worst possible evil. We have a chance to rise above fear and darkness and let light shine. We have a chance to let love conquer where hatred runs free. I stand here today and ask you to join me. If you can find the courage within, please offer up your services. Be it with a bow, an ax, a sword, or any other weapon you can wield against evil, please come forth and fight. I cannot promise to lead you into a battle where no one is harmed, nor can I promise that all your lives will be spared, but I can promise to fight alongside you and to see that evil falls. I can promise to lead you with love in my heart and a belief that we can beat this monster. I ask those willing to join in an army of honor, loyalty, and happiness."

Murmurs and whispers could be heard from all directions. She stood there watching and wondering if she had reached any of them. One man, a little older than Drake, spoke out from the crowd. "Why should we follow you? What gives you the right to lead this army? Won't there be kings and queen's armies fighting? Why do we need to leave our home when others will fight this battle?"

The crowd grew louder with a resounding "Yes, why should we follow you?" She was losing them.

Drake squeezed her hand, and for whatever reason, she felt like he was telling her it was going to be okay. She looked within again, searching for the answer, and there in her heart she knew what she had to do. "You have every right to question me and to question why I am to lead you into a battle of blood and death." The crowd's roar became a hushed whisper as she spoke. "I am no better than any of you, and I look not to lead to have power over any of you. It has been foretold that the armies of the world's kings and queens will not reach the battlefield. They will fall long before, because they fight under the order of another. I give no orders. It is your choice to fight. It is your choice to believe in love and life. I wish to fight with you as an equal, side by side, learning how to wield a sword just as you do, but I also wish to be a weapon. You see, I have been given a gift by Ariadne, a gift that will allow me to sacrifice myself if need be to ensure that we are victorious."

With that, she closed her eyes and brought forth her power. She let love surge her veins, let her heart open to Drake and feel that love flow through her. She started to glow soft lavender, and the people backed away and gasped. She let her light shine bright and brilliant. There were oohs and aahs coming from the crowd. She felt Drake hold tight her hand. She brought her arms up over her head toward the heavens, not letting go of Drake. She let her magic fly up into the sky. It shot off her fingers like fireworks. She thought of the symbol that meant the most to her and let that take shape in her mind's eye, and the image of a heart surrounded by angel wings formed from her sparks. It hung in the air even after she dropped her arms.

She opened her eyes. All were silent; all eyes were on her. The man who had questioned her dropped to one knee. "Please forgive my dismay, my lady. I meant no disrespect. I gladly follow you into battle if it is my life that I must give to serve so be it."

A small family stepped forward. Rhea recognized Sarah and little John as they came through the crowd. Sarah's husband spoke. "This woman is an angel of mercy. She showed kindness when it was needed most. She healed my son, John, even though my wife had no means of paying for her service. She showed John magic. Because of her, my son lives pain-free. I owe this woman much, and if it means marching into war against abominations, so be it. My wife vowed there would be a way for us to repay her, and here is my chance." He dropped to one knee and looked at Rhea. "I give you my services and my word to fight for what is right in the world. It is small thanks compared to that of what you have given my family."

Rhea was touched. This little family was willing to sacrifice for things beyond their realm. "It was an honor to spend time with your son and lovely wife, and as I told her, no payment was necessary, but I am grateful to you that you stand here today willing to help me fight. I hope to be able to share more magic with your son another day."

John beamed when he saw Rhea. He tugged at his father's sleeve. "Papa, it is the fairy queen." Tears fell down Rhea's cheeks at this. She smiled sweetly.

At this, others followed and took one knee and offered their allegiance to her. Before long, the entire crowd was on their knees; she had an army. She stood there watching this scene unfold, her heart overflowing. Drake was the last to declare his loyalties. He, too, got down on one knee with her hand still in his. "Lady Rhea, I offer you my sword in this battle, and I will fight at your side, not as a man, but as the man who loves you and will see that you survive this war so that I may one day take your hand in marriage. I fight beside you in the name of true love. Let evil hear my battle cry as it rings out, forever and for always, that I, Drake, am completely in love with Rhea of the light." He kissed her hand, and the crowd cheered. It was in that moment that she felt like their queen and she had finally found her king.

She heard Ariadne's voice in her mind. "Beautifully done, my daughter. Believe you are a queen, and a queen you will be." Rhea felt elated.

She spoke to the crowd and told them what she knew and what was to come. She spoke to them of strategy and learning to wield weapons. She spoke to them of listening to their heart and believing good will triumph. She offered to have her army gather in the coming weeks at the little inn for training and plotting.

The crowd finally dispersed somewhere around nine thirty, and she was left alone with the man who knew not yet that she loved him. She lay down on the grass and looked up at the stars, and he sat down beside her. "Drake?"

"Yes, Rhea."

"Did you mean what all you said in your proclamation when you pledged your allegiance?"

He looked at her, moonlight reflecting in her eyes. "You need not doubt what I said. If they were not true, I would not have spoken them. I am a man of honesty and good intentions."

She nodded. They lay there in silence for a little while. She liked that they didn't always have to be talking and could just enjoy sharing the same space. "Drake, can I ask you something?"

"If I say no, will it make a difference?" He cocked his head and gave her an impish smile.

She rolled her eyes at him. "No, it really won't make a difference," she said teasingly.

He nodded and smiled. "I didn't figure as much. Ask away, my lady, although I must say, I have never met a woman who asks as many questions as you do." There was a hint of mocking in his voice, but she didn't care.

"I suggest you get used to it. If you plan on sticking around, you are going to have to understand that I will dig deep and I won't settle for surface-level answers. I will get to the heart of the matter. Therefore, questions are mandatory." She stuck her tongue out at him. He chuckled. This feisty female was becoming more and more enticing. He was going to have to kiss her again very soon. She continued, "Drake, what did you say to all those people to get them to follow you here tonight?" She turned her head and looked at him, her heart screaming at her to stop thinking and give love a chance, but her mind needed to be put at ease.

"Rhea, I know you have no reason to trust me and that our time together has been very short, but I love you, and that I know to be true with all of my heart. I have never known what it feels like to love anyone as I love you. I will do whatever it takes to prove that to you. I told them that the angel who has swooped in and stolen my heart needed all the help she could get. I told them the truth that I was under your spell and that I was begging them to hear what you had to say. Apparently, the fact that I have never really been in love before was enough to convince them to come." He took her hand.

She thought about all that he said. She let his words mull around in her mind, mind and heart always at war. She pushed down doubt and thoughts that caused her to second-guess this man. She pushed down her need to analyze everything little thing. She locked down feelings of mistrust and betrayal. She remembered Ariadne's words, and she listened to her heart. She squeezed Drake's hand and rubbed his knuckles softly with the tips of her fingers. This man had put his own heart on the line to carry out a promise that he made for her. No one had ever been that selfless when it had come to her. The only one who had even come close was Feeorin, and his motives were not selfless.

Her words came softly and delicately. "Thank you, Drake. Sincerely, thank you." Her words touched his heart. She was warming up to him. He rolled to his side and put his arm around her, pulling her into him. She lay there in his arms. She could feel his heart beating against her own, the rhythm much the same. The synchronicity of it was as if they shared but one heart. It was warm and comforting, almost safe in his arms. She hoped that she was not opening herself up for more heartache and hurt; she hoped for once that she wasn't playing the fool, but she wouldn't know unless she tried. Looking at him looking at her, she reached her lips up to his and gently kissed him. She could feel him smile as their lips met. He pulled her into him closer and held her tight. She allowed herself to give in to his strength and let her body meld to his. She put her arms around him too.

As the kiss deepened and they became more entangled in each other's embrace, the air around shifted, swirled, and Ariadne hovered above them. As they were locked in lovers' kiss, she bound them together by unbreakable thread linking them forever. This thread severed the bond that was created years before with Travis. It would sever the bond of romantic love from Feeorin, and it would last through this life and any that should follow her. He was to be hers forever. They would withstand any and all challenges that they faced together, and they would come through it stronger. For never was there a more perfect match than this unlikely pair. He needed her to show him what it meant to be loved for who he truly was, and she needed him to save her from herself and the internal web of chaos that she had created. Ariadne watched her chosen one and the man destined to be her hero fall in love before disappearing once again without a trace. She knew Drake would not defy or betray Rhea as so many others had before. She was pleased that the earth angel had listened to her prophecy. She had spoken to a crowd of strangers with the strength and dignity of a queen, and she opened her heart to the only man who was ever worthy of its love. Rhea would surely shine in the upcoming months before this war, and Drake would be at her side reminding her of her brilliance. Ariadne was pleased with herself. She knew that these two would be tried and tested and that they would question each other more than once, but she also knew they would work through it and love truly would prevail. That would be enough to set Rhea free from her tormented internal prison; that would be her driving force to conquer the undead.

That night on a blanket of seasoned grass in the meadow, Drake and Rhea made love. It was the first time either of them had ever felt what it meant to truly be loved by another through physical contact. As their bodies combined and their flesh touched, they spoke to each other what could never be expressed in words. They shared true love's flame, and their souls joined, becoming one, not knowing where she ended and where he began. Entangled naked flesh, warmth of tender fingers, strangers' bodies were finding their way together as if made for the other. He entered her with ease, his throbbing member filled her drenched womanhood to the deepest sanctum of her womb. Waves of tormented passion rode through her. Never had a man merged with a woman the way that Drake merged with her. A soft, sensual mutter escaped her lips. As an expert ship rides the waves, their bodies rode the pleasure higher and higher. He brought her to orgasm more times than she could count. The moment climax came for both at the same time, and she would swear the heavens shattered above and time stood still. Mind-blowing, earth-altering bliss was all she felt. They lay still in each other's arms dripping in desire. It was the first time that anyone had ever truly made love to her.

Without knowing why, she whispered three little words to the man that lay next to her: "I love you." She said it so quietly he almost didn't hear her, but it brushed against his ear and the nape of his neck, sending delicious shivers down his spine, and brushed against his heart.

"I love you too," he said without hesitation. Nothing in his life had ever been more real. He loved this woman with all his might. His arms wrapping tighter around her, she rested her head on his chest, and they lay there covered in his cloak. For just that moment, all was right with the world, and the earth angel had found her home.

About the Author

Raven Gregory: mother, wife, yoga instructor, certified medical assistant, fond of baking sweet treats, lover of books, believer in magic and happily ever after. Raven is married to the love of her life, she has two amazing sons and an amazing stepson. They live in Corpus Christi, Texas, originally from Flagstaff, Arizona. Raven started writing at early age. She was published in a poetry book at the of age twelve. Raven has dreamed of writing a novel for as long as she can remember. She writes what she knows and from the heart. Raven believes that love is the greatest power on earth, and her books follow this theme. Though romance is the dominating trait in her writing, Raven knows that a good story comes with conflict, both from within the main characters and from the outside world. She believes that through struggle and strife, a good outcome will arise. *An Angel's Heart* is her first novel and is the first book in the *Ray of Light* series. Raven hopes that you enjoy her writing style and that some parts of her stories will speak to you on a personal level.

CPSIA information can be obtained
at www.ICGtesting.com
Printed in the USA
JSHW031156120222
22821JS00001B/15